A LITTLE BIT KIN

OTHER BOOKS IN THE
DANIEL BYRD ADVENTURE SERIES

MOUNTAIN JUSTICE

A DANIEL BYRD ADVENTURE

A LITTLE BIT KIN

PHILLIP W. PRICE

Alpharetta, GA

AUTHOR'S NOTE

I was employed by the Georgia Bureau of Investigation for over twenty-nine years (twenty-nine years and ten months to be exact). Being the lead investigator on many homicides, I built walls to protect myself from the toll that dealing with death can take on a human being.

What I couldn't ever learn to shield myself from was the emotional damage investigators experience after dealing with living victims or the families of dead victims.

Those times when I had to be party to someone's private moments, on the worst day of their life, were the hardest part of my job. There is never a way that you can make those moments less painful.

The locations and characters described in this book are an amalgamation of counties and cities in which I worked. The geography described for the area is accurate, and the relationships of the various localities are grounded in reality.

The characters are composites of individuals I have known and worked with throughout my career and beyond. In 2002, the Cherokee Sheriff was a good friend, Roger D. Garrison, who is nothing like the character portrayed here. Nor is the character of GBI Director a representation of either Buddy Nix or Vernon Keenan, lawmen I consider to be friends. The individuals who inhabit this work, both the good guys and the bad, are taken from a variety of people, locales, and life events.

Most of the methods and protocols described in this book are valid and appropriate for the time. However, this book is not a history book, nor is it a textbook; it is a work of fiction.

PROLOGUE

OCTOBER 26, 2022
EL PASO, TEXAS

Daniel Byrd felt like he could stretch a mile. He had been sitting in the seat for almost two hours, and his flight still had about another hour left. His journey was bitter-sweet.

The flight left around noon, so he had fought traffic to the Atlanta airport. He checked in at the gate, discreetly showing the Gate Agent his credentials identifying himself as a Special Agent of the Georgia Bureau of Investigation. He completed the required "flying armed" paperwork, grabbed a rushed breakfast, and got into the gate area just in time to be called to board. Once he had settled in, he tried unsuccessfully to nap.

Napping wasn't in the cards, he decided. He double-checked his motel reservations and the times on the invitation he had received. Just the names on the invitation brought memories flooding back. Nineteen years seemed like they had passed in the blink of an eye. The retirement invitation made him ponder his own future. And then reflect on his past.

He had to wonder if the sacrifices he made were worth it. The sleepless nights, the lonely vigils, and the lives he had seen destroyed. And he wondered about his choices. About his solitary life, and the women he had known. He wondered how his life would have been different if he had pursued a normal job.

He still couldn't control the flinch when there was a loud noise around him. Sometimes he would duck without thinking. And the nightmares still came, although they were less frequent.

He rarely went outside his home without a gun, a residual effect that he suspected had to do with being shot at more than once. And he hated to sit in a restaurant if he couldn't see the main doors.

Cop life, he thought.

He pondered the friendships he had enjoyed, the friends he had made, and the friends he had lost.

He was still thinking about those old times when the plane began its descent. He tightened the seatbelt and waited for the wheels to touch. It couldn't come soon enough.

When he had a chance, he stood in the aisle of the commercial jet. He had to be careful that his handgun wasn't exposed as he reached up for his bag. Slowly, the passengers made their way out and Byrd was among the last to deplane. Byrd was stiff; sitting for so long was more difficult every day. He wondered how much longer he could continue to carry a badge. How much longer he would be contributing to the job.

The Captain and the senior Flight Attendant gave him a subtle wink as he passed them. They were both aware he was an Officer flying armed. He had noticed earlier that he was the only person on the flight wearing a suit and tie.

Byrd walked off the airplane and made his way up the jetway. He noted the sign welcoming visitors to "Texas's Only Major City with Mountains." The terminal was not much different than any other Byrd had passed through in the past. Byrd pulled his carry-on bag and followed the signs to the exit, then walked out into the high desert heat.

Hot—but it's a dry heat, people had told him. He laughed to himself. *My oven is a dry heat, but I don't hang out in it*, he thought. Byrd used his smartphone to summon a rideshare car.

The mountains advertised at the airport were beautiful. This was not his first time in El Paso, and he always enjoyed the scenery. Byrd had visited the city for both business and pleasure. Business had brought him to the city where drugs flowed easily across the porous border that marked the boundary between the US and Mexico. El Paso was one of the primary ports of entry into the United States, and the busiest in the area.

Byrd thought about the times he had spent in this city and the surrounding desert, working with Texas State lawmen. During his time in Texas, he made several good friends.

When a black sedan pulled to the curb, Byrd confirmed the license plate number and then crawled into the back. He checked his watch, did the math in his head, and figured it was just after one in the afternoon.

They left the airport and swept around the south side of the city. The ride was short and uneventful.

When the driver came to the address, he looked back over his shoulder, questioning. "Are you sure you want this place?" the man said with a heavy Spanish accent. "You want the place where they give the driver's license? It is in another place."

Byrd just nodded. "This is the place I want."

The driver pulled past the sign reading "TEXAS DEPARTMENT OF PUBLIC SAFETY" and to the front entrance of the low, tan building. Byrd climbed out of the black sedan and pulled his bag to the door.

Holding his credentials in his hand, Byrd badged his way past the front desk and was pointed to a conference room. When he entered, a man in tan trousers, a white shirt, and a tie seemed shocked to see him. The big man wore the gold circle-and-star badge of a Texas Ranger Major.

Byrd had worked cases with Clete Petterson on more than one occasion. The big man, tanned from working in the West Texas sun, strode over to greet him.

"Hey, my old friend. I can't tell you how happy I am to see you!" Petterson said.

Byrd hugged him, and the two stood for a second before stepping back to look at each other.

"You don't look much different, except your hair has almost all turned white."

Byrd laughed. He pointed to his friend's shaved head. "Clete, it looks like yours turned loose." Byrd had always thought that *Clete* was one of the most Texan names he'd ever heard.

Petterson laughed. "Yep. We both have a lot of miles on us."

Byrd pushed his bag into a corner. "While I'm here, I hope we can hit the Cattleman's Steakhouse. The sunsets out there are spectacular."

Petterson nodded in agreement. "Yes, a trip out to Fabens is in order. And maybe a lunch at Rosa's Cantina. Did I ever take you there?"

Byrd raised an eyebrow. "The place in the Mary Robbins song? We went there once, but we had to rush out. Who could imagine a meal being interrupted by a drug deal?"

"Yes," Petterson said. "Home of some real Mexican food, not that Tex-Mex stuff you boys get back in Georgia."

Byrd looked leery. "All I remember is the salsa and chips. But I'll be happy to try it again, as long as there is no *menudo*. I'm not eating that part of a goat. I didn't try to feed you chitlins when you came to Georgia!"

Petterson slapped Byrd on the back. "Okay, gringo. But we are going to get you some real tacos!"

Byrd nodded. "Sounds good. I try to eat at least three times a day."

Petterson raised his eyebrows. "Hey, didn't I hear that your pregnant Intelligence Analyst had to hold a guy at gunpoint for you?"

Byrd shook his head. "Nope, but the truth is just about as bad." Byrd explained, "I took the Office Analyst out with me since I had no intention of getting involved in the search warrant my Agents were about to serve."

Petterson pressed. "That's not what I heard. And I got it from a reliable source."

Byrd frowned. "That's how rumors get started. We had gone out to the house my guys were searching. Our analyst was ready to deliver, and I thought she might enjoy getting out of the office. We rolled up just as the subject ran. I told her we would drive around the neighborhood to see if we could spot him. Then, who should run out in front of us but our suspect!"

Petterson laughed at the thought.

"I jumped out of the car after putting out on the radio that we needed backup."

"You asked for backup?" Petterson asked.

Byrd laughed. "Even I use common sense sometimes." He continued with the story. "I'm on the side of the road with this suspect at gunpoint. I grab my cell phone and dial 911. The call goes through, but I can't hear them, and they can't hear me. I didn't know it, but the Bluetooth in the car was grabbing the call. The 911 operator thought we were fighting and sent the cavalry. Cops came from everywhere."

"I'm sure they were worried about a man of your age fighting a suspect!"

"That wasn't the worst part. When my Analyst's husband found out, he was mad as hell!"

Byrd looked around the room. There were a couple of dozen men and women in Highway Patrol uniforms, and as many more in white shirts and ties, the unofficial uniform of the Texas Rangers. He saw several troopers around the wheelchair-bound governor of Texas. Byrd was surprised at the officials who were there, but he was looking for one face more than any other.

The two lawmen were working their way across the room. Petterson stopped and introduced Byrd now and then to a friend or relative. About halfway across, Petterson stopped to introduce Byrd to a teenage girl with long dark-brown hair and a gangly young boy. Byrd immediately saw the resemblance to Petterson and his wife. "This is my daughter, Alma, and our son, Guerrero."

Byrd shook their hands warmly, but the teenagers were more interested in the celebrities who were in attendance.

Byrd looked back at Petterson. "I appreciate the chance to celebrate your retirement. This is a great day for you. I look forward to a day like this myself."

Petterson nodded. "I hope I can come to your celebration." He grabbed Byrd's elbow and led him toward the other side of the conference room. "But somehow," Petterson continued, "I have a feeling it's not just me you're here for. Am I right?"

Byrd smiled. "Yep. But a double retirement gives me lots of reasons to be here."

Byrd stopped and stood still. Suddenly he caught a glimpse of the trooper he was here for, and in a blink of an eye, Daniel Byrd was propelled back to 2003.

CHAPTER 1

VALENTINE'S DAY

FRIDAY, FEBRUARY 14, 2003
BLUE RIDGE, GEORGIA

Daniel Byrd was sitting in his government-issued Ford Expedition, listening to the police radio in the hope something might be happening. But nothing was. He had turned off the "good-time" radio, saddened by the details emerging about the destruction of the space shuttle, *Columbia*.

He glanced over at the man in the passenger seat. Byrd knew his credentials carried the name Jackson Farmer, but he was known as Doc Farmer. Jackson became known as Doc when a letter came to the GBI Regional Office addressed to "Joseph S. Farmer, MD." No one in the office had ever heard of a Joseph Farmer, but the connection was made. Farmer, not wanting to be outdone, had told the group of Agents who tried to harangue him that he was a graduate of the Hong Kong School of Chiropractic. From then on, Jackson was known to all as Doc Farmer.

Despite Doc's knowledge of the travails a body could suffer from poor life choices and bad habits—not from medical school but from watching countless autopsies—he was smoking an unfiltered cigarette. He did, however, courteously keep the smoke directed toward his open window.

Doc sported wavy, iron-gray hair, combed back from his receding brow. His eyes were blue, and there always seemed to be a twinkle behind his glasses. He was dressed in a white shirt with a tie, chinos, a heavy jacket, and a GBI mesh raid vest.

Between puffs on the cigarette, he looked toward Byrd and asked, "Son, how many hours do you think we've spent sitting in cars waiting for something to happen?"

"Too many, Doc. I guess you did a lot when you worked for the Revenue Department?" Farmer had joined state service once his hitch in the Air Force was over. He was hired by the Georgia Department of Revenue, the old-school Revenuers. The State had employed the Revenue Agents to track down illegal moonshine manufacturers, but the need to find and smash liquor stills had faded. After his Revenue job had been eliminated, Doc and a few others were transferred to the GBI.

Doc had been thirty-five when he went through GBI Basic Class, seven years older than the next oldest student. He had run with the kids, as he called them. But the class-work was different, harder for a man who had dropped out of college to join the military. He was the rare GBI Agent without a four-year degree, and he was acutely aware of that fact. When he graduated from GBI school fifteen years ago, he had been diligent in turning in the best paperwork in the office.

Farmer nodded. "Yep, too many. I need to be back at the office working on one of my case files. But I guess we get paid the same to sit here and wait."

He crushed the cigarette out and rolled up the window. They were both feeling the chill in the air, and the temperature was predicted to drop below zero after sundown. A light rain had started about an hour ago, and Byrd had to run the wiper blades every ten minutes so they could see. *Who the hell thought it was a good idea to do a dope deal on a day like this?* Byrd thought.

They were parked in a church parking lot in a once-busy part of northern Fannin County. Once the Zell Miller Mountain Parkway had been completed through the heart of the area, this crossroads had become quiet.

Byrd looked at the radio control head again, hoping for something to happen. They could see a Fannin County Detective car with two occupants on the opposite side of the church. Their fellow Agent Tim Atkinson had set up a drug buy using a confidential informant. Doc Farmer, Daniel Byrd, Atkinson, and Fannin County Investigator Russell James would then execute a search warrant at the house. The four Officers would have raised eyebrows if anyone had traveled the road, but so far, the highway was deserted.

Their timetable was dependent on many things, not the least of which was the informant's ability to see drugs in the house. A previous buy had been enough to secure a search warrant, but the Agents didn't want to knock down the door if there weren't any drugs there.

The informant had been in the house for almost an hour. Enough time to use drugs or to engage in a sex act with the dealer—two things they had specifically instructed her not to do. The minute hand on Byrd's watch continued its slow progress.

"You got plans tonight with that hot redhead in the DA's Office?"

Byrd flushed. Then he shook his head. "I'm not allowed to see her till the court case is settled on her ex-husband." Byrd and Rose Mitchell, the Secretary for the District Attorney, had been swept up in an investigation on corruption in Gilmer County, the county just to the south of

Blue Ridge. The case had resulted in Rose's husband going to jail and the Sheriff and Chief Superior Court Judge going to the morgue. As primary witnesses in the case, Rose and Byrd had been discouraged from having contact outside the District Attorney's Office. And since Byrd wasn't one to step out of line, he hadn't talked to her except for business.

Farmer leaned back in the seat. "Well, a young man like you must have plans of some kind on Valentine's Day."

"Doc, I don't ever seem to have the time to get involved with anybody. You know we don't meet a lot of people outside the courthouse or the jailhouse."

Farmer shrugged. "Get one of these ladies you locked up out on bond, she'll appreciate the hell out of it. Hell, you might set them on the right road by taking some young lady in and turning her life around."

Byrd smirked. "Very funny. But that's better than going on some dating site on the computer."

Farmer laughed, and his laugh was all the way to the core. He shook and slapped his right thigh. "You're a treat to work with."

Byrd gave him a puzzled look. Doc laughed again. "Son, your life is more fucked up than a football bat."

Byrd had to laugh, too. "I can't argue with that."

Byrd sat forward as a little car, mostly rust-colored, pulled up to the Fannin County car. At first, the two GBI men were alarmed, but then they recognized the driver. They watched as the informant got out of the car and bounced over to the window where Atkinson sat. They carried on an animated conversation for several seconds.

"She saw dope," the radio squawked. They both recognized Atkinson's voice.

Byrd grabbed the radio microphone, as he watched the

informant's car drive away. Speaking into it, he said, "Same plan as before? Y'all go to the front door, and Doc and I go around back?"

Atkinson acknowledged the rough plan. "She says the dope is in the cabinet above the refrigerator, and there are two ugly dudes in the trailer. Both of them were sitting in the living room playing a video game."

Byrd pulled the truck into drive. Like so many drug deals Byrd had participated in, they were short-handed for this type of raid. He followed the unmarked Fannin County Crown Victoria out onto the paved road, then seconds later onto a dirt road. They were moving quickly down the red-clay path when Byrd recognized the trailer home on the left coming up.

The Fannin County car nosed into the yard near the door, and Byrd pulled to the right, pointing his truck toward the backyard. He came to a stop near the corner of the single-wide.

Byrd ran his left hand up and laid it palm-down on his chest. This move made his seatbelt quickly retract without catching on his gun, handcuffs, or his credential case in his shirt pocket.

As he dropped out of the big truck to the ground, he heard Atkinson and James pounding on the front door. Byrd could hear him yelling, "Sheriff's Office! Search warrant! Open the door or we'll break it down."

Seconds later, and simultaneously, Byrd heard the front door crash and the back door slam open against the outside wall. Two men launched out the back door at a dead run. Both the runners were dressed in jeans and boots with no shirts. Byrd was ready and lowered his right shoulder. He quickly rammed the second man and pushed him to the ground.

He heard Farmer run up behind him. Byrd pushed himself up and, without looking back, said, "Doc? You got this one?"

As he scrambled off the first suspect, he heard Farmer pushing the cuffs on the drug dealer, but Byrd was already running headlong after the other man. The ground behind the trailer was soft, and the terrain dropped off sharply.

Byrd used his right hand to hold his gun in place, so it didn't flop around at his side. He could see the other dealer about three yards ahead of him. His dress shoes didn't provide much traction on the wet ground, and the dealer's boots gave him an edge.

Byrd pushed hard to catch up, but his feet kept sliding in the mud, and he would have to grab at the small trees on his path for control. Byrd made some progress as the dealer, a bigger man than Byrd had realized, was running out of steam.

The man stumbled on the hill and was trying to keep on his feet as he fell into a stream. The water was about knee deep, and the dealer ended up sitting back and going under the fresh mountain water.

Byrd jumped into the stream and immediately regretted it. The water was much colder than he had expected. The stream was deep in a hollow and so the water was seldom warmed by the sun.

Byrd suddenly felt the dealer grab his right arm and try to pull him under the water. No matter how hard Byrd tried, his foot couldn't keep traction in the rushing waters. The bed of the stream was littered with small, smooth rocks. Byrd couldn't find an anchor to hold himself in place. When his foot slipped, the world turned upside down as his head dipped under the frigid water.

Byrd fought the instinct to open his mouth for air. His

head was spinning from being turned upside down, and his eyes stung as he struggled to keep from drowning.

The big man punched at Byrd's face, but the water blunted the blow. Byrd was having a hard time not sucking in water. He managed to put his left arm down onto the stream bed and used it as a brace, grabbing the dealer's crotch with his right hand and pulling down as hard as he could. Byrd leveraged his own body back to the surface.

Byrd gasped for air, then he got a firm footing and pulled the dealer onto his feet. Once he did, his assailant rose to his full height, towering over Byrd. The man was big in the shoulders, and taller than Byrd by several inches. The big man was winded, but not out of the fight.

Byrd didn't have time to think—he grabbed the dealer by the head. Once he had the big man's head locked in, Byrd twisted his hips, pulling the dealer around and off his feet. Byrd kept twisting his body around and the man slammed into the water. Byrd stepped over his attacker, pulled the man's right arm out straight, and applied pressure to the suspect's elbow. The dealer quickly begged for mercy.

Byrd kept the armbar in place and guided the man out of the water and onto his face on the bank. Byrd felt around for his handcuffs, then realized they had been lost in the struggle. If he didn't cuff him, the second Byrd's guard was down, the dealer would take off, or worse, start the fight up again. Byrd's chest heaved, and his eyes stung from the icy water. He decided to sit down on the middle of the man's back and wait.

After Byrd got his breath back, he called out, "Anybody up there?"

"Danny," he heard Farmer shouting, "are you okay?"

Byrd took a deep breath and started coughing. When

he could, he said, "I'm down here with the second guy. We had a little tussle, and we're both soaking wet."

Byrd heard someone crashing down the hill. Only then did he realize how truly steep the hill was. He could see Tim Atkinson clutching from tree to tree to get down the slope without falling. When he got to Byrd, he handed him a set of handcuffs.

"What happened to yours?" Atkinson asked.

Byrd pointed to the stream. "I think I lost them when we went whitewater rafting."

Atkinson helped Byrd pull the big man to his feet. Byrd was beginning to shake from the cold. "Are you going to give us any trouble getting out of here?" Atkinson asked the big man.

The dealer flexed his arms, trying to break the cuffs. "You assholes are going to pay for this."

Atkinson grabbed the front of the man's shirt and tugged him down to his height. "You don't seem to get it. If you give us a hard time on the way back up this hill, we'll all end up at the hospital."

The man growled, "Is that a threat?"

Atkinson shook his head. "No, dipshit. It's a warning. We can't keep it from happening if you try to jerk away from us. All we can do is try not to fall all over each other."

"I'm your prisoner. That means you have to take care of me," the man said between chattering teeth.

Atkinson nodded in agreement. "Right you are. And if we need to get a wrecker to lower a cable down here and drag you out, we can. But I think it would be simpler for all concerned if you just worked with us to get out from down here."

"I ain't done nothing. What are y'all doing here anyway?"

"On behalf of the State of Georgia, we are here to deliver your valentine," Byrd said as he stood shivering.

Suddenly the big man turned to Daniel Byrd, his eyebrows contorting in confusion. "Hey! I know you."

Byrd looked him over. After a moment, Byrd recognized him. "You're Brandon Fisher. The meth cook."

"Meth dealer now. I got tired of getting blown up."

Byrd was surprised. "What the hell are you doing out of jail?"

Fisher frowned. "I'm a 'nonviolent offender' is what my Lawyer told the Judge. Judge Pelfrey thought I would be a good candidate for prohibition. I been clean for a while."

Byrd smirked. "It's 'probation,' Einstein. And that is some bullshit. When we get you to the jailhouse, we'll find out if you're clean. Meth will show up in your system for forty-eight hours."

"Well, I'm just a victim of a broken system. I can't help if I fall off the wagon, now and again," Fisher replied.

"You're a laugh a minute," Byrd said as he and Atkinson pushed the dealer up the hill.

Fisher grumbled, but he started stumbling up the mountainside with Atkinson and Byrd pushing him along. Once they were at the top, Byrd helped him into the trailer where they could both get warmer.

Doc Farmer stood by the door and looked at the two soaking-wet men. "Y'all are one hell of a sight."

Byrd smiled and shrugged. "He wanted to teach me how to swim."

Farmer nodded. "How'd that work out?"

"Not good." Byrd pointed at the man with his head. "But I did manage to find Bigfoot."

Farmer turned away. "At least your trip wasn't wasted."

Byrd pulled a wooden chair as close as he was able to the coal oil heater in the living room of the trailer. Byrd sat back in his chair trying to get warm while the other lawmen searched. He would do prisoner control until a uniform car could get there to take the two dope dealers to jail. Fisher was exhausted and did little more than groan as he sat slumped on the other side of the heater.

Once a uniformed Deputy arrived, Byrd helped shuffle the two men out to the patrol car and get them into the back seat. Byrd slammed the door and gave the Deputy the driver's licenses he had found on the men. Once the suspects were tended to, Byrd went to his car and found a heavy coat to put on over his still-wet clothes.

Atkinson and the Fannin County Investigator were cataloging the different drugs found in the main bedroom. Farmer motioned with his head for Byrd to come over.

When Byrd was close enough to whisper to, Farmer said, "Son, what in the hell were you thinking?"

Byrd seemed confused. "I was thinking I needed to catch that son of a bitch. Is that wrong?"

Doc shrugged. "Not if you plan to retire someday. If you want to go out under a state flag, then that's just fine. Me, I plan to live a long time after I retire, and the way you're acting ain't the way to do it."

Byrd was on the verge of giving a flippant answer but thought better of it. He stood there with Farmer, silent.

Doc put his arm around Byrd's shoulder. "Son, you're a good Agent. But you have got to learn that you're not the Lone Ranger. That's why we come out here as a team. So one of us doesn't get hurt."

Byrd hung his head. He knew he tended to work alone when he could, but he valued Farmer's criticism. "Thanks, Doc."

"Son, you got a long way to go in this job. Take your time. Don't rush headlong into everything. It'll still be there."

Byrd nodded, then met his eye. "Can I buy you a cup of coffee? I feel like I owe you."

Doc gave him a puzzled look. "Where at?"

"The jail."

Doc laughed. "That coffee's free."

Byrd smiled. "That's about what I owe you."

Doc poked Byrd in the ribs. "You're going to need your money anyway. You'll have to pay for that set of handcuffs you lost today."

Byrd groaned. "Aw, fuck! A twenty-dollar set of cuffs, and I'll do fifty-dollars' worth of paperwork to explain how I lost them. Government at its best."

Doc laughed his all-body laugh. "You won't do."

Byrd laughed, too. "Maybe I'll do till something better comes along."

Byrd had expected the conversation with Special Agent in Charge Will Carver to be unpleasant. He had called the office as soon as they got to the Fannin County Jail. Byrd was able to get into a small office with a phone, where he could explain himself without an audience. He sat at a small metal desk, still soaking wet, and dialed the office number.

"Was there a problem with the search warrant over in Fannin?" Carver asked upon answering.

Byrd swallowed hard and then began to recount the events of the afternoon.

The line was quiet as Byrd told his version of the short chase. Once the young GBI Agent got to the end of the story, Carver spoke up.

"Did you test Fisher?"

Byrd knew what he was asking. "Yep, we had his Probation Officer pee test him at the jail. He failed spectacularly. Meth. Which is what we found in the house."

"Do you think your friend the Judge had anything to do with him being on the street?"

"She was watching out for him when she was his Lawyer. I think he was the Judge's meth source. It wouldn't be a stretch to think she helped him stay out."

"Just keep your distance from her. She will be gunning for you."

"I'll do what I can. She has most everybody up there under her thumb."

"Then be sure you record her if you can. If she gets you alone, she'll try to twist whatever you say."

"Last time we were alone, she tried to get me to sleep with her. I'm not sure you want to hear that recording."

Carver wasn't amused. "I'm not laughing."

Byrd was contrite. "Sorry, Will." Byrd paused for a second. "Will?"

"What now?"

"Happy Valentine's Day."

Byrd heard the phone click as the line went dead.

CHAPTER 2
WAKE-UP CALL

Byrd was sound asleep when his home phone rang. It took a full ring for him to figure out what the noise was before he sat up straight in bed. He grabbed the receiver and brought it to his ear.

"Hello?" he said.

"Were you asleep?" He recognized the voice of Rose Mitchell.

"No," he said, trying to wake up. "What time is it?"

"So, you *were* asleep. That's what I figured," she taunted.

"I worked late last night. I was called out to a death investigation up in Blue Ridge. I got back home about three this morning." Byrd rolled out of the bed and stretched as much as the phone cord would allow. He looked around for his alarm clock and saw it was 7:45 a.m.

"Dammit, Rose! I thought it was later in the day with the way you were talking. What are you calling for so early?"

"Don't be cussing at me!" She laughed. "Judge Pelfrey wants you in court in Jasper at nine. She wants to have a hearing on the confession you got on the arson case in Ludville. She called my boss before seven. She was cussing up a storm and said you better be on time. Mr. Mason said he would cover for you as much as he could, but you better get on up here as quick as you can."

Jerry Mason had a better chance of running interference for Byrd as the District Attorney for the Appalachian Judicial Circuit.

"I guess she will be trying to catch me short. She probably wants a little payback out of my hide." Byrd had been the Lead Investigator in a case that uncovered Judge Pelfrey's father had been deeply involved in the theft of government funds.

"My guess is that is exactly what is going on. So get your ass on up and get to the courthouse." Rose paused. "And come by and see me when you get out. I'll be in the Jasper office today."

"You bet," Byrd said as he hung up the phone.

Byrd had been transferred to a GBI regional office in 2001 and was thrown into a corruption investigation in one of the northern counties in the territory. As a Regional Agent, Byrd was expected to respond to any of the fourteen counties in the region to assist the local law enforcement with everything from bad check cases to homicides. The region Byrd was assigned to—Region Eight in GBI parlance—was one of the most active in the state for violent crimes. That was fine with Daniel Byrd, who loved working criminal cases.

He rolled out of bed and stood on the cold floor. Just two days ago, the overall temperature for the day was in the high seventies. Last night the temperature dropped below freezing. *You've got to love a Georgia winter*, he thought.

Byrd's apartment, located near the middle of Canton, was small and highly functional. Some would call it Spartan. Byrd lived on the second floor of a complex that was locally known as "alimony hill." If you weren't collecting it, you were paying it. Byrd was doing neither, but he rented there just the same.

Byrd got in the shower and ran the water as hot as he could stand. He had gotten home in the early morning with the smell of death still on his clothes and hands. He had worn rubber gloves but could still smell the gasses the body was releasing when he got there. It soaked into your pores, your hair, your clothes. *Or maybe I just think I smell them*, he thought. He washed his light brown hair, cut just a little long, with vigor and then ran the washcloth around the back of his arms and the back of his head. It wouldn't be the first time he had missed blood transfer that ended up on his own skin.

He climbed out of the shower and toweled off. After a quick wash of his face, a shave, and a brush of his teeth, Byrd grabbed his court suit from the closet. It was charcoal gray, matched with a white poplin shirt and a dark blue patterned tie. He wanted to be sure he looked his best.

Byrd always kept his clothes from the day before, laid out with everything he needed in the pockets, so he could respond quickly to a late-night call. He transferred his keys, change, and a couple of twenty-dollar bills in a money clip. He put his credentials in his shirt pocket, gave his hair a brush, and headed to his car in less than thirty minutes.

He took a look at himself one last time on the way out the door. His blue eyes were tinged with red, and he looked haggard. He shrugged to himself, grabbed his black overcoat from the hall closet, and headed out the front door.

When he stepped out, the sun was almost blinding. The cold air slapped him in the face, and his breath swirled in a fog around him. His mouth tasted bad from the drinking the night before. The young girl—Byrd had learned she was eighteen—had taken a full bottle of her grandmother's pain medication. She then cut her wrists and bled to death. This had been his third death in as many days. This one, and the one two nights ago, were probably suicides, but Agents were trained to treat every death as a homicide.

The middle death, a Saturday night argument between lovers—witnesses could not agree on whether they were married—was a murder. The suspect admitted to Byrd that his girlfriend had "been disrespectful" and he had hit her with a hammer to shut her up. Once she was dead, his family tried to argue her death was the result of illness. Even though the scenario was unlikely, the District Attorney expected all possible defenses eliminated or explained.

With all the death he had witnessed over the seventy-two-hour period, Sunday night—or technically Monday morning—had seemed like a good time to have a strong drink before bed. The exhausted Agent had mixed a strong vodka martini. Vodka, gin, and an olive plopped in. He drank with gusto, and the slight buzz helped the next martini seem like a good idea. The vodka helped sleep come faster and the nightmares come less frequent.

He locked his apartment and jogged down the steps to the common parking lot. His white Expedition was parked nearby. The windows were covered in frost, and it took a full two minutes for the truck's heater to start clearing the windshield. After clearing a porthole in the front window, he drove out of the parking lot and headed north.

The clock on the outside of the Pickens County Courthouse read 8:55 when he parked. The courthouse was an imposing structure. With walls and floors glistening white, it was hard to forget you were in the marble capital of the United States.

He radioed his newly promoted Office Investigative Assistant, Machelle Stevens, who pretty much ran the GBI Regional Office, and told her he was out at the Pickens County Courthouse. Then Byrd hustled to the courthouse entrance, using his badge to bypass the metal detectors. The Courthouse Security Deputy smiled and said, "Master Badge. Don't leave home without it."

As he pushed through the back door of the courtroom, Byrd saw Judge Pelfrey rush into the courtroom and take the bench. She paused for a moment when she saw Byrd in the back of the room.

Jerry Mason, sitting at the prosecutors' table inside the bar, noticed the look that settled on the Judge's face before looking over his shoulder to see Byrd. Mason smiled.

Mason was typical of the overworked District Attorneys in the rural parts of Georgia. He had to juggle trials in three counties, with the same number of Judges. As a former cop, Mason was popular with the law enforcement community and had a pretty good relationship with most of the judiciary in his circuit. He usually dressed in dark suits with bright red ties, and today was no exception. A big man whose weight had grown with his blood pressure since he had taken the job, Byrd had been surprised to learn Mason had a background with the US Special Forces.

The Judge took her seat. She was wearing the standard black robe zipped to the chin. Her blonde hair hung down to her shoulders. She looked directly at Mason. "I certainly hope you're ready for this hearing. We need to move this case along." She chose to ignore Byrd, keeping laser-focused on Mason.

Mason stood up and addressed the Judge. "Your Honor, the State is ready."

Lane Sims, a local Attorney, stood for the defense. He

tugged at his collar near the knot of his tie and said, "The defense is ready, Your Honor." His client, barely old enough to shave, was hunched over in the seat beside Sims. He was dressed in jailhouse oranges.

The Judge looked around the room, finding Byrd with her eyes. She spoke to Mason while staring at Byrd. "Call your first witness."

Mason cleared his throat. "Hmm. The State calls Agent Byrd to the stand."

Byrd stood uneasily and walked to the witness stand. He kept his eyes dead ahead and ignored the Judge as he stood in front of the bench and took the oath. Then he stepped into the box and took a seat. He was acutely aware the Judge was less than a yard from his right ear.

Mason stood at the table. "Please state your name for the record."

Byrd locked onto Mason's eyes. "Daniel Byrd."

"And how are you employed?"

"I am a Special Agent with the Georgia Bureau of Investigation. I am assigned to the Region Eight Office in Gainesville, Georgia."

"And, Agent Byrd, were you so employed on the eighth day of December of last year?"

The Judge interrupted Mason, "I believe we are all familiar with Agent Byrd and his employment. Since this is a hearing to determine if the statement the defendant in this case is alleged to have made will be admitted at trial, we can dispense with Agent Byrd's vita for the moment. Let's just move on to the meat of the questions."

Attorney Sims shot to his feet. "Your Honor, I object to any shortcuts that might prevent me from perfecting the record in this case for later appeal."

The Judge craned her neck to Sims, and he visibly

recoiled. Her face was red, and her eyes narrowed. "Mr. Sims, I'll decide how things go in my court. And it would behoove you to wait to see how I rule before you worry about perfecting the record."

Sims was wary. His head bobbed up and down. "I just assumed that Your Honor would—"

Judge Pelfrey raised an eyebrow. "Don't assume anything in my courtroom, Mr. Sims." She shifted in her seat.

Sims nodded. "Yes, Your Honor." Sims dropped into his seat and looked over at Mason for some clue as to what was happening.

"Fine," she spat. Judge Pelfrey turned to face Daniel Byrd. "Agent, did you take a statement from this defendant in which he admitted guilt."

Byrd turned and faced Judge Linda Pelfrey. They locked eyes, and Byrd was apprehensive for a moment. "I did, Your Honor."

"And were there any other witnesses to this alleged confession, Agent Byrd?"

"No, not in the room. But the statement was recorded by me at the time. I collected the audio recording as evidence. That tape has been turned over to the District Attorney and to the defense counsel."

"And you expect this court to take your word on this matter, Agent Byrd?"

"I would think that the recording would stand on its own merit."

"How does this court know you didn't edit or change this statement? Why should I think this recording is even of this defendant?"

Suddenly the young man at the defense table stood. "It was me, Your Lordship. I heard the tape yesterday. My Lawyer played—" Before he could finish, Sims dragged him into his seat and shushed him.

Judge Pelfrey ignored the defendant and kept her attention on Byrd. "Agent Byrd, did you create a web of lies that resulted in the death of my father? A man who served this community for over thirty years before his untimely death?"

Byrd's mind was racing. *What would be the proper answer?* he thought. *Your dad killed himself to keep from going to prison, so that seems pretty timely, Judge.*

Mason was on his feet. "Objection. The court's question is incompetent, irrelevant, and immaterial."

Judge Pelfrey was red-faced. Her words shot back like bullets. "Do you know what you are doing?"

Mason walked around in front of the Prosecutor's table. "Your Honor, I think you have decided the outcome of this hearing without listening to the State's witnesses."

The courtroom was silent. The Judge was almost shaking. Her face was bloodred, and her hand was quivering as she raised her gavel. *Bam! Bam!* She hit the bench.

Judge Pelfrey leaned forward. "Mr. Mason, if you plan to let your case stand on the testimony of this liar, then you may want to rethink your strategy." She turned to face Byrd. "Isn't that what you are, Agent? A liar and a scoundrel."

Mason shouted, "Objection, Your Honor."

"On what grounds?" Pelfrey roared.

"Your question to the witness is improper. Your evaluation of him as a witness is improper. And I am putting the court on notice that I will appeal any adverse ruling in this case based on the stated bias of this court."

This time, Byrd was surprised the gavel didn't break. *Bam! Bam! Bam! Bam!* "I'll see both Attorneys in chambers," the Judge shouted. She looked around and made eye contact with Daniel Byrd. "Agent Byrd, you need to stay your ass in the witness chair. Is that clear?"

Byrd sat uncomfortably. He looked to Mason for a life-line. "Yes, Your Honor."

She stood and gave Mason a pointed look. "Mr. Mason, instruct your witness to remain in his place for the duration of our conference." She motioned to Mason and Sims. "My chambers. Right now." Then she turned and stalked through the door.

Mason and the Defense Attorney worked their way around the end of the bench and stepped into the back hallway.

Byrd let out his breath and slumped in the chair.

Mason came back into the courtroom in less than ten minutes, but it seemed like an hour to Byrd. Mason went directly to the front of the witness stand.

Byrd shook his head. "How long is this going to last?" he asked.

Mason shook his head. "She realizes she let her mouth get the best of her. She wanted to expunge the record of this whole hearing—if you can call it that. She got pushback from both of us, so she decided to recuse herself. She was really planning on jumping your ass today."

Byrd climbed down from the witness stand and asked, "Then do I need to hang out here, or can I go?"

Mason thought about that for a minute. "Why don't you go wait in my office? When she takes the bench again, I'll see if I can get you dismissed."

Byrd shrugged and brushed his hair back with his left hand. "Sounds good. At least in there I can use the phone and get something done." Byrd took the back door to the hall leading to the District Attorney's Office.

He found Rose Mitchell sitting at the front desk. Rose had her red hair pulled back into a bun. She was wearing a suit and pants and was holding a phone to her ear. When she finished the call, she stood and walked over to Byrd.

"Well, hello, stranger," she said. "You should have come in here first."

Byrd smiled. "I wish I had. Do you have coffee?"

Rose pointed at the pot in the waiting area. "Of course. I know you cops can't function without it."

Byrd grabbed a foam cup and filled it. He took a long drink of the burnt coffee. "Any idea when your divorce is final? The GBI will be closing the cases on the Sheriff's Office crowd when they plead guilty. I heard that might happen as soon as the end of this month."

Rose nodded. "In the mountain way. All the main folks seem to have skated."

Byrd thought that over. "The mountain way, huh? I guess that does kind of sum it up. All the cases in Gilmer County dropped because Mason thinks no jury will convict them. The cases in Fannin County on your husband and his buddy are going full speed ahead."

"Ex-husband," Rose interjected.

Byrd nodded. "Your ex-husband. Certainly not the brains of the operation."

Rose laughed. "That's a fact."

Byrd glanced around the room, being careful there was no one who could hear his next statement. "I still can't believe that Mason let Linda Pelfrey skate on that case. Hell, if he had even charged her, she wouldn't be a judge. Except maybe at the county fair."

Rose shrugged. "People excuse a lot up here if it means a favor they can collect on down the line. She still held enough power and influence to protect herself. Something her daddy had probably counted on."

"I hear your ex and his codefendant plan to plead guilty."

"Yep, all their charges will be adjudicated. And Givens will never go to trial. He'll enter a plea and take some jail time, but he'll probably do less than a year in prison. I'll be glad to have all that behind us."

"Does that mean we can go out again?" Byrd asked.

Rose bent her head down slightly so she was looking up at him. Byrd had forgotten how captivating she could be when she wanted to be. But just as suddenly as her eyes locked on his, she turned away. "We'll have to see how things go," she said. "Between college and the kids, I have a pretty full plate."

Byrd felt the awkwardness of the moment. He wasn't sure what to say, so he just let everything hang in the air.

Rose had been hired into the District Attorney's Office as a Secretary with only a high school diploma. After she filed for divorce, she started college in Jasper. Mason had promised he would help her get into law school if she had the grades.

Byrd took off his overcoat and suit jacket and hung them on a coat rack. Then he found a comfortable chair near the wall with a good view of Rose's desk. He sat and put both hands behind his head, letting himself relax more than he was usually able to, resting his hands far from the gun on his right hip.

Rose sat down at her desk and grabbed a file she was working on. She pushed it aside and propped her chin on her left hand, elbow down on the desk. She wanted to get the tension out of the air. "I guess it seemed like the day that everything would be over and we could both move on would never come. I hope you didn't mope around this whole time waiting on me." Her laugh was thin.

Byrd couldn't deny it. He had dated a few girls during their forced separation, but none had worked out. One had tried to get Byrd to try cocaine and thought it was terribly funny when he told her he would arrest her if she brought any of the white powder into his apartment. Another had thought being a Special Agent was the same as being an Insurance Agent or a Travel Agent. She almost fainted when he brought her to his apartment and took his gun off in front of her. And there was a Canton Police Officer who seemed to be flirting with Byrd at times, but nothing had come of that. Byrd had no doubt Rose had relationships too, but he didn't feel he had the right to ask about them.

"Will you be around long enough to buy my lunch today?" Rose asked.

Byrd nodded. "As far as I know, I am here for the day. I may run down to the Sheriff's Office and check in. But no reason we can't grab a bite to eat."

Before the words were out of his mouth, the office phone began to ring.

Rose grabbed it on the first ring. "DA's Office." After a moment she said, "Hey, Machelle. I'm doing great. What can I do for you today?"

She listened, and after a moment, her eyes cut to Byrd. She offered the phone to him. "Your office is looking for their best Agent. When they couldn't find her, they started looking for you."

Byrd frowned. "Very funny," he said.

"The boss is looking for you," Machelle said. "He wants to see what's going on with you having to rush to the Pickens courthouse."

"He must have a pretty good idea," Byrd said.

"Uh-huh, he figures it's that crazy Judge. Is that about right?" Machelle sounded amused.

Byrd dropped his voice. "She's crazy enough to have this phone tapped."

Machelle sounded unimpressed. "Hold on. I'll get Will on the line."

The wait was short, and then Will Carver, the Special Agent in Charge of the Gainesville office, was on the line. "Are you in jail?"

"Nope. Not yet," Byrd responded.

"So, was this rush to Jasper over your favorite Judge?"

"Yes. She tried to hold a hearing on an arson case where I got a confession. Rose from the DA's Office gave me a call and I got here just in time."

"Did the Judge give you any problems?"

Byrd glanced at Rose. "I'll do a memo for you, but she called me a liar and a scoundrel from the bench."

Carver paused for a moment. "Hmm. I think you need to get to your office in Canton as quickly as you can and write out a report. The Director will want to see it as soon as you get it done. Can you do that?"

Byrd looked at Rose. She seemed to sense their lunch date was going to hell in a handbasket. Byrd said, "Yes, sir. I'll head that way now." Hanging up the phone, Byrd looked at Rose.

Rose sighed. "I have a feeling I will be having lunch alone."

Byrd stood and nodded. "I'm afraid so. But maybe we could do something tonight. How 'bout I call you later today?"

Rose stood and gave him a peck on the cheek. "We'll see. I don't have class tonight, but I'll have to see if my parents can keep the kids."

She wasn't meeting his eyes and Byrd felt the brush off. It hung in the air, but it wasn't quite the kiss of death he feared it might be.

Byrd walked out of the office and skirted around to the courtroom. When he stuck his head in, Jerry Mason was talking to a witness, and the Judge was nowhere in sight.

"Mr. District Attorney, is it okay if I run back down to Canton?"

Mason looked up. "Sure." He nodded. "The Judge went back to Ellijay, so you should be good for the rest of the day."

Byrd let the big door close and headed back to his government car. In just over thirty minutes, he was in his office at the Georgia State Patrol Post in Canton. He established the secure connection with the GBI computer network and typed out a report on the hearing with Judge Pelfrey, then sent it to Will Carver. He knew if there were no typographic or grammatical errors, it would go straight to the Director.

An allegation against a sitting Superior Court Judge was a very sensitive matter, and the GBI treated it as such. Memos and reports were closely guarded, and the particulars of the case weren't even known to the other Agents in the office.

Byrd waited till noon and still hadn't heard from his boss. He took up the offer of a couple of the local troopers and went with them to lunch. They went to a local barbeque place and exchanged gossip about what was going on down at the Capitol. And, sure as death and taxes, when Byrd walked back in the Post, the GSP Radio Operator said he should call his office in Gainesville right away.

Once Machelle transferred the call to Carver, there was little preamble. "I read your memo. I don't think anything will come of it, but we need to document everything she says to you like that," Carver noted.

Byrd thought about the Judge's words earlier that day. "I guess you're right. But who would have thought she would have pulled a stunt like that? I sure wasn't expecting it. But I would have thought her calling me a liar in open court would at least get her admonished or something."

"I briefed the Director. He just said to remind you to keep your distance from her. He, nor I for that matter, can predict where any complaints will go."

Byrd understood their concern. "Boss, I get it. I just got pissed when she called me a liar!"

Carver laughed. "She can't be the first woman to do that!"

Byrd laughed, too. "You're right. And certainly not the last."

Carver grunted. "Right. Just make sure you stay as far away from her as you can. If the Director thinks it is significant enough, he'll make a formal complaint to the Judicial Qualifications Commission. You know how Lawyers are though, always ready to give a terribly wordy argument about why one of their own should be defended. This is going to be a close call. We may have to give her more rope and hope she hangs herself with it."

Byrd wasn't getting his hopes up. "Or we give her enough rope and she goes into the rope business."

Carver grunted. "This ain't my first rodeo, either," he said. "If I hear anything out of headquarters, I'll let you know." Carver hung up.

Byrd figured he might as well catch up on his paperwork since the day was already shot. He planned to dictate an investigative summary about today and review completed reports online. Maybe he would call Rose, but she didn't seem like she would be waiting by the phone.

Byrd was concentrating on a report from last Friday when his office phone rang. He grabbed the receiver.

"GBI, Agent Byrd."

He recognized the voice on the other end immediately. His Assistant Special Agent in Charge, Scott Andrews, had been promoted to some high-profile job in headquarters. Andrews's replacement was Christina Blackwell. Tina had worked all over the GBI before being promoted to the Gainesville office. She was a respected veteran Agent.

"Danny?" she said.

"Yep. What can I do for you, Tina?"

"You're going to love me for this."

Byrd groaned. He didn't know what was coming, but he could tell he was going to hate it. "You know I ended up with three death investigations this past weekend. I just got finished getting investigative summaries in on a suicide I worked up in Pickens, and I have two more to get dictated as quick as I can."

Tina tutted. "You're the GBI's James Brown, the hardest-working man in our office. All suicides?"

"One was a smoking gun, or I should say a smoking *hammer* murder. The other two were pretty obvious suicides."

The new ASAC didn't want to sound indifferent to his problems. "That is a pretty tough weekend."

Byrd knew there was a "but" coming.

Blackwell continued. "This is something in your neck of the woods, and it comes from the Governor's Office."

Byrd groaned again but louder. "Come on, Tina. I'm up to my ass in alligators here."

"I know that, but everybody has to do their part. We have a background that needs to be done for a judicial appointment. And one of his references lives in Canton. I can't send someone else to do it when you're right there."

Byrd gave in. And deep down he didn't want another Agent coming over in his territory, any more than any other Agent would want him in their area.

"How soon does it need to be done?"

"Today, if you can."

"Tina, what have I ever done to you?" Byrd whined.

"The information should be in your inbox. And it is a quick one. The guy you need to interview is the new Cherokee County Sheriff. Have you met him yet?"

Byrd was cautious in his answer. "Only in passing. I don't really know him."

Blackwell caught the tone. "I hear he's something. He has new-Sheriff syndrome: everybody loves me and I can do whatever I want."

Byrd had heard the same thing. "That's the talk on the street. But I haven't had any problems with him."

"Yet?" Blackwell questioned. "Well, the interview shouldn't take long. Dictate it and get it done. We have some of the Agents running down other interviews, but we need to have it in the Governor's Office by Friday." Blackwell tried to sound encouraging.

"Will this get me out of the doghouse?"

"It can't hurt. Carver likes you. He just doesn't want you running around like some cowboy. He told me you ran off by yourself to tackle the Jolly Green Giant."

I like cowboys, Byrd thought. "I was just focused on the guy who ran. I guess I got tunnel vision. I'll do better next time, I promise."

Tina Blackwell didn't respond.

After several seconds, Byrd sighed into the phone.

Byrd was glum. But there was no getting around it. The Governor had been burned on a political appointment earlier in the year, and now he expected the GBI to vet each of the applicants to appointed positions.

He was seeing his dinner plans evaporate. The Cherokee Sheriff was notorious for being hard to catch in the office. "I'll get on it, Tina." Byrd didn't sound enthusiastic.

Blackwell softened her tone. "I know this sucks. But we have to get this done."

"Don't worry, I'll get it knocked out as quick as I can. I know you had to dump it on somebody."

"Don't consider it a dump job. I'm sure I'll have to give you one of those soon. This is just a chore. Let me know if we can do anything else to help you out."

"Thanks, Tina." He hung up the phone.

Byrd looked up the phone number for the Cherokee Sheriff's Office and dialed the number. His day wasn't going as planned.

CHAPTER 3

HOME COOKIN'

MONDAY, FEBRUARY 17, 2003
CANTON, GEORGIA

Mark Goodwin was waiting patiently in his kitchen. Patience was a trait most in his vocation failed to master. Patience and methamphetamine didn't go together. But he only made the magic, he didn't partake. At least in his mind, he didn't partake. The reality was the low-rent gear he wore to keep the poison off his skin was almost worthless. His body was taking chemicals in from the air, from contact with the cooking pots, from just about everything he touched. Thus was the burden of a life creating pleasure for others.

He looked like he had been up for a couple of days, which he had. His hair was wild, and he had several days' growth of beard. He was dressed in a pair of worn jeans and a long sleeve T-shirt, which hung on his skeletal frame. The trailer he was living in was barely warm enough, making it a step up to living outside. He knew, having slept outside most of last winter. *Winter in Georgia isn't supposed to be this cold*, he had thought.

He had been prepared to cook for a couple of hours, but his woman was taking her time with the ingredients. She had been gone all night and most of the day, but Mark wasn't surprised. It took time to get just the right things to make a batch of premium, almost pure methamphetamine. He knew the pseudoephedrine was the most important part of the cook and the hardest ingredient to get in bulk. Most drug stores were wary now and were prone to call the police if someone bought too many packages. That's why Krystal liked to do as much shopping as she could in the middle of the night, when clerks and other staff were indifferent to her.

He knew the yield was slightly less than one gram of meth for each gram of pseudo. If he was smart, a day's work would keep them afloat for the next month and still let him pay off some of the money he owed.

He put his painter's mask aside and took off his rubber gloves again. He looked for a minute at his wrists where they hung out of the shirt sleeves. He had a number of burn scars from where the scalding hot phosphorus had jumped out at him when he introduced the iodine too quickly. And his hands were gray and scarred from the other mishaps that happened too often to count.

He was anxious, not from meth but from the anticipation of cooking again. Cooking meth was his life's greatest achievement. He had barely finished high school and bounced around from dead-end job to dead-end job. He was flat broke and had moved into a tent on the side of an interstate highway when a guy he met asked him to help with a methamphetamine cook.

The man had said Mark could make a lot of money, and to someone flat broke, any amount was good enough. Mark had watched with fascination as the man took an assortment of household products, none of which were illegal, and produced some of the purest methamphetamine on the planet. Sure, Mark had to take his word for it. Mark wasn't a user. But the stuff sold like hotcakes, and the man doubled his money in less than forty-eight hours. Meth was a hot commodity in the mountains of North Georgia and a sure-fire moneymaker if you could get your hands on it.

Mark's best customer had been Brandon Fisher, a big redneck from Blue Ridge. Brandon had finally blown himself up so many times that he finally approached Mark. Brandon had moved most of Mark's product, but Mark had a plan to make even more money. He knew larger dealers in the Metro Atlanta area were hungry for the mountain meth and could move larger amounts.

Mark didn't know, or care, that methamphetamine use in the mountains of North Georgia dated back several generations. The chicken industry relied on manual labor to catch chickens and get them to market. This work needed to be done at night, and the men who performed this difficult chore discovered levomethamphetamine. The product wasn't as strong as the pure amphetamine tablets and capsules preferred by long-haul truckers of the era. The "West Coast turnarounds" favored by truckers could result in schizophrenia, while levomethamphetamine was much less harsh. A true background in chemistry, a substantial investment in equipment, and specific difficult-to-obtain ingredients were required to make the grainy powder that bolstered energy. In 1980, a primary ingredient—phenyl-2-propanone—was banned in the US and levomethamphetamine was soon impossible to find.

But the market was still there, and a recipe for meth manufacture using ephedrine was resurrected. The procedure involved the reduction of ephedrine using iodine and red phosphorus. The simple process required no special equipment, no special skills, and produced the more powerful dextro-methamphetamine. Essentially, the same recipe was handed down to Mark.

Mark offered to help out again and made a mental note of all the steps. He used his payment to get his own materials for a chemistry experiment which would have made his high school chemistry teacher think twice about what she said about his abilities in science. He started cooking over a year ago, and since then, Mark had discovered he was a natural.

Within a few months, he had a place to live, a woman, and a fairly steady income. Life was good to him once he discovered his secret talent. But only if he had just a little better understanding of basic math or basic economics. The batches he was making were good stuff, but he always seemed to be short on money.

When he first started cooking, he had accumulated his own customers. They would line up for the top-rate meth Mark Goodwin was known for. His name was on the lips of every geek monster in central North Georgia. But he was never able to make any money off his product. In fact, he was steadily sliding into a financial hole when one of his friends introduced him to a middleman in Marietta. The guy offered to take every bit of his work—the street name for meth—off his hands. And he had introduced him to Wilmer Westbrook. Westbrook had given Mark enough money to get himself back on his feet.

At one time he thought maybe Krystal was stealing from him, but she was so cute and horny all the time, he didn't have the heart or the balls to confront her. He knew Krystal did the hard part, and the riskiest part if you didn't count being blown up. She worked a route from drugstores to big-box stores to country convenience stores. It wasn't unusual for her to loop up into Tennessee or over to Alabama. She would buy pseudo where she had to, steal it where she could. Her goal was to get as near to a pound of pseudo as possible.

Earlier today, Mark's pulse had quickened when he thought he heard her coming down the rough driveway. It had turned out to be a delivery truck headed for one of his neighbors. Delivery drivers were always getting the four trailers on adjacent lots confused. The drives were unmarked and looked so similar that Mark had made the same mistake a few times.

Then, around mid-afternoon, her little Honda came storming down the dirt drive and slid to a halt at the trailer. Anytime a car came near the front of his house, Mark made sure to look out through the slats on the taped-up window. Wilmer Westbrook had come by more and more often, asking Mark to pay him back the money he was owed. Mark was dodging Westbrook until he could put some money together to get Wilmer off his back.

Mark was happy when he saw Krystal jumping from the car into the cloud of dust she had created. She was a doe-eyed woman with a petulant smile and mousy-brown hair. She ran to the trunk and pulled out several bags containing what he hoped was more pseudoephedrine than last time.

She loped across the yard, headed to the little metal steps up to the front door as he opened it for her. She pushed past him and threw the bags on the couch in the living room. Without speaking she turned and went back toward the car. He followed her out and was stunned at the second bag of pseudo she pulled out. He saw two complete cases of over a pound each of the decongestant.

When she saw the look on his face, she stood with a big smile. "Can you believe I got two whole cases?" she asked.

Mark just shook his head. "Wow, girl. That is the most pseudo I've ever seen in one place. How the hell did you manage this?" He looked her over. She was dressed in a puffy silver-colored coat, jeans, and a tank top. She twisted around and stood on one foot with the other toe touching the ground. Her brown hair was pulled back in a ponytail, and he had to admit she was one of the prettiest girls he knew. He regretted getting her hooked on meth, but that was what had brought them together.

She leaned into him and kissed him long and hard.

"Now can you tell?" she asked.

It dawned on him. He thought about spitting but decided it wouldn't make any difference. And it would probably just make her mad. "You blew somebody."

She nodded enthusiastically. "Two, to be exact. I found these good ole boys running convenience stores out in the middle of nowhere in the middle of the night. I got to sweet-talking one of them and he offered to sell me as much as I wanted for a blow job. After that, I went to the next place and just told him straight up what I wanted and what I would do for it."

Mark shrugged. He had to admit she was good at what she did. In the meth world, she was known as a "smurf." A smurf is someone who goes from store to store buying or stealing the prime ingredient of methamphetamine, pseudoephedrine. Each case was good for almost a pound of meth. Between the individual packs of decongestant and the cases she had procured, they had enough to manufacture almost two pounds by his estimation.

He put his puritanical issues aside and smiled at her. "I don't deserve a woman like you!" He helped her grab the last boxes and get them inside. As he walked her back inside, out of the bitter cold, he was doing math in his head.

Mark figured, taking away his expenses for the cook, he could end up with around twenty thousand dollars. Enough to get them into a better life.

"Do we have enough of the other stuff to make all this into crank?" Krystal asked. She had spent enough time with Mark to know some of the other ingredients were as hard to get as the pseudo.

The red phosphorus was hard to come by, but he had found a chemical supply store in Chattanooga where he was able to score two cans of a pound each. Krystal had spent a whole day last week buying bottles of tincture of iodine and more bottles of hydrogen peroxide. Those two were easy to get since most people didn't know what they could be used for. He had plenty of red devil lye and acetone on hand. *Yes*, he thought, *I think I can do this.*

He gave Krystal a big hug and tossed her the coffee bean grinder he had bought at an overpriced coffee shop. "Hell, yeah!" he said. Then the phone rang.

Krystal stopped in her tracks as the phone on the wall started to ring. Mark didn't want her to answer—it was time for her mother's afternoon call.

Krystal ran to the wall. She picked up the handset. "Hello?" She said as she turned away from Mark. Krystal knew Mark resented the relationship she had with her mom.

After several seconds, she sighed. "I knew it was you, momma."

Ramona Page didn't care for her daughter's lifestyle and made no bones about it. "I see you're still living in that death house."

Krystal's mother had learned to whisper in a sawmill. Mark tried to ignore her caustic remarks, but he heard them just the same. Ramona had a voice like fingernails on a blackboard.

"Momma," Krystal said, "Mark knows what he's doing. He's not going to blow us up."

"Right," Krystal's momma retorted. "And I guess those poison gases he makes are fine for you two."

"Momma, I don't worry about him. If you saw him working, you would think he was some kind of scientist."

She sniffed. "A scientist, my ass!"

Mark frowned. "Bitch!" he said as he tried to ignore the noise.

"Momma, we just got a big haul of cold medicine. We are about to be rolling in money. We'll have enough meth to pay all our bills off, get the cable turned back on, and maybe go for a trip."

"What about the feller in Canton he owes money to?"

"I should have never told you about him. We'll have more than enough to pay him."

Momma wasn't convinced. "I thought you said that he had threatened to hurt you if you didn't pay up soon."

"He just wants to get paid back is all. And we got the money coming to do that. Mark says that we can get this cook done in a day or two and start raking in the money."

"Are you talking about Wilmer Westbrook? Is that who you owe money to?"

Krystal lowered her voice. "Momma, I ain't supposed to tell you about that."

Her mother was quiet for a minute. "Well, I guess I won't worry if it's Wilmer that Mark owes money to. I'm a little bit kin to his momma."

Krystal was surprised. "Do you know him, then?"

Mark waved at Krystal and motioned for her to cut the call short. Ramona's raspy voice was giving him a headache. Krystal ignored him.

"Not much. He was always the sorry one in that family.

They say that him and his wife are running around on each other. That they throw sex parties and such." Ramona paused for a second. "And the son of a bitch never invites me to any of them parties," she laughed.

"He does kind of give me the creeps. He tries to talk me up and wants to get high with me. But I never did that."

"Well, just see that you don't. Him being kin to us, you get pregnant and them kids would come out with webbed feet or something."

Krystal rolled her eyes. "Momma, you've got a wild imagination."

Momma ignored her. "I know men, I can tell you that. I've done been married to more than I can count. Now, you mind that Mark pays what he owes and don't take any chances with that Wilmer Westbrook. He may be a wimp, but he's sneaky. You just watch him!"

Krystal nodded. "I will, momma. Now I need to get to work pulling these pills so we can start the cook."

Ramona understood. "Okay. You stay safe and be careful. And get your momma a taste when this batch comes in."

"Of course. I'll get you the first eight ball we cut."

"Love you, darling," Krystal's mom said as she hung up the phone.

Mark sounded impatient as he pointed at the coffee grinder in her left hand. "Are you ready to start now?"

She clapped and then sat on the floor with the pills and the coffee mill to begin the task of grinding the pills into powder. This part of the process would take more time than the rest. The blister packs made the procedure slow and tedious. It would be several hours before the pills were all out of the packaging and turned into powder.

Mark prepared the acetone bath the pseudo powder

would be immersed in. The solvent was pungent, but he was immune by now. Like a house painter, he almost didn't smell the chemical. Mark gave the room a once-over. There was a space heater running in the corner of the kitchen, providing very little heat. He worried the highly flammable chemicals he used could ignite, but it was too cold to cut the noisy heater off. The sun had gone down less than an hour ago, and the temperature would soon plummet.

He used the kitchen table to sort out the ingredients and then sat in a rickety chair to begin the conversion of the tincture of iodine into pellets. The process wasn't particularly difficult but it was time-consuming. Mark looked at his wristwatch and decided they could have everything in process by midnight. They could rest some and then start the actual cook the next morning.

He looked to Krystal, who was concentrating on the pill grinding. "Baby," he said, "we are about to get into the big times!"

She looked up and gave him a lopsided smile. Then she went back to twisting the blister packs.

Daniel Byrd's appointment with Sheriff Haggin was for three thirty in the afternoon. He decided to go over early in case the Sheriff came back to his office.

Byrd headed to his truck, and as soon as he left the building, he could tell the temperature had dropped. Since he had on a brown suit, which wasn't warm enough for the cold weather, he pulled an overcoat from the backseat and threw it on.

He drove to his interview with Albert Haggin, the newly minted Sheriff of Cherokee County. Byrd was curious how things would go. He had had little contact with

Sheriff Haggin but heard he was full of himself. It was telling that the Sheriff of the largest county in his area had not called on the GBI once since he was elected to office.

Byrd made the short drive to the Cherokee Sheriff's Complex, located just outside of Canton. He parked outside the jail and found his way to the Sheriff's suite. Haggin's Secretary offered Byrd a seat and explained the Sheriff wasn't expected in until five.

Byrd was perplexed. "I called earlier and made an appointment. I thought it was you who told me he would be in by three thirty."

His Secretary rolled her eyes. She coughed and said, "He just called on his cell phone to tell me he was handling some errands. He must have forgotten you would be here. He said he would be back no later than five."

This wasn't the first time an elected official had stood Byrd up. He took it in stride and chose a seat against the wall where he could see all the doors. After finding a magazine from the last century, he made himself comfortable.

Byrd sat quietly reading the magazine, which featured articles about the 1996 Olympics in Atlanta, checking his watch occasionally, and waiting to see the Sheriff come down the hall.

He was surprised, at a quarter till four, when the Secretary stood and beckoned him toward the closed door to the Sheriff's personal office. He had seen her answer the phone several times but hadn't gotten any indication that one of the callers was Sheriff Haggin.

"He must have a back entrance," Byrd stated the obvious, as she opened the door and stood aside.

Haggin stood up from his desk, extended a hand, and smiled broadly. "Sorry, I was running late. A Sheriff has lots of duties that pull him in several directions."

Byrd tugged on his left ear. Byrd didn't want the politician to get under his skin. "No problem, Sheriff. Everybody has to be somewhere, and on a day like today, your office is nice and warm."

Byrd watched Haggin's expression carefully. Haggin had wanted to make a point and looked disappointed when the GBI man didn't seem annoyed. Byrd had heard Haggin frequently made appointments and then came in late. He liked people to wait on him, as a way of impressing upon them how important he was. And how unimportant they were.

Haggin sat back behind the overlarge desk and put his feet up. Byrd noted that the cowboy boots Haggin wore were an expensive exotic hide.

Haggin asked, "What can I do for the GBI today? We don't see many GBI folks around here. We like to handle our own affairs."

There was a more comfortable-looking couch behind him, adjacent to the rear door to the office, which Byrd ignored, instead sitting in one of the two chairs in front of the desk. Byrd noted the office walls were covered with all sorts of personal mementos.

"Sheriff," Byrd started, "we haven't met, but I am the GBI Agent assigned to your county. I know you have your own detectives, but I'm always willing to help out any time you might need the GBI."

"The county is sure growing," the Sheriff said, beaming. "We employ over two hundred deputies. We do our best to serve this population with the people we have. We don't call on outsiders to do the job my people are sworn to do."

Byrd smiled. "I understand. We don't come into an area to take over; we come in to help. We come any time we're needed, always happy to offer assistance."

Haggin nodded. "We are still getting things sorted out with my administration. It takes a while to get things the way you want them. But our detectives are top-notch. If you need anything here, you make sure to let me know."

Byrd sat forward in the chair. "I have never had a problem getting what I need from your records department. Anytime I come looking for copies of old cases, they are great."

"That's good to hear. How can I help you today? I understand you needed to see me personally."

Byrd nodded as he opened his folio to take notes. "That's right, Sheriff. When I spoke to you on the phone, I mentioned I was working on an investigation you might give me some help on."

Haggin screwed his face up as if he were concentrating on what Byrd was saying.

When Haggin didn't speak, Byrd continued. "But I'm not here to drum up business. I have a background investigation on someone who put you down as a reference. It seems you went to high school with him."

Haggin seemed to perk up until Byrd mentioned the candidate's name. Byrd assumed they were not close in school. Without a whole lot of preambles, Byrd began going down the list of canned questions required on a Governor's Appointment Background investigation.

Haggin sat at his desk, seeming to admire the plaques and certificates displayed on the wall.

As Byrd went through the list of required questions, he noted the Sheriff's halfhearted answers. He didn't expect the Sheriff to offer up any dirt on the applicant, whether he liked him or not.

Once Byrd had finished his list, he stood to leave. "Sheriff, I appreciate your time. Let me know if there is ever anything I can do to help you."

Haggin thought about that. "I'll sure do that, Agent Byrd. And same here, I'm always happy to help you State boys anyway I can."

"You can call me Daniel. I live here in the county, so I'd love to work around here if you need it."

"My deputies do a good job of keeping up with the crime around here, but we always are on the lookout for help." Haggin changed the subject. "I've met your Director, Buster Hicks, several times. He seems like a good man."

Byrd nodded. "Director Hicks has always treated me fairly."

Haggin pointed to a signed photo of Georgia's current Governor. "I can pull some weight with Governor Franks, too, if you ever need it. I'm always here for the voters in this county." Haggin inclined his head toward Byrd. "I assume you are registered to vote here."

Byrd nodded. "Yep, signed up as soon as I found a place here to live."

"Is there a Mrs. Byrd?"

Byrd laughed. "Just my mother."

Haggin turned in his chair to look out the window at the jail construction. After staring out the window for several seconds, he said, without looking at Byrd, "You know, the people of this county love me."

Byrd didn't know what to say to that so he stood up to leave. As an afterthought, he extended a business card to Haggin. The Sheriff took it without comment.

Byrd watched him put the card on his desk and then turned to go.

He did not come away with a good feeling about the top Law Enforcement Officer in his home county. Glancing over his shoulder as he walked down the hallway that led outside, he imagined the Sheriff throwing his business card into the trash.

Byrd winced at the cold air as he left the Cherokee County jail and made his way toward his government ride. But Byrd stopped in his tracks when he saw a green Department of Natural Resources truck parked next to him. Willie Nelson stepped down from the truck and came toward him. Willie was a Ranger for the DNR and had worked with Byrd in the past.

Byrd stuck out his hand and shook Willie's vigorously. "I heard DNR moved you down this way, but I thought you were working out of the Calhoun office. What are you doing over here?"

Willie zipped his green uniform jacket up and motioned to his truck. Byrd had no intentions of standing in the cold air for too long, and the two men climbed into the green State vehicle. Willie had left the truck running, so the heat felt good to them.

After they were both seated and the doors were closed, Willie turned to Byrd. "You're right. I have been working out of the Calhoun office for a couple of years now. Since right after your little dustup with the Gilmer County constabulary."

"I hope I didn't get you in trouble," Byrd said, looking concerned.

Willie smiled. "Nope. Just the opposite. DNR was concerned that I would have issues trying to work in the mountains. They offered me a transfer anywhere I wanted."

Byrd was impressed. "Wow. They were willing to do that?"

"Yep. My wife's family is from Woodstock, so we were able to move down here and live near them. It was a blessing to us."

Byrd felt relieved. "That's great. It sure is good to see you. I don't think I would have survived that night if it weren't for you."

Willie looked embarrassed. "I did what they pay me to do." He paused, looking around the parking lot, and then continued. "I wanted to let you know something that isn't public yet."

Byrd raised his eyebrows. "Your wife is pregnant again? Raising four kids on a State salary isn't hard enough?"

Willie shook his head. "I sure hope not. No, it's about us living in Cherokee County. I'm guessing you just met the Sheriff?"

Byrd nodded. "Yeah. He is a piece of work."

Willie nodded in agreement. "His first term has been a disaster. His deputies, who do a damned good job, are on the verge of leaving en masse. He is a horrible leader, and he probably won't get much support from the public for his reelection campaign."

Byrd frowned. "Is he crooked? Do you know about any criminal conduct?"

"That's not why I wanted to talk to you. Word on the street is he has problems in his Criminal Investigations Division. They call it CID. The guy in charge is weak as hell. They don't have any experience among their detectives and are having trouble with making arrests. And when they make one, they can't make them stick in court. If they get into something over their heads, they may try to get you involved and use you as their scapegoat."

Byrd laughed. "He won't be the first elected official to try that. But thanks for the warning."

"I didn't pull you in here just to tell you that. But I do get a lot of inside information about what is going on in the department." Willie paused again, looking around. "I wanted to let you know that a group of people in the county have asked me to run for Sheriff at the next election."

Byrd was stunned. "Would you do that? You'd be giving up your retirement and any other benefits."

Willie nodded. "The people here deserve someone who has their best interests at heart. I think I can do the job. And I would be the first Native American Sheriff in Cherokee County. What a thing for our people to put one of us in the role of the highest Law Enforcement Officer of this county. A county your people took away from my people almost two hundred years ago."

Byrd raised his hands. "I didn't have anything to do with it."

Willie laughed. "You know what I mean."

Byrd laughed, too. "And I'm happy for you. I hope you win. That would be awesome."

Willie nodded. "Any chance you might quit the GBI and be my Chief Deputy?"

Byrd looked out the car window. He liked Willie but had no desire to get involved in politics. "I like my job, and I would have a problem being tied down in a single county. Right now, I'll keep all this under my hat. I'm guessing the DNR will force you to resign as soon as you announce your intentions."

"They will. I'll be living off Beanee Weenees for a while. But it will be worth it. I think I have a good shot at the job."

"Does it cost a lot to run for office? I've never had any interest in that side of things."

Willie nodded. "I probably couldn't do it alone. The people who came to me to run are going to pay my way. Everything is above board. We have a Lawyer to make sure we are fully compliant with the election laws. I will be knocking on every door in the county if I can."

"Well, Willie, I don't know much about the current Sheriff, but I know damn well that you'll be an improvement for the folks in this county."

"I hope you can say that after I've been elected. I plan to be the best Sheriff this county has ever seen."

Byrd shook his hand again. "That's great. I wish you all the best."

Wille smiled as Byrd stepped down from the DNR truck. "You're a voter here, aren't you? Just be sure to get out and vote."

"Will do. When is the election?"

"November of next year. Not that far away. I'll probably kick off my campaign about a year from now. I'll need every vote."

"I won't forget. And stay in touch. If I had known you were living in Woodstock, I would have come by for another home-cooked meal."

"You're always welcome. I'll see you soon."

Byrd climbed in the white truck and waited for the heater to put out some warm air. He had just pointed the GBI Expedition north when he looked at his watch. It was almost five p.m. He had forgotten to call Rose back to see if they might have dinner.

He wheeled the truck into the first place he saw a pay phone, then dialed the number by heart and waited as it rang. He was hoping no one would answer and he could deal with it tomorrow, but she picked up on the second ring.

"District Attorney's Office. How may I help you?"

"Hey, Rose. It's Danny." His tone said it all.

"Some big crime come up? No time for dinner? I can tell by your voice, so what's the deal?"

"Rose, I'm sorry. I got hung up with an interview straight out of the Governor's Office and have to get it finished right away. I'm under the gun, so I need to start it tonight."

Rose was matter-of-fact. "Well, this is the only night I'm

free for a couple of weeks. We can try to get together some other time but no promises."

Byrd tried to explain. "I'm sorry. I don't want to miss the chance to get together, but I don't have a choice."

He was going to explain further when Rose interjected, "No problem, Danny. I have to go now. Some other time then."

Byrd didn't think that sounded good, but he was stuck. He was going to say something else when he heard the click of the phone hanging up.

He climbed back to his truck, glum at the turn of events. He examined the list of individuals he would need to interview for the background. *Might as well get started*, he thought. He had just pulled out of the lot when he heard a call on the GBI radio.

"Nine Oh-eight to Eighty-nine." Nine Oh-eight was the call sign for the GBI regional office in Gainesville.

He picked up the radio microphone. "This is Eighty-nine. Go ahead, Nine Oh-eight."

The voice of Machelle Stevens came back over the radio. "Can you go to Fannin County? They have had an attempted rape at one of the elementary schools. The victim is standing by at the Fannin County Jail."

Byrd's day wasn't getting any better. "Tell Fannin I have a forty-minute ETA and tell Eighteen I'll give him a call when I have the details."

Will Carver came on the radio. "This is Eighteen. Thanks, Eighty-nine. Let me know if you need help. I can have Doc come your way."

Byrd simply replied, "Ten-four."

Byrd pulled into the parking lot at the Fannin County Jail as the sun was setting. He dropped out of the seat from the big Ford and started for the back door but decided to turn back and get his overcoat as the temperature dropped with the sun.

When he got into the jail complex, he was met by Fannin County Investigator Russell James. James was a veteran of the Gulf War and a hometown boy. He was well-liked by everyone in the department, and Byrd had nothing but respect for the man.

"Sorry to drag you out on this, but this could be bad if we don't get someone in custody really quick," James said as he led Byrd to the jail visitation room that doubled as an interview room.

Byrd walked into the room and saw a pretty woman of around thirty sitting at one of the tables. She stood, turned, and extended her hand. He saw that she was also very pregnant. Byrd shook her hand, then said, "I'm Daniel Byrd. I'm with the GBI."

She smiled. "Mr. Byrd. My name is Constance Smart. You can call me Connie."

Byrd motioned for her to sit back down. Then he pulled a chair over and laid his notepad on the table. "Connie, before we get started, do you need anything? Water, or food? I'm sorry you had to wait here on me."

She shook her head. She seemed tense, which was no surprise to Byrd. Any assault can be traumatic. Sexual assaults were even worse. Byrd knew them to be more intimate and could result in lasting psychological trauma for the victim. He imagined it was worse when the victim had to protect themselves and their unborn child.

"Connie, do you mind telling me what happened?"

She sat ramrod straight and held her hands in her lap. "I am a teacher at Blue Ridge Elementary School. I stayed late today to prepare for our Winter Carnival that we hold for the kids each year." She leaned forward and said, "You see, Mr. Byrd, some of our students don't have winter clothes and we take donations and pass them to the families in need."

Byrd nodded. "I understand. And you can call me Danny. No need to be formal."

She cleared her throat. Byrd noted her breathing was slow and even, as if she were working to keep it that way. She settled back and continued her story. "I was in my classroom working on some posters. I knew most of the other teachers had gone home, but I only needed a few more minutes to finish. I guess it was about five o'clock when I heard a noise in the hall. I got up to look when this young man burst into my room and lunged at me."

Byrd was taking notes as she talked. "How was he dressed?" Byrd asked.

"White tennis shoes," Connie said.

"What else?"

"That was all," Connie said. Then she corrected herself. "Well, he had a bandana over his face. He had curly blond hair and looked like he couldn't be much older than twenty."

Byrd looked up from his notes. "That was bold of him. Was he armed?"

She shook her head. "I didn't see a weapon of any kind. He stood looking at me for a moment, and then he came toward me. But when he got close, I knew I had to fight back."

"Could he have been a student?"

"I teach fourth grade."

"Fellow teacher or somebody else who worked there?"

She thought about that possibility. "I don't think so. When he made his escape, I heard an old truck start up. It looked like it came from an old roadbed beside the school."

"Okay, what happened after he came at you?" Byrd was careful to keep his voice soft and empathetic. He wanted to make sure she knew he was on her side.

Connie blushed and looked at her hands. Byrd felt uncomfortable for her. For a victim of such a violent assault, she was holding up really well.

"He tried to put his arms around me. Well, I had just seen this mystery movie where a woman was raped and killed. The victim fought back and was able to get some of her attacker's DNA under her fingernails before she died. So I grabbed him on the cheek and dug in. I wanted to be sure the police had evidence to work with."

Byrd nodded. *She was tough as nails*, he thought. "Did you get a look at his face when you dug into his cheek?"

Connie's face was red. She coughed again. Then she continued. "Not those cheeks. I grabbed him by the butt cheek with my right hand and I grabbed his, uhm, man things with my left hand."

Byrd was trying to follow what happened. "You mean you had his testicles in one hand and his butt in the other?"

Connie began to cry quietly. "I thought he was there to kill me."

Byrd gave her a moment to recover. She was twisting a tissue in her hands and staring at the floor. Byrd waited until she looked up to speak. "What you did was exactly right. It probably saved you from a physical attack. What happened then?"

"I was twisting with my left hand."

"The testicles?" Byrd asked.

"Yes, and digging in with my right hand."

Byrd kept his eyes down. This lady was a warrior.

"What happened next?"

"He asked me to stop. It was more like begging me to stop. But I didn't trust him."

"I can't say I blame you. Go ahead," Byrd said.

"Then his voice got weaker. I started to feel sorry for him. I twisted his man things as hard as I could and then pushed him away. He ran out the door and down the hall. None of the other staff got a good look at him."

Byrd asked for any other details she may have noticed. When she finished with her story, Byrd closed his folder. "Mrs. Smart, you did an awesome job dealing with this guy. Has your Doctor checked you out?"

"I called his office. They are going to see me in the morning as a precaution. The young man didn't hit me or anything. But he did scare me to death. I'm sure my blood pressure or whatever went sky high." She sighed deeply, probably relieved to have the story out. "I would like to go home now. I have a two-year-old who is, I'm sure, running my husband ragged."

Byrd smiled. Then he met her eyes and held them. "Please let us know if you think of anything else. What you have been through is horrible. We are going to do everything we can to bring this man to justice." She nodded and looked at the floor. Byrd cleared his throat, and she looked back up. "You may feel on edge for a while. That's natural, but it will help you to talk to someone. Even if you think you don't need to, it will help."

James spoke up. "I'll make sure the DA's witness advocate reaches out to you. They will pay for a professional counselor to meet with you."

She nodded and mumbled, "Thanks. To both of you."

Byrd got her contact information for his report and then escorted her out to her car. When he came back in, Russell James was shaking his head, then said, "He picked on the wrong teacher."

"He sure did. Do you have any idea who the suspect might be?"

James nodded. "We won't be able to be sure until in the morning, but we went out to where the truck was parked. You could see the tracks. Whoever was parked there lost a few pallets off the truck when they drove off."

"Is there anything unique about the pallets?" Byrd asked.

James smiled. "They have yellow highway paint on them. We think they came from a place down in Ellijay that makes the stuff."

Byrd checked his watch. "The place is probably closed now."

James nodded. "Yeah. Without some kind of confirmation from the company, I don't think we have probable cause to make an arrest. I figured we could hit it first thing in the morning."

Byrd mulled it over. "I think we have a lot of digging to get probable cause for a warrant."

"There's a young man who lives in Mineral Bluff who works at the paint factory, and his mother is the school janitor," James said. "We think he might have something to do with this, but we'll need more to pick him up. His name has come up with some peeping tom incidents in the community where he lives."

Byrd raised an eyebrow. "Sounds like he could be our guy. Do you think he would be a danger to the community? We might pitch it to a judge, even if the PC is slim."

James shook his head. "He won't be in much condition to do anything tonight. He is probably at home with an ice pack on his crotch."

Byrd nodded. "I guess you're right about that. I'll meet you back here at around eight."

"I'll have coffee on."

Byrd walked out into the dark parking lot, wrapping the overcoat around himself, and climbed into the truck.

He was headed home to an empty apartment and couldn't shake the feeling his job was the cause of his loneliness. He wondered if any relationship with Rose was over. Or if they ever actually had a relationship. Rose was a free spirit after her divorce, which was one of the things about her that Byrd had been attracted to.

This seemed like a good night for a stiff drink. He was tired, hungry, and lonely. He turned the heat up in the truck and did the same with the radio. Byrd made his way to the Appalachian Parkway and headed for his empty apartment.

CHAPTER 4

POUNDING THE PAVEMENT

TUESDAY, FEBRUARY 18, 2003
CANTON, GEORGIA

Wilmer Westbrook was angry. He slammed his fist on the kitchen table where he sat. His wife, Gail, turned with a start.

"What in the world is wrong?" She was dressed in blue jeans and a flannel shirt since the thermostat in the house was turned down to save money. She had just turned thirty in January, and she and Wilmer were saving up for a trip to Orlando she wanted to take before they had any children.

Wilmer was less than a year older than her. As an average-sized man with medium brown hair and a beard, he wouldn't stand out in a crowd. Westbrook stood up and walked over to the back door of the ranch house and looked outside. "That fucking Mark Goodwin is holding out on me."

He leaned an arm on the doorframe looking out at the backyard. His house was off a quiet street just outside the Canton city limits. Everything behind his house was dense pine trees with the occasional oak. It gave him a sense of privacy.

"Didn't you give him several thousand dollars to get going with?" Gail asked.

He nodded. "Yes. And he paid me back for a while. He is one damned good meth cook, but he has a hard time keeping his money straight. I've propped him up and tried to let him do his thing, but the last three months he hasn't come through. And I know he's making money. I saw Krystal last week, and she was geeking to beat the band. Her hands were shaking so much she could thread a sewing machine while it was running."

Gail, being the supportive wife she was, walked up behind him and gave him a hug. "Meth people are just so unreliable. You know that. What can you do to get him back on track?"

"I thought it was a good investment. He had a plan laid out and told me how much he would pay me back every month or so." Westbrook shook his head.

"Don't people have any honor anymore?"

Westbrook frowned. "I'm not surprised. I just wish he hadn't done it. We've been drawing in good money propping up these meth cooks, and I knew at some point we'd have to make an example of somebody." He sighed, looking out the dirty window. "I just wish it wasn't Mark. I kind of liked him."

"Are you going to hurt him?" Gail asked.

Westbrook was thoughtful for a moment. "Not me. But he is going to be hurting. I can't let this stand."

Gail didn't seem convinced. "Will that do the trick? What about the other ones who owe us money? Will they think they can fuck us over?"

"I guess I'll just have to send somebody over to beat the shit out of him. Send a message." He shrugged. "I figure he's putting some money back. Can't blame him, but I can't let word get out that somebody can get by without paying me back. It's like the Bible says: fool me once, shame on me; fool me twice, everyone thinks I'm a fool."

Wilmer feared that he was not up to doing violence to Mark Goodwin. Wilmer had never been a scrapper growing up, and he knew he wasn't much with his fists. But he didn't want Gail or anyone else to recognize this weakness.

Gail was quiet. She walked back over to the sink and resumed cleaning a baking pan. "I understand, honey. I wish it didn't have to be this way, but I understand."

He continued looking out the door. "This business is built on trust. I can't take him to court and enforce any kind of agreement. All I can do is what I got to do. If word gets out that I'm a pussy, none of these guys will pay up."

As Gail continued to clean the pan quietly, Wilmer looked around the house. Their life was comfortable; the house was small, but it was nice. His truck was almost brand-new, her car was in good shape, and they had just bought a new camper trailer. He could have worked at the family hardware store, but he had hated the early hours and the stupid customers who came in and acted like he should fall at their feet to get them to spend a dime at the store. His brother had done it. Kissed mom and dad's asses to scrape by until the store was all his. But his parents had influence in the community and the Westbrook name was respected. The new Sheriff had enthusiastically taken the campaign contributions his father had offered, and Wilmer had been able to skirt the law a few times. The political connections, particularly with the Sheriff, were useful when the law came sniffing around Wilmer's operations.

Wilmer had been a partyer in high school and didn't want to be stuck in that life. He had forged a different path. He considered himself a drug user but not an addict. He invested in the drug business but wasn't like the trash his clients sold the shit to. And he really couldn't say he was surprised this had happened.

He looked for any sign of deer in the backyard. He was looking for something, some kind of sign this was the right course of action. He thought having Mark killed might send a stronger message, but Mark was one of the best cooks he knew. He shook his head and wondered what the best course of action was.

"Honey, do you think it would hurt our business if I have Mark put down?"

Gail turned around to face him. "You mean have him killed? Are you thinking you're the Godfather or something?"

He was stone-faced. "Some people call me 'Moneyman.' I like that respect."

She scowled and said, "That would sure send a message, but it would throw a kink in our long-term plans. His work is some of the best around, and you know as well as I do he can make money if he can get his shit together."

He shrugged. "I know. I wish I didn't have to deal with this. I was hoping we could have a mini-vacation this weekend."

She nodded. "Are we still planning to take the trailer down to the lake?"

He thought about his options. "Yes, I think we will. It will be good to get away. Are Melvin and Dolly still in?"

"I'll check and make sure. And Melvin said he would bring some primo weed he had. Being in the camper will be like a huge hotbox. We should be able to get really high."

He paused, thinking about getting high with the other couple. Dolly was sure a looker and he hoped things went the right way. Even if they didn't want to swap, watching them would be a real turn-on.

After a second, he dragged himself out of his reverie.

"Gail, does your jailbird cousin still work for your brother at the car wash?"

"Roger? Yeah, unless Leon laid him off. Things are always slow at the car wash until the end of March or so. I don't know everything Roger's done time for. I think one of the reasons he went to prison was for beating his wife." Gail looked at Wilmer. "But you know he's the one that's kind of slow?"

Wilmer came over to where she stood and hugged her. "He won't have to be a genius to do what I want done. I need somebody to put the arm on Mark and make him scared to hold out on me. You're right about having him killed." He raised his eyebrows. "After all, 'thou shalt not kill'! At the end of the day, I still have to live with myself. So, tuning him up a little is probably the way to go. I can't afford to do it and have something come back on me, but an ex-con might be just the ticket to set things right."

Krystal Page was pushing the little Honda hard as she headed south on the interstate toward Cobb County. Mark had sent her out to buy some more supplies. She was headed to a horse supply store near Woodstock to get a tincture of iodine. Pharmacies sold the product by the pint, but equestrian stores sold the mixture by the gallon. Then she would look for a drugstore to buy an equal amount of hydrogen peroxide. This would take a couple of hours.

Mark had told Krystal he was headed to Chattanooga to try to get another pound of red phosphorus. Their two shopping trips would take most of what they had been able to save. Extra pseudo meant they needed an equal weight in other chemicals. The two hardest to find, after the cold pills, were red phosphorus and iodine.

He had hinted to her this cook would put them in really

good shape. She didn't do any of the sales or get involved in that side of their growing business, but she knew they were in bad shape financially. Mark had spent too much money on getting good cookware and mixing bowls, the kind that could stand the heat of a cook for more than a couple of times. He was investing in the business, he assured her. His enthusiasm was contagious. Numbers and logistics weren't her strong suit, anyway. She was the Sharon Stone of the business. She imagined that her looks and allure would carry the day if she were questioned.

Her Honda was nice and warm, and when she pulled up in front of the horse store, she dreaded getting out. This was a legit business, with several employees who looked at her with suspicion. There would be no trading blowjobs at this place.

The building looked as if it had been built like something in her daddy's favorite cowboy TV show. It was a single story with a low porch across the entire length. The wood was almost gray with age.

Krystal had a sense of dread as she sat in her car glancing around the parking lot. All the other vehicles in the parking lot were either big pickup trucks or high-end SUVs. There were two Land Rovers parked right beside the doors. Last time she had been here, some big-money bitch from Alpharetta had complained to the staff about her. *Well, fuck her and her blonde helmet hair,* she thought. Krystal knew, however, that she looked and felt out of place here.

Krystal exhaled hard, switched the car off, and swung the door open. The air bit at her as she stepped out and crossed the gravel lot to the building. She pushed through the swinging doors with her head down. She remembered where the big bottles would be and made a beeline for them. She had to walk past the front counter and through an area packed with western wear and riding gear for women. *At least I don't have to wade through the hats and boots to get over here,* she thought.

There were a couple of women in the clothing department who were examining the western gear. They were dressed in tight jeans and expensive-looking tops. They gave Krystal a hard look as she passed nearby. Krystal pegged them as being the owners of one of the Land Rovers. *Don't give me the stink eye, you rich bitches. You suck dick for a living too. You just get paid in credit cards and cars,* she thought.

She grabbed a box with four big gallon bottles and struggled to the sales counter. The old man behind the counter looked her over through narrowed eyes. The equestrian supply businesses were beginning to realize methamphetamine cooks were coming to them for certain items.

"Is that all you need today?" the old man at the counter, who Krystal knew also happened to own the store, asked her.

"Yep," she said without meeting his eyes.

The man frowned. "Your horse must be in bad shape to need all this iodine. Did your vet tell you to buy all this?"

She shook her head, with her eyes still down. "We're just stocking up."

"What kind of horses do you have?" he asked her.

"The regular kind," she replied without thinking. She immediately regretted she hadn't thrown out a breed. She had watched old western movies with her dad, and had heard of Palominos and Paints. Either one would have been better than her answer.

The old man shook his head, disgusted. But what she was doing wasn't illegal. He stood quietly for a moment, then, as he put the items through the cash register, he added, "I guess you mean the kind with four legs?"

Krystal kept quiet and passed the cash over to him without waiting for the cost. Krystal then grabbed her change and lugged the jugs of liquid out to the Honda.

Daniel Byrd pulled into the lot beside the Fannin County Jail and parked. He climbed out of the Expedition and made his way inside to the coffee pot. As he was pouring a paper cup of the steaming hot fluid, Russell James joined him.

"Anything new come up?" Byrd asked.

"Nope. Are you ready to go?" James asked.

"Sure," Byrd said. He headed back out into the morning cold with Russell James trailing behind.

"Do you know where we're going?" James asked.

"Is it Roadway Paint Company? I've seen it right off the parkway south of Ellijay."

The lanky James climbed up into the truck. "That's the place."

Byrd started the truck and pulled out of the lot. As they waited in traffic, he looked over at James. "That lady last night is one hell of a fighter."

James chuckled. "She sure is. I bet our boy felt like he had walked into a weed eater."

Byrd drove and drank from the coffee cup. "This guy you think might be our suspect, has he been in trouble before?"

James looked out the window as they crossed into Gilmer County. "We have had complaints that people in the community think he's a peeping tom. We tried to catch him, but never could."

"That would fit the profile. How old is he?"

"Twenty-two, I believe."

They exited the parkway and saw the facilities for the highway paint manufacturer in sight. Byrd parked in the visitor's lot, and the two men went inside. Byrd displayed his credentials to the receptionist and she quickly rounded up a manager.

The manager of the plant was short, completely bald except for a small fringe of hair, and looked like his day had started off badly without their help. He asked Byrd what he could do for them.

Russell James spoke up. "We found several wooden pallets with yellow highway paint on them that made us believe they might have come from here. Would you have any idea how those got out of the plant? Do you sell them?"

The manager shook his head. "We don't sell those. Too much liability, according to our attorneys. But they do sound like ours. Do they have splashes or what?"

"Some splash and then you can see the rims where big buckets sat on the pallet," James offered. James pulled a Polaroid photo from his file and showed the manager.

"That would be us. Let me see if I can find out anything on how they got out of the plant." He moved off at a brisk pace and the Officers were left to stand in the lobby.

They didn't have to wait long. The manager came back at the same brisk pace. "Well, I feel better. We definitely don't sell the pallets. What we do is give them to one of our employees who lives up in Mineral Bluff. His family burns them for heat. We let him have the ones that are too old to be serviceable. He hauls some off about once a week."

"Can you give us his name?" Byrd asked.

"Sure. His name is Clancey Dixon. He goes by 'Slim.' Do you need his address? I think he lives with his mom and dad."

James smiled. "Thanks, but I know right where he lives."

The manager smiled. "Well, that will be helpful. He didn't come in today, so I guess that's where he is."

Mark had used the interstate to get to the chemical supply place in Chattanooga. He wasn't worried about getting stopped on the way up. But he didn't want to take a chance on some cop pulling him over with a pound of red phosphorus in the car. He planned to take the back roads all the way home.

He had borrowed his neighbor Old Man Grimes's rusted truck for the journey. The man next door was in his late fifties and had no love for the younger couple. But the offer of twenty dollars was enough to seal the deal. Mark just had to be back before Old Man Grimes left for the evening shift at the chicken plant.

Mark pushed the old truck hard, keeping his speed right at the limit. He was in a hurry to get there and get back. He had called his man, a dock worker at the business, and told him what he needed. The guy had set a time he would barely make, if there were no traffic issues.

He rolled into the big parking lot across the street and looked for a pay phone. He found one near the front of a discount store and called his contact. When he came on the phone, he was gruff.

"You're late, Mr. Wizard."

"I had to borrow a truck to drive from this old man next door. I'm right across the street. I can come to you, or you can come to me." Mark was breathless with anticipation.

"I'll be there in just a minute." There was a pause on the line. "And the price has gone up."

Mark felt a sinking feeling in his stomach. The dock worker was a big stupid asshole, but he was the best source for red phosphorus he had run across. Mark wasn't surprised to hear the lunkhead wanted more money. The heat was on everywhere for the ingredients he needed. "How much?"

"A hundred more."

"Dollars?"

"Yes, dollars. Are you an idiot? What the hell else would the price go up in? I don't get this shit from China. I ain't tradin' in Yen."

"Shit, man! I don't know if I have enough with me."

There was quiet on the line. "You need to come up with it then, Jack. I ain't runnin' no charity here. The DEA came by the warehouse last week givin' us the rundown on what this stuff is used for. I already had this box put aside for you, but next time it'll be a lot harder to get anything out of this place."

Mark huddled in the phone booth, counting the cash he had with him. He would be twenty-five dollars short. "I only got seventy-five. I can trade you some product, though, if you're interested."

"Don't that shit make you out-of-your head crazy? I don't want nothin' like that."

"It gives you energy is all."

"Yeah, well, I got energy."

Mark thought for a minute. "It'll also make your dick hard all night long." Mark knew meth made Krystal all juiced up and horny as hell. And after a cook, he did have lots of stamina, but it didn't count if he didn't smoke it or shoot it.

"What?"

"Me and the old lady can screw for hours. It's some kind of sex potion. It just makes you and her both want to screw like rabbits."

Another long pause on the phone. "Okay, I'll take the seventy-five and a sample of the goods. *But just this time!*"

Mark pulled a sample out of his wallet and cut off a taste for the bastard. If he didn't need the phosphorus, he would have given him a piece of cement from the parking lot. The ancient lot had bits and pieces everywhere as the light poles slowly crumbled. To someone who didn't know any better, you could pass the debris for whatever you wanted. But the guy was his best source.

Mark looked at the empty wallet and hoped there was enough gas in the old truck to get him back home.

He climbed back in the truck to wait with the engine off. The heat would have been nice, but he couldn't afford to bring the truck back empty. He didn't need to worry though. Almost as soon as he was seated in the truck, he saw the big man coming across the street toward him. Mark stood back up and waved.

The hulking dock worker was walking briskly, and his breath was condensing as it blew from his nose. He looked like a steam freight train running on a deadline.

Mark mustered his best smile. "You got it?"

The man pointed to a vacant lot next to the warehouse. "In a box over there. I didn't want nobody to see us meeting." The big man looked all around. "You never know where the DEA is hiding."

Now Mark glanced around, specifically for cars with extra radio antennas or black-wall tires. But it wouldn't have mattered if there was a fleet of marked patrol cars in the lot. He needed the chemical, and he would have run through fire to get it.

Mark handed over the cash, including the extra seventy-five. Then he made a show of pulling the jewelry bag out. He proudly showed it to the dock worker.

The man looked at the bag. The contents looked like wet sand. For a minute he seemed poised to return it. "How the hell am I supposed to use this? I ain't puttin' a needle in my arm!"

Mark shook his head. "Just sprinkle a little in food. You can give it to your wife that way. She won't know what hit her till she starts getting all sexed up. Same for you. Just like salt, sprinkle a little on top."

The dock worker seemed skeptical, but he took the bag and stuffed it in his pocket. Without another word, he turned and paced back across the street. And Mark climbed back in the truck after retrieving the box. Soon he was making his way toward US 411 for the drive back home.

Byrd and James drove back to Blue Ridge as quickly as the traffic would allow. James located the Chief Magistrate in his office in the basement of the courthouse. He swore out an arrest warrant for Clancey "Slim" Dixon. As soon as the warrant was signed, he jogged back up to Sheriff Oliver Farr's office on the main floor. Byrd was in the office with Sheriff Farr, bringing him up to speed. He had also used the office phone to call Will Carver and briefed him on the case.

James was breathing hard when he came into Farr's office. "Oliver, did Danny tell you what we have?"

Sheriff Farr stood up from behind his desk. "He did. I sure do hate that the Dixon boy did that. His family is dirt poor, and he has never been worth much to them. I thought when he got a job at the paint company, he might get himself right."

James shook his head. "I told you he was the one who was peeping in windows around Mineral Bluff. And I think he may be the one who wagged his wiener at a school bus last week down near the Gilmer County line."

Byrd remembered that James and Farr had known each other since elementary school and had graduated high school together. They could speak frankly to each other. "Damn it, Russell. I just wish we could have headed this off. I feel like I've let some folks down."

"Oliver," James responded with some heat, "there is no way we could have seen this coming. Up until now, the stuff with the Dixon boy was just talk. Trust me, we've done all we could."

Farr hung his head.

James looked to Byrd. "Do you think we need more help to pick him up?"

Byrd shook his head. "I think we'll be fine. But you might want to put something out to the Road Deputies. If they see him, stop him and call us."

"I'll let Dispatch know from your car. You have our dispatch channel in it, don't you?"

Byrd nodded as they headed out the door.

James directed Byrd past the elementary school where the attack took place and then north toward Mineral Bluff. James indicated for Byrd to turn down a rough-looking dirt road. They bounced around for less than a mile before James pointed out a small wooden house near the road. The house sat off the ground on concrete blocks, and there was a chimney belching smoke on the right side of the worn-looking structure. Piled outside the house, up near the chimney, were dozens of pallets with yellow highway paint splashed on them.

Byrd parked in the roadway, just past the house. The men climbed down without exchanging words. Byrd had worked with James enough that they didn't need to say anything. They knew the drill.

James took long steps across the front porch of the little

house. He took up a post beside the front door on the door-knob side. Once he was in place, Byrd walked as lightly as he could up to the front door and then pounded on it with his fist.

"Sheriff's Office. Come to the door, please."

They heard movement inside the house. James stepped back and was going to move around to the rear of the house when the front door opened.

A gangly man with curly blond hair stood at the door, in jeans and a heavy flannel coat. James walked back over to the door and said, "Slim, we need to talk to you."

The boy hung his head and walked back into the house. James stayed close to him as Dixon walked over to the fire-place.

"What is this about?" Dixon asked.

"Were you at Blue Ridge Elementary last night?"

Dixon shook his head, but his face flushed and his ears were beet red. "No. I don't know nothin' 'bout what hap-pened up there."

James walked close to Dixon. "You don't need to start out lying to me. This can go a couple of ways, but lying is not a good option for you today."

Dixon kept staring at the fire. "I didn't do nothing."

Byrd moved closer. "There's one way to prove it to us," Byrd offered.

Dixon turned. "What's that?"

Byrd pointed to his jeans. "Drop your pants and show us your butt."

Dixon laughed nervously. "Are y'all some kind of freaks? I don't have to show y'all my butt."

James spoke softly. "If you didn't do anything, this will prove it. Anyway, we'll check it out at the jail."

Dixon lowered his pants. When he did, Byrd saw the

lacerations on his left butt cheek. They were red and looked like they might have become infected. Byrd tugged the pants back up and held them until Dixon fastened them back.

James said, "Slim, you're under arrest for the sexual assault and sexual battery of Constance Smart. Do you understand?"

Dixon stared at the floor. He nodded and said, "Yeah. But I never meant to hurt her! I'm not a bad guy. It's just that meth makes me so horny. That stuff is the devil."

Byrd shook his head. Mountain families were being torn apart by the home-brewed meth that had become so common.

James interrupted. "Let me read you your rights first, okay?"

Byrd watched as James read from the card supplied by the Sheriff's Association. When James finished reading, he took his handcuffs and pulled Dixon's hands behind his back.

Byrd patted his pockets, finding a set of truck keys. "Do you want me to leave these keys here?"

He nodded. "Yeah, momma and daddy can use the truck while I'm in jail."

Russell James held Dixon's elbow as they started outside. "Is your mother working at the school today?"

Dixon said, "Yes, sir."

"You want me to have someone get word to her that you'll be at the jail?"

"Thanks," Dixon said as they went outside.

"How often are you using?" Byrd asked.

Slim hung his head. He muttered, "I'm usin' about an eight-ball every few days."

"Who's your plug?" Byrd asked.

"I can't tell on nobody," Slim said.

"It's Brandon Fisher, isn't it?" Byrd asked. When he saw Slim's eyes go wide, he knew he had hit the nail on the head. "That's what I figured."

Slim was suddenly animated. "You can't say nothing about Brandon. Me and him are cousins."

"Your secret is safe with me," Byrd said.

Byrd locked the gray, weathered front door and pulled it closed. Then the three men rode in silence to the Fannin County Jail.

CHAPTER 5

JAIL BIRDS

WEDNESDAY, FEBRUARY 19, 2003
CANTON, GEORGIA

I am fucking freezing, Roger Sturdevant thought as he ran water on the front tire of the almost-new sports car. He had been in prison so many years he couldn't even name the brand of the hot-looking red import. He just knew he wouldn't last much longer with these wet feet in this weather. His cheap shoes weren't up to the job he had chosen. Really, the only job he had been able to get.

Roger grew up in Georgia, but after several stays in jails around the state and one trip to the State Prison, he migrated to Texas in his early twenties. Texas turned out to be the wrong place to ply his criminal lifestyle, and the prisons in Texas were rougher than in Georgia. Roger had come back home with his tail tucked between his legs.

He looked over at his friend, or as close as he had to a friend, Ricky Cochran. Everybody called him Lumpy from his early days in the criminal justice system when he had fought a Louisiana Deputy Sheriff. The Deputy had deposited him in the county jail with lumps all over his head. From that day, he had a lifelong nickname. Like Roger, Lumpy Cochran had been a petty criminal who had worked his way up the food chain. Mostly county jails in

Louisiana, but when he sought refuge in Texas, Lumpy made the mistake of shooting a store clerk during an armed robbery. He had been lucky when the clerk survived, but the Texas Judge and jury had no love for Louisianans who came to Texas to rob honest people. He had been lucky to get twenty-do-ten in Huntsville Prison.

Lumpy had gotten out of prison on the same day as Roger in Huntsville, Texas. Roger planned to go back home to Georgia. Lumpy had no place to go, but he had some distant family in Georgia. Lumpy was willing to head east. Roger then bought a beater truck with the few dollars he had and gave his friend a ride to Canton. Lumpy liked the tag on the truck. The Texas license plate, 6677QM, had a double lucky number. They had shared the cost of gas. Roger's mom and dad had agreed to let them both stay in their house if they worked. But Roger hadn't counted on this kind of work. *Who the hell washes their car in this kind of cold*, he thought? *Rich assholes.*

Now they both had warrants from Texas for parole violation. Apparently, the folks in Texas expected them to live up to the terms of their release. One of which was to notify the State of Texas about a change of address.

Lumpy wasn't much happier. Both had cold feet and cold hands. Even when the water came out of the hose warm, it took just a few seconds for it to become cold to the touch. Lumpy had grown up in Louisiana and had no love for this cold weather.

Lumpy threw the sodden gloves to the side and stomped his feet. "Man, we need to find another way to make some money. This is bullshit!"

Roger was a born follower. Whatever Lumpy said was good with him. He had never held a steady job anyway. Then he thought of Jimmy Lee, the owner of the car wash.

As soon as they walked away, his parents would throw them out on the street. "Lumpy, we gotta stay for a little while. Otherwise, we got no place to stay. I don't want to have to sleep in my truck. And they ain't room for both of us anyway."

Lumpy shook his head. "I can't do this much longer."

Roger nodded. "Me neither. But we got to hold out a couple more days till we can get a stake."

Lumpy's eyes narrowed. "I guess you make some good points. But we need to find some money pretty quick." He looked at Roger for a reaction. "Do your folks have any money hid that you know of?"

Roger felt alarm bells go off. He knew Lumpy had claimed to have done a couple of murders while they were in prison. He hadn't paid a lot of attention to him. Lots of folks on the inside claimed to be killers. But Lumpy had a look in his eyes that made Roger think his stories might hold some truth.

Roger shook his head. "They ain't got shit. Hell, they can barely pay the power bill when it's cold like this. I don't figure they got any big stash of cash at that house."

Cochran nodded. He thought about things for a minute. "You in for a stickup?" Lumpy asked.

Roger shrugged. "I got caught in Texas trying to rob a service station. They called it armed robbery, but I just had a BB gun. I ain't afraid to do a job here if we can scope it out first. I'd want to know we had a good chance of getting away and maybe go down to Florida."

Lumpy looked around him. The line was slow at the car wash, and he didn't see anyone looking his way. He pulled a small bottle of bourbon from his hip pocket and took a drink. He offered the bottle to Roger, who took a pull.

Lumpy stuck the bottle back deep in his pocket and said, "When we get done today, we need to find a place around that would be some easy pickings."

Roger grunted. He still couldn't gauge whether he was mostly talk or not.

Roger was what people in the South called "country strong." He was descended from a long line of laborers. He stood over six feet tall, and his shoulders were broad. His dark brown hair was cut short, and he constantly wore a baseball cap with a Chevrolet logo on the front. He did so despite the fact his green and white truck was a Ford.

Lumpy was about the same height but much thinner. His hair was jet black and so thick it seldom looked groomed. In the years prior to his last hitch in prison, he had developed a taste for cocaine. He wanted the money to pick his habit back up where he left off. Lumpy was not the kind of man to easily give up on a bad habit. In fact, bad habits were his wheelhouse.

Roger picked up the wash bucket as easily as if it were empty and dumped the bucket of dirty water as they walked into the small office together to get warm. The room was about the size of a small bedroom, and the space heater in the corner kept it very comfortable. Roger was happy to be inside, at least until the next customer rolled in.

The owner, Leon Meier, was hunched over a stack of bills, examining each line. Meier was not a man born to labor. He was balding and wore thick glasses. He was about the same age as the two ex-cons, but otherwise, they might have been from opposite ends of the universe.

Lumpy moved over close to Meier and bumped his shoulder. Roger recognized the move as a prison yard attempt at domination. Meier looked up, startled. He was a born coward, but this wasn't his first time working with convicts. He knew when to take a stand and when to ignore things. He went back to his books.

Meier's eyes glanced at Roger's and Lumpy's shoes. "There are some boots in the back that you men could wear. They aren't new, but they are still waterproof. They'll be a sight more comfortable than the shoes you have on," Meier said. He turned back to his work without waiting to see what the men did.

The two ex-cons stood near the heater for a little while longer, then shrugged to each other and turned to leave. Once outside, Roger said, "Anything will be better than these shoes I got on."

Lumpy sneered. "I'd like to wipe that smile off his face. Him sitting in that nice warm office, and us out here freezing our asses off."

Roger shook his head. "We can't start anything with him. We owe him for letting us work. And he's my cousin."

Lumpy laughed. "You think we owe him for this shitty job? Freezing out here for minimum wage, and occasionally one of these ritzy motherfuckers gives us a five-dollar tip. Fuck him and the horse he rode in on, I say!"

Roger had called in a favor for this job, poor as it might be. He didn't want anything coming back on him. "You can quit if you want to, but I need a job."

Lumpy shook his head. "When I go, I want to take some cash with me."

Roger wasn't as stupid as he seemed. "Maybe you ain't noticed, but the only ones taking any cash is us. We get a tip here and there, but all the company business is on credit cards. Nobody much takes cash anymore. All that changed while we was inside."

Lumpy took the information in. After a couple of seconds, he nodded. "I guess you're right about the cash." He opened the door to the back room and saw several pairs of firemen boots. He grabbed a pair and sat on a bucket to try them on. "But cash or not," Lumpy continued, "I sure would like to beat that man's ass. He puts my teeth on edge."

Lumpy turned to Roger. "Ain't you kin to him? Ain't that how we got these jobs? How come you can't make that prick treat us better? I sure would like to take him down a notch."

Roger ignored him and found a pair of boots that fit him. *I don't have no desire to go back to prison, and I ain't about to let you fuck that up*, Roger thought.

The two stood up in their new footwear and walked back out to the car line as a black Porsche roadster pulled in.

Sheriff Albert Haggin didn't want his staff to bring him problems. He couldn't seem to get it across to his command staff that he expected them to fix things and not bring him down with talk of problems. In the short time he had held his office, he had spent a considerable time worried one of the decisions he was forced to make would come back to haunt him.

He saw himself as a political animal, not an Administrator or a Lawman. A Sheriff had to get elected and reelected. Haggin felt like he had to compromise to keep his job and didn't see the finer points of the law to apply to someone in his position. And he enjoyed rubbing elbows with people in power. He figured he could do whatever it took to keep his own power, if only he didn't have to deal with his staff. He was half listening to the man talking. Haggin was proud of himself and what he had accomplished, and the walls told the story. At least, they told part of it.

Two years, one month, and twenty days ago, he had

taken office as the Sheriff of Cherokee County. Haggin had won by a comfortable margin, running against a two-term Sheriff in a county that was growing by leaps and bounds. His predecessor had overspent his budget, buying toys for himself and his command staff, and had neglected his duties to the point the voters flocked to vote against him. But the "voting against" concept was lost on Haggin, who was convinced the voters had come out in record numbers to vote for him.

Haggin had been a Detective with the Bartow Sheriff's Office, never having supervised a soul in his life. But he was a glad-hander, with a ready smile, and he spouted platitudes like a candidate for national office. He had been willing to campaign hard to get the previous Sheriff ousted. He visited houses every evening, begging for a vote, he said would bring needed change to the rapidly growing population.

Now he had a multi-million-dollar budget and was about to move into a new, modern jail facility that would rival anything in metro Atlanta.

The trappings of the office, his official warrant of authority signed by the Governor, the pictures of him with various officeholders around the state, and the accolades on the wood and bronze plaques on the wall, were the only things keeping Haggin from collapsing in a heap on the floor. On his face was a thousand-watt smile but, in his heart, he knew he was in over his head. And no number of trophies would help.

Haggin was an average-sized man. He was fit and trim, and his hair was always immaculate. Haggin felt compelled to wear boots to make him look taller, and was self-conscious of his need for thick glasses. The county's insurance would not cover laser eye surgery, but he was putting cash aside to rid himself of the hated glasses as soon as he could.

Haggin had become more erratic as his self-doubt grew. Last week Haggin had forced one of his top Captains—the only female—to resign after his affair with her became common knowledge. He told everyone he knew, except his wife, that he was spending time with her on the couch in his office. Once the relationship became a major liability, he demoted her to Sergeant and moved her to the jail. He reminded her the jail was not a punishment. She opted to resign and look for a Lawyer but hadn't served the Sheriff with papers. Yet.

Captain Craig Weislowski, Cherokee County's Chief Investigator, came into Haggin's office determined. He was almost six-four and the Sheriff didn't like for the two to be in pictures together. Weislowski was still learning some of Haggin's habits and needs. Even though Haggin needed constant reassurance and was short-tempered in most matters, he knew Weislowski had his back.

Haggin ignored his subordinate, stood from behind his desk, and walked to the window, looking over his empire. The new jail was almost finished, and his office looked out on the concrete tower that would soon house hundreds more men and women than the county's current capacity. Haggin put his arms on the frame of the tall window, wishing his boots didn't hurt his feet so much.

"Sheriff," Weislowski started. Haggin liked to be called Sheriff. "We are having problems with our Detectives."

Haggin snorted. "Then fix it. That's what you get paid to do."

Weislowski pressed on. "None of our Detectives have any experience. And we're getting hit with burglaries every day. They don't have any clue what to do."

Haggin walked over and propped a hip against his desk, standing over Weislowski, who sat on his couch. Haggin wasn't going to take responsibility for Weislowski's problems. "What do you want me to do? I can't make the people *you* picked any smarter."

"We could try to get the GBI to help us out with these burglaries. But I figured you would rather not bring in any outsiders. I don't know what else to do."

"Do your damned job. I hired you to run investigations. Do it!"

Weislowski pushed on. "We just need some help. If my guys had a little guidance, I think we could figure it out. But the pressure is going to mount if we don't make some kind of progress. And I'm talking political pressure."

Haggin walked to his office door, slamming it shut. He didn't want his Secretary to hear this conversation. Haggin sat back down in his chair and considered pushing the button under the desk that would activate the video recorder he had installed. He decided that was a bad idea. *Some conversations should never be heard again*, he thought.

"You need to pick up the pace. If I am voted out of office, I don't have anywhere to go. The Sheriff in Bartow County has made no bones about me being done in his county." Haggin sighed. "And the same goes for you. If I'm done, you're done. We have to hold onto these jobs, or we go in the breadline."

Weislowski nodded. "I know that. That's why I'm coming to you. I don't want this coming as a surprise. We just need to get somebody in here who knows how to conduct an investigation."

Haggin squinted at Weislowski. "Why do I think you have someone in mind?"

Weislowski pressed on. "I have a guy who was fired by Atlanta PD. He was one of their best Detectives, but he got caught on a wiretap tipping off a bunch of bookies."

The Sheriff shook his head. "How the hell am I going to hire a guy that Atlanta PD fired?"

"He was a Captain. APD let him resign. He left APD and went into private investigations. He kept his training current and still has his Officer's Certification. He could go to work on day one."

Haggin narrowed his eyes. "I feel a 'but' coming on."

Weislowski looked away. "He wants to be hired as a Captain."

Haggin snorted. "That's what you are. I guess we can just let him take your job, and let you go to the jail."

Weislowski didn't care for this turn of events. He sputtered, "Like it or not, we need him. He can turn things around. And he has another Detective who is willing to come along. Two people with real investigative experience would put us over the hump."

Haggin had to admit, it was probably a good idea. He met Weislowski's eyes and held them. "What did the other one do to get run off by Atlanta? Rape a kid or something?"

Weislowski laughed nervously. "They're a she, and she got caught cheating on a certification test. The local news got hold of it and she got busted back to the road from being a Detective. She wants to get back in that game."

Haggin shrugged. "She wants rank, too?"

Weislowski winced. "I promised her Sergeant."

Haggin tilted his head to the side. "I guess we can do that, but then what do I do with you?"

Weislowski's reply was almost a whisper. "Make me a Major over Investigation."

Haggin snorted again. "Is this about getting you more rank?"

Weislowski shook his head. "No, but I want to stay where I am. I worked hard to get you elected. I would like to see things go in a direction that would mean we could both coast into a second term. Being the head of CID is a good deal."

Haggin laughed. "Damn straight. An unmarked car. Plain clothes every day. What more could you ask for?" He stuck his index finger out in mock surprise. "Oh, yeah! To be a Major."

Weislowski sat quietly.

Haggin returned to his chair. "Okay, you're a Major. But no pay raise. You can keep your job, but I'm going to hold off on any money until I see if this works out."

Weislowski stood, stretching from the tension.

"I'll let you know when they can start."

Haggin gave him a pointed look. "You haven't promised them a salary amount, have you?"

Weislowski shook his head in the negative.

"What's your plan if we have some big crime before we can get them on board?" Haggin asked as Weislowski stood by the door.

"We could ask one of the neighboring Sheriffs to give us a hand. Do you know any of them well enough to trust them to keep that out of the news?"

Haggin scowled. "No. That wouldn't work. A neighboring Sheriff isn't going to want to be left holding the bag if we have a murder. It might make them look bad. As bad as we would look asking for their help."

Haggin looked around his desk, finally finding the card he was looking for. He handed Daniel Byrd's business card to him. "In the meantime, call this guy from the GBI if we have any problems. He lives here in town."

Weislowski looked at the card. "I thought you didn't want the GBI's help?"

Haggin blustered, "Not for a bunch of burglaries, but if

we have a major rape or something, we can't afford to screw it up."

Weislowski muttered, "I got it."

Haggin frowned. "The GBI Director has said at every Sheriff's Association meeting that his agency is willing to come in and help with major crimes. This guy said they would support our staff, not take over. We might end up seeing if he is a man of his word."

Weislowski opened the door and hesitated for a moment. "You know that all of this is because I'm trying to look out for you."

Haggin laughed bitterly. "It's just a coincidence that it also helps you. We've been lucky that no major crimes have happened since we took office."

Weislowski shrugged, knowing there was nothing he could say. Weislowski's wagon was irrevocably hitched to Haggin's.

Haggin hung his head. "Get this fixed before it hits both of us between the eyes."

Weislowski left the office door open as he crossed the hall to his own desk.

Wilmer Westbrook pulled up to the car wash and parked his truck without getting in the line. Wilmer had never met Roger Sturdevant, but he wasn't about to pay his cousin-in-law for a wash. He locked the truck and walked over toward the line.

"Buddy, you need to pull your truck around here and we'll get you all cleaned up," Roger said, waving Wilmer toward the car wash lane.

Wilmer motioned Roger away from the office doors. "Are you Roger?"

"Who are you?"

Wilmer stuck out a hand. "Hey, I'm Gail's husband, Wilmer. We've met before, I think."

Roger looked Wilmer over and then pulled out a cigarette. He lit the cigarette and blew out a big cloud of smoke before he answered. "Can't really remember you. Say you're married to Gail Meier?"

Wilmer nodded. "Yeah. Gail Westbrook now. I'm Wilmer Westbrook. We met right before the last time you went off to jail in Texas."

Roger corrected him. "I went to *prison*. May not sound different to you, but it is for me. Prison makes jail seem like preschool."

Wilmer rolled his eyes. "Sorry, Your Lordship. I didn't mean to belittle your service to our country."

Roger shook his head. "Most folks don't know, I guess. You need to talk to Leon?"

Wilmer tried to draw Roger farther away from the building. "I really wanted to talk to you. About some work I thought you might be able to do. Something I need done. Something that would be a onetime thing, to make you a few dollars."

Roger took a step back. "I ain't looking to go back. I just got out and want to stay out."

Wilmer shook his head. "I don't want you to do anything that will get you back into trouble. I just need a job done that's off the books."

Roger paused as he puffed on the cigarette and tried to find a place where the wind wasn't hitting him.

Wilmer was reluctant to put the job out here if he didn't think Roger would do it. He looked all around and then back to Roger for some kind of acknowledgment. "I need a little job done that involves collecting a debt. A drug debt. I need somebody who can keep their mouth shut. I hear you might be the right man."

Roger seemed surprised but didn't immediately respond.

Wilmer continued to glance around. "How about we take a little ride?"

Roger shook his head. "I can't afford to lose this job. I need to stay here."

Wilmer thought about it. "How about I clear it with Leon?"

Roger shrugged. "Just as long as I don't get fired."

Wilmer walked into the office, still in view of Roger.

Leon stopped and looked at Wilmer. "You needin' your truck washed?'

Wilmer smirked. "I got someone for that. I just want to talk to one of your workers for a minute."

Leon leaned back in his chair. "Which one?"

"Your cousin Roger," Wilmer said.

Leon shook his head. "He's on the clock. Talk to him tonight, after he gets off."

Wilmer frowned. "I've got things to do. Why can't I just talk to him while he's standing around with his thumb up his ass?"

Leon glanced out the window. Then he shrugged. "You're right. He's not doing a damned thing right now, but I pay him to be here when a customer shows up."

Wilmer threw a fifty-dollar bill on Leon's desk.

Leon smiled. "You've got him for thirty minutes."

"You pay him a hundred an hour?" Wilmer shouted.

Leon turned back to his work. Without looking up, he said, "Tick tock."

Wilmer Westbrook stomped out the door and motioned to Roger to follow him. "Come on. We're on the clock. I need to have you back in twenty minutes."

Roger followed Wilmer to his big four-wheel-drive truck and climbed into the passenger side.

Wilmer fired up the truck but didn't move. He turned

to Roger. "I have a couple of friends I have been loaning money."

Roger sat in the passenger seat, staring straight ahead.

"Are you hearing me?" Wilmer asked.

Roger just nodded. He didn't look over at Wilmer, who figured it must be some kind of prison thing.

"I don't want them hurt. I just want somebody to go to their house and get my money. I figure you can help me with that. Act tough, holler at them some, and get me my money."

Roger might not have even heard him. He continued to sit, staring out the windshield, watching the trees whip around in the bitter wind.

After what seemed like five minutes to Wilmer, Roger asked, "How much?"

"He owes me five thousand. If you can get it, I'll give you two hundred for your trouble."

Roger shook his head. "I get one upfront. If this thing doesn't work out, I still get paid the other hundred. Whatever money I recover for you, I get ten percent of."

Wilmer Westbrook was shocked. He didn't think Roger could think that far ahead. He wouldn't underestimate him again. "How 'bout I give you one upfront and then another one when you bring me the cash? That cook might not have any money at his house, you know."

"Or he might have a king's ransom stashed. You wouldn't be willing to pay anything if you thought there wasn't money there," Roger observed.

Roger turned to face him for the first time since they got in the truck. "Five hundred if I get all the money he owes you. Partial amounts, which would be out of my control if they spent your money, would still cost you ten percent." Roger waited for a reaction. "I won't do any rough stuff, just some yelling and what not? You're not going to expect me to do any harm?"

Wilmer shook his head, insulted. "Absolutely not! These are people I know. And he is one of the best meth cooks around these parts. I just want them to pay up and then keep paying me like he promised."

"Okay," Roger relented. "One hundred up front, and one hundred after we do the deed. But, that's one hundred on the back side whether there is any money or not."

Wilmer grunted in agreement.

"Does he have guns?" Roger asked.

"Not that I've ever seen. He lives with a girl named Krystal. I'm kin to her."

"Don't them meth labs blow up from time to time?"

"Well, I mean, they can. But I'd just wait till he ain't cookin'. I hear you can smell the shit cooking from a mile away."

"What does it smell like?"

Wilmer made a sour face. "Cat piss and chemicals."

Roger cracked the door. "When do you need this done?"

Wilmer gave it some thought. "Are you still living with your mom and dad?"

Roger nodded.

"I'll see you there Friday after you get off from work, then I'll take you over and point out the house they live in."

"I get off at three this Friday. I got to work early the next day."

"Okay, I'll be at your folks' house by three thirty."

Roger grunted and dropped to the ground without using the step rail.

Wilmer watched him move off. He knew that Roger could be talked into doing what he wanted. He just wasn't sure he could do it alone. Wilmer sat with his truck in reverse for a couple of seconds, trying to gauge his options. He was still pondering what his options might be as he took the ramp onto the four-lane highway home.

CHAPTER 6

WE HAVE A DEAL, LADIES AND GENTLEMEN

FRIDAY, FEBRUARY 21, 2003
CANTON, GEORGIA

Mark Goodwin took off the painter's mask he had been wearing for a decade and a half it seemed. He had been up for over twenty-four hours and was nearing the end of what he thought would be a legendary cook. He didn't know anyone around the area who had cooked this much meth at one time.

Meth manufacturing was not a complex series of chemical reactions but was more closely like cooking a cake from a recipe. It's just that the ingredients are much more likely to kill you. Mark had been extra cautious as he worked through each part of the cooking process. But his pots and cooking vessels were only good for about a couple of ounces at a time.

It was taking about two hours per cook to get to the point of having meth oil, the golden-brown honey that was the next-to-last step. He looked at the assortment of plastic containers of brown liquid scattered around the kitchen. The oil was pure meth, but users weren't interested in the honey. They wanted methamphetamine hydrochloride.

That was the brownish powder that came after he bubbled sulfuric acid through the honey.

Mark had worked straight through, being extra careful with his mixing. He knew that he should have enough ephedrine to make over two pounds of finished product, but he had to take into account the mistakes he would make along the way. Still, as he looked over the kitchen, it appeared he would be very near the two-pound mark. He estimated the yield would be about twenty-eight to thirty ounces. Enough money to buy them out of trouble and a night or two in Pigeon Forge!

Goodwin was parched and realized he hadn't had anything to eat or drink in several hours. He opened the worn-out refrigerator that had come with the rented trailer. He took out a jug of water and drank from the bottle. After several seconds of chugging the cold water, he sat down in a kitchen chair. It was only then that his exhaustion hit him like a wall.

"Krystal," he called out, "I'm done with the last cook. All we've got to do now is salt it all off." Krystal had been staying clear of the kitchen to avoid any of the dangerous phosphine fumes created during this part of the process. But she had been willing to drag trash in large bags out onto the back porch of the trailer.

"Thank God!" Krystal exclaimed. "Do you think it will be okay if I put my clothes back on?"

He peeked around the corner and saw her wearing a cheap raincoat and nothing else. He was puzzled. "Sure, I guess. Why did you take them off to begin with?"

"I didn't want my good clothes burned again. You remember what happened last time I helped?"

Mark nodded. He had added the iodine too quickly to the hot red phosphorus. The result was hundreds of red burn spots on his and Krystal's clothes. "Sorry, babe."

"No problem. But this coat blew open one of the times I was dragging trash out, and that old man you borrowed the truck from is watching us like a hawk now. I guess he's hoping he'll get another peek."

"Shit!" Mark said. "The next part will stink to high heaven. We don't need him sniffing around, literally, while we finish this all up." He pointed at the golden liquid in the various plastic vessels.

The final reaction was a simple two steps and, other than the occasional chemical burn, painless. But the gassing off that occurred when the table salt, aluminum, and acid reacted with the meth oil smelled awful.

Mark thought out loud. "I had hoped to do it out on the back porch after midnight. But the old man stays up late a lot of nights."

"Can we do it inside?" Krystal asked.

Mark shook his head. "It'll stink this place up so bad we won't be able to stand it."

Krystal was pulling on a pair of jeans. She checked the clock on the wall and realized it was only mid-afternoon. "What else can we do?"

Mark gave it some thought. "Our best bet is to wait till all the lights are out in his trailer, then we can finish most of this batch up. It might take us two nights, but I think we can get this ready to sell by Sunday."

Krystal had put on her bra and a flannel shirt. "I was hoping we could get this done sooner. I sure would like to get the heat back on in this trailer."

Mark understood. He was dressed in a T-shirt and jeans, and his feet were bare. He hadn't wanted to ruin any of his clothes, either. "Baby, I promise you that we'll be in high cotton when we get done with this last step. I'm going down to Marietta to meet a guy who has the money to take a pound of this off our hands."

"How much will we clear?" she asked.

"We should clear between eight and ten thousand dollars for a pound of finished product. We can pay Wilmer Westbrook what we owe him and get some things for ourselves."

"Is a pound all that came out of all that pseudo?"

"Nope. All that running around you did got us enough to make about another pound of meth. We got lucky with being able to use some clean ingredients. All this ought to be rocket fuel. Them boys in Marietta are going to love it."

Krystal smiled. She liked to think she was part of the process. She twirled around. "Damn, it would be good to go out to eat at a drive-through or someplace. I sure could use something besides canned soup."

He grabbed her and pulled her tight. "Baby, I'll take you out to get a steak when we get this work sold."

She kissed him hard. "While we wait till that old man goes to sleep, let me show you how I got all that cold medicine."

Her eyes were twinkling, and she reached down to rub his crotch. *She was around enough of the cooking process that she got high*, Mark thought. *And meth makes her horny as hell.* The thought crossed his mind that maybe she had intentionally exposed herself to their neighbor. She had a great body even though the meth was starting to make her rail thin. She had approached him about stripping when their finances were at their lowest point, and he knew she got off wearing her cutoff shorts in the summer.

He smiled back at her. *Why not*, he thought, *we have the whole afternoon.*

Daniel Byrd passed the gold dome of the Georgia capitol as he headed east on Interstate 20 toward GBI Headquarters.

He was pushing his Expedition as hard as he could without attracting a traffic cop or a trooper. Traffic was light by Atlanta standards, but he knew it would be a parking lot trying to get home.

When he pulled into the main parking lot, he looked around for Will Carver's Crown Victoria. He saw it parked near the front. He hustled across the lot and through the large main doors. He showed the guard at the security desk his credentials, was passed a proximity card for access, and then turned to go into the section of the building occupied by the Investigative Division.

Before he made it more than a couple of steps, the guard called out. "Agent Byrd!"

Daniel turned toward the man behind the desk. "Yes, sir?"

"You're supposed to go up to the Director's Office on the second floor."

Byrd shook his head and mumbled under his breath. "Aw, fuck."

Byrd felt his stomach muscles tighten. He had hoped he could avoid the second floor. Machelle, the Office Secretary for Region Eight, had called him on the radio and said to meet Will Carver at headquarters around two p.m. Byrd checked his watch. He was fifteen minutes early, which meant he was five minutes late.

He waited for the elevator with one of the Crime Lab Scientists who occupied the other side of the building. She was from the serology section and had helped him luminal a death scene for blood last year.

"Agent Byrd," she said, "What brings you to the epicenter of all knowledge?"

He laughed. "I always wondered what this big building was. I'm happy to know it has a function." He extended a hand. "Nelly, isn't it?"

They boarded the elevator, and Byrd pushed the button for the second floor.

"That's me. Are you in trouble? Usually, the Agents stay away from the second floor."

The question didn't help the rumble in Byrd's tummy. "I don't know for sure. But I would rather be somewhere else."

She nodded with understanding. They boarded the elevator and made the short trip to the second floor. Once the door opened, Nelly turned to her left and Byrd went right, toward the Director's Suite.

He took a deep breath and walked into the first office. A middle-aged woman dressed in a smart-looking navy-blue suit sat at the desk just inside. Byrd assumed she was the gatekeeper for the Director. Rita Weaver was the Director's Administrative Assistant. She sat, back straight, watching the door that was the gateway to Director Hick's office. Rita was the epitome of professionalism. Not recognizing Byrd, he assumed, she stood and said, "May I help you find someone?"

"I was sent up here. The guy at the security desk said I was to go to the Director's Office."

He got a forced smile. Rita stepped around her desk to guide him back into the hall. "I'm sure you misunderstood. The Director is in a meeting right now. Let me see what we can do for you."

Before she could usher Byrd out the door, Director Quinin "Buster" Hicks stepped out of his private office. "It's okay, Rita. He's expected."

Hicks stuck out his hand to Byrd. They shook, and Hicks said to Rita, "This is Agent Byrd. He's down here from the Gainesville office for a little meeting."

Rita nodded and smiled at Byrd. This time the smile was genuine.

Byrd followed Buster Hicks into his private office and around to a couch. Hicks pointed Byrd to one end and then sat himself at the other.

"Thanks for coming, Daniel," Hicks said.

"My pleasure, I guess. Machelle made it sound like this meeting wasn't optional."

Hicks laughed. "I guess I've forgotten how I felt when I got called to the boss's office. You're not in any trouble."

"This time!" Byrd interjected. Byrd tried to relax, without much success.

Hicks must have sensed the discomfort. "Do you prefer Daniel or Dan?"

"Either is fine, sir. My friends call me Danny. My business cards and credentials say Daniel. But I also answer to Dan."

Hicks laughed. "Thanks for clearing that up."

Byrd tugged at the knot of his tie. "Call me Dan, Director."

"Well, Dan, how are things up in the mountains?"

Byrd was careful not to say anything that might get him in trouble. "Busy, sir. We have a pretty heavy caseload of violent crimes in our area. But I really like that there is plenty to do."

Hicks nodded. From what Byrd knew, Buster Hicks was a Georgia native who had joined the FBI after a hitch in the military. When the Director's position came open, he threw his name in the hat. Hicks was still learning the challenges of being in an appointed position in an agency that should stay as far away as possible from politics. "I didn't realize what kind of autonomy GBI Agents had when I was young. I got out of the Army and went back to college. I got my law degree and then applied to the FBI. I didn't have anything to compare the job to. Knowing what I know now, I would have applied to the GBI."

Byrd was incredulous. "The FBI wasn't a good job?"

Hicks shrugged. "Sure, I had a great time. But we had to run everything we did through an Assistant US Attorney. We couldn't get a search warrant signed without their okay. And God forbid if you wanted to make an arrest. No, you have far more latitude to do your job than any Federal Agent."

Byrd nodded. "I guess I haven't worked around any Feds enough to see that side of things."

Hicks looked wistful. "I busted my ass at Quantico. Came out fourth in my class. Second on the firing range, and tops in physical fitness. With my background, I figured I'd get a posting with lots of criminal work. That didn't happen, and I got sent to Denver to work on a background squad that spent most of our time clearing people for a top-secret facility in the mountains."

"Really?" Byrd said. "That sounds interesting."

Hicks shook his head. "Nope. Not even close. Mostly work that could be done sitting in front of a computer. Then you go out and talk to all the neighbors and ask the same questions over and over again."

"You couldn't get out of that?" Byrd asked.

Hicks continued. "I did, after two long years. Got transferred to a violent crimes squad. I liked the work, but as a Federal Agent, like I told you earlier, you have to get the US Attorney's Office to approve anything you do."

"I guess that slows you down," Byrd said.

Hicks looked grim. "It does. We had a twelve-year-old girl who was kidnapped. We thought she was with her dad. Turned out that wasn't so. We were slow to get on the real kidnapper's trail, so by the time we figured out where he was, we were playing catch-up. We got him cornered in a motel outside of Durango. We surrounded the place but didn't know which room they were in. The manager was trying to figure out the room number for us, but the place was full of tourists. The SAC wanted to get a master key and go room to room, but the Assistant US Attorney told us there was no way we could justify breaking into all those rooms. The government would be liable. We'd all lose our jobs."

Byrd was aghast. "With a kid in danger?"

Hicks nodded. "Damn straight. The SAC was pissed. He called the local Sheriff who did what needed to be done. He and his folks went door to door. It took a while, but they found her. She had been raped and strangled. The ME said that she had only been dead about an hour. We sat on our hands for almost three hours. She died while we waited."

"I guess heads rolled over that. Did the US Attorney get in trouble?" Byrd asked.

Hicks's eyes were moist. "Nope. The SAC got transferred, and his career was over. Anybody on the scene that day who was a supervisor got jammed up for their part in calling in the locals. The rest of us got letters of censure from the Bureau."

Byrd shook his head. He started to comment when Will Carver rushed into the room. "Sorry, Director. I got hung up downstairs with Inspector Mason."

Hicks shifted gears and the spell was broken. Byrd hadn't anticipated that Hicks would ever let his guard down with a Street Agent.

Hicks sat back down on the couch, while Carver dropped into a vinyl-covered guest chair. Carver looked at Byrd and said, "Good job on that assault in Fannin the other day. You handled that very well."

Director Hicks nodded. "I heard about that. Quick work and a good arrest, it sounds like." Hicks shifted in his seat. He pointed at the little refrigerator in his office.

"Do either of you want a water or a soda? We are waiting for the Attorney General to get here."

Byrd and Carver declined the offer.

Within minutes, Rita Weaver stuck her head around the door. "Sir, Attorney General Villegas is here."

A compact bundle of energy that was Georgia Attorney General Jonathan Villegas came into the room at a run, shaking hands with everyone. All but Byrd seemed to be friendly with him.

"General Villegas, this young man is the reason for this meeting. He is Agent Byrd," Hicks said, by way of introduction. The man acknowledged Byrd and shook hands again. Byrd wasn't sure if Villegas was "General" because he was Attorney General, or because, Byrd knew off the top of his head, he was a General in the Georgia National Guard.

"Well, Agent Byrd, these folks here at the Bureau have put you in one hell of a bad situation."

Byrd wasn't sure what the General was referring to. Will Carver spoke up. "General Villegas, we haven't briefed him on the talks we've had about Judge Pelfrey."

Villegas nodded. "We might as well get everything out on the table then. And all of you can call me Jon. No need to be formal, right, Buster?"

Hicks smiled. "Jon and I studied law together at UGA. He was a little younger than me, but we had several classes together."

Hicks stood and closed his office door, and then addressed the group. "Daniel is in a precarious spot right now. He continues to be assigned to an area where one of the Superior Court Judges, and many of her political allies, would like nothing better than to see him strung up by his balls, at least figuratively. And the Judge will, no doubt, become aware that we are looking into her."

Carver leaned forward. "Jon, she has called Byrd a liar in open court and tried to get his testimony impeached before he even testified. We can't let her act like this. I think we have a duty to address her actions."

Villegas nodded. "I read the report that y'all sent over to my office. I also got a copy of the latest report this morning. That's why I thought we should meet."

Like watching a tennis match, Byrd sat, turning his head left and right as one or the other of the high-ranking officials talked about his life and career like he wasn't in the room.

Hicks sat back down. "I have no intention of letting her run an Agent out of the office he's assigned to. But I know that it will be hard to get her canned. She just got reelected."

"*Elected*," Carver interjected. "She was appointed in 2001. She ran for the office for the first time last year."

Hicks leaned back. "That just makes her surer of herself. She won a popularity contest."

Carver pointed at Byrd. "Danny isn't a dummy. He has been taking notes anytime he and the Judge had any interaction. And I'm with the Director. The GBI doesn't need to let a Judge, who should be in jail right now, push one of our people around."

Villegas nodded. "I've spoken with the new Governor about this situation, but he doesn't feel like he is strong enough to go after her this early in his administration. He took office only a month ago, and the legislature is in full swing. He isn't going to battle over this matter without more to go on."

"I understand the Governor's reluctance, but our man is hanging out here in the wind," Hicks said.

"And I'm on notice," Villegas said. "If they lock him up on some bogus charge, we will be all over it. They won't be able to hold him long. We'll have Lawyers beating down the courthouse doors, filing motions, and using the full force of the authority of the State."

Byrd finally interjected. "But I would be in jail while this is all going on?"

"Not for long," Villegas said.

Byrd stood up. "But in jail. Not being released by some order from you or the Governor?"

"I can only do what the law allows. But I don't think Judge Pelfrey is completely off her rocker. She knows the State would come after her if she put you in jail on trumped-up charges."

Villegas seemed convinced. But Byrd wasn't. "You haven't looked into her eyes. When she is tweaking, she is liable to do anything."

Hicks touched Byrd's arm as Byrd sat back down. "Danny, we are not going to leave you hanging. I have spoken to a Judge on the Court of Appeals. If it comes to it, we will have a writ issued to have you released. It's already drawn up, and ready if something goes wrong."

"I don't look good in orange," Byrd mumbled.

"What was that?" Villegas asked.

Carver redirected the conversation. "So from the perspective of the new Attorney General, what can your office do with the Judge?"

Villegas shook his head. "Not much. She is a loose cannon, but she hasn't broken any laws. She probably will at some point, but I can't go after her for calling a GBI Agent a liar."

"What will it take?" Hicks asked.

"More than this," Villegas replied.

"How much more?" Hicks countered.

Villegas shrugged. "Hard to say. We just have to keep an eye on her."

"Can we get her drug tested?" Byrd asked.

Villegas shook his head. "She won't consent, and we don't have anything close to enough for a search warrant. Hell, we'd probably have a hard time getting a Judge to sign a search warrant for a drug test if she showed up on the bench high."

The room went quiet, and Byrd figured the meeting was winding down.

"Gentlemen," Hicks said, "we're just going to keep talking in circles. Will, can you explain our strategy to Dan while I address another matter with the AG?"

Byrd and Carver stood and made their way outside. They rode down the elevator in silence, dropped their proximity cards at the security desk, and then made their way to the parking lot.

Once in the open, Byrd turned to Carver and said, "Why do I feel like my pants are unzipped?"

Carver squinted into the sun. "Danny, you know you have a target on your back in her courtroom. Just stay on your toes. She knows that we're gunning for her, too."

"But it looks like her gun is a lot bigger than ours right now."

"She can't run over the State. She's a big fish in a shrinking pond."

Byrd winced. "Which makes me an even smaller fish. The kind bigger fish swallow whole."

Carver smiled. "Even more of a reason not to run off on your own. We have more than one Agent in the GBI."

Byrd didn't see the humor. But he nodded and said, "Will, I'm sorry to be a problem for you. I really am."

Carver shook his head. "Buddy, you're a challenge, not a problem. You have it in you to be a great Agent. You just need to work on trusting people, letting them help you."

Byrd met Carver's stare. "Thanks. I probably need that more than either one of us knows."

Carver put his hand on Byrd's shoulder. "Call Doc. I know that you and he are close and he'll come out to help you anytime you need it."

Carver turned toward his car. Byrd stood in front of the building, looking up at the windows to the Director's Office. Byrd was surprised that Hicks had opened up to the young Agent like he had. Maybe Hicks sensed that Byrd needed to hear what he had to say, too.

CHAPTER 7
ROAD TRIP

FRIDAY, FEBRUARY 21, 2003
CANTON, GEORGIA

Wilmer Westbrook pulled into the driveway of Roger Sturdevant's house. He was a few minutes late but figured Roger was looking out the window, expecting him. He didn't want to deal with Roger's parents anyways, so he sat in his truck with the engine running.

Roger burst through the door of his parents' carport. He walked quickly toward Wilmer's truck. He was wearing warm clothes and had a knit hat pulled down on his head. Wilmer was happy to see that he was thinking ahead. No point in making it easy for anyone to identify him in Wilmer's truck.

Wilmer watched Roger climb into the passenger seat and buckle up.

Wilmer was driving like an old man, signaling far in advance and staying five miles under the speed limit. Not being noticed was difficult enough in Westbrook's big truck.

Roger had a piece of scratch paper and was taking turn-by-turn directions as they traveled. Thanks to Wilmer's pace, he didn't have any trouble with street signs. Wilmer was impressed that Roger had thought to take notes.

Roger and Wilmer had barely spoken during the journey, but as they neared the place they were looking for, Wilmer's mood changed. He leaned into the steering wheel, focused ahead and concentrating. They turned off the state highway and were traveling on a major county road when Wilmer asked, "How much do you know about meth cooks?"

Roger turned to look at Wilmer. "Not a lot. I served time with a fellow who had cooked some meth. He would charge folks to teach them how to do it. I heard later that the ones who tried his recipe blew themselves up. Seems like he forgot to teach 'em a step or two."

Wilmer nodded, never looking away from the road ahead. "Those boys that are good cooks can make some dynamite meth. But they need front money to buy all that poison they use to make it. That's where I got involved. They can't do business for shit. It takes folks like me who can bring money to the table. I'm like a banker."

Roger seemingly listened.

Wilmer continued with his explanation. "I got a couple of boys that I give seed money to so they can cook. Some are better than others, but this tweaker we're talkin' about here is a master at turning all these different chemicals into meth. His stuff is pretty close to one hundred percent pure. Strong stuff."

Roger nodded. "Do you ever use his stuff?"

Wilmer cut his eyes over. He mumbled his answer, "I don't touch that stuff. I mean, I might have tried it but it ain't my thing." Wilmer drove on without speaking. When they turned off the road onto a dirt route, Wilmer slowed even more. "Roger," he said as he stopped the truck, "these folks are okay, but people have to know that they got to pay me back. Otherwise, I'm out of business." Wilmer turned to Roger. "My old man loaned money to a man who wanted to open a garage. The feller was one of the best mechanics in this area. But he didn't know shit about running a business. He fixed every car that came into his shop as good as new, but he ran that business into the ground."

Roger spoke up. "What did your old man do?"

Wilmer laughed. "Nothing. He just let it go. From then on, everybody in the community who needed money came to my old man with their hand out. Old man never got over that boy, the mechanic. He wanted to do good, but it turned out bad for everybody."

Roger said, "I guess you don't want to go down that path?"

"No, but I want this cook making money. I don't want him thinking he can get away without paying, but I really just need you to put him in the right state of mind. I don't want him hurt, just scared." Wilmer looked at Roger with an ugly smile. "Maybe tie him up and screw his girlfriend in front of him. She's hot."

Roger shook his head. "That ain't my thing. I'll not misuse a woman like that."

Wilmer shrugged. "Your call. Just an idea."

Wilmer let the truck roll forward, and then they turned down a path with several trailer homes along it. Wilmer pointed at the third trailer on the right as they drove on past. When they got to the dead end, Wilmer maneuvered the big truck around, and they rolled slowly back out. They crawled past the rear end of the little Honda, and then, Wilmer stopped on the road.

Wilmer climbed down from the pickup and walked up to the door.

A common side effect of meth use is the need for repetitive motion, whether it is as simple as scratching or turning a screwdriver to running a vacuum cleaner over the same spot for hours or, in this case, sexual intercourse.

Mark Goodwin and Krystal Page were having meth sex. Meth sex is distinguished from other sex by the required intensity. This is not romantic sex where couples connect on an emotional level; it is mechanical and visceral, with the participants seeking stronger and stronger stimulation.

Mark didn't like to be in a position that kept him from looking out the living room window. Other than the energy, a major meth side effect is paranoia. And when he saw Wilmer Westbrook's truck roll by the front of the house, he immediately disengaged and ran to the front window. Standing in the shadows to the side of the window, he shouted, "Shit, Krystal! I think that's Wilmer. He must be coming for the money we owe him!"

Krystal jumped up and joined him. "He didn't pull in. Are you sure it's him?"

Mark nodded. "That's his big ol' truck. I'd know that thing anywhere. It looked like there was somebody else with him."

Krystal looked worried. "You reckon it's him and Gail?"

Mark shook her head. "Looked like another dude."

"You don't figure he came to put the strong arm on us, do you?"

Mark hit the side of his head with his fist. "Damn it. If he would wait just a couple more days, we could pay him off."

Krystal stood back from the window. "You think he might take product?"

Mark shook his head. "He never touches it. He uses a dab, now and then. But he won't get around any sales or anything like that. That's why I have to go to these guys in Marietta to move it."

Suddenly, Krystal jumped backward and tried to hide behind a couch. "He's coming back. It's the same truck!"

Mark dropped to his knees and crawled to the edge of the window. "Shit, it is!"

"Should we go out and try to get a little more time?" Krystal offered.

"Buck naked? No, but we should get dressed in case he pulls up and wants to come in."

Mark was grabbing his pants and shirt when the truck slowly rolled down the dirt path and stopped behind Krystal's car.

Krystal ran into the bedroom and slammed the door as a bang came from the front door of the trailer.

Mark cracked the door and peeked out. "Hey, Mr. Westbrook."

Wilmer stood with his hands on his hips. "We need to talk. Can I come in?"

"Krystal and me was just playing around and she ain't decent."

Wilmer shrugged. "Don't matter much. It's not any warmer in there than it is out here."

Mark laughed a nervous laugh. He held the door as Wilmer shifted from one foot to the other on the stoop.

"When do you plan to pay me, Mark?" Wilmer asked from the front stoop.

"I should have the money on Monday. I promise. I can pay you everything I owe you." Mark had no intentions of letting Wilmer inside.

Wilmer spat on the porch. "There ain't no way you can come up with all that money. And if you got that much coming, why don't you just give me a payment now?"

Mark shuffled his feet. "We got enough pseudo to make a big batch. We are flat broke now, but I got a deal to come up with your money by Monday. Tuesday at the latest!"

Wilmer shook his head. "Mark, I want some good-faith money today. You have got to have something."

"I can give you product if you want?"

Wilmer's laugh was harsh. He squinted through the crack in the door. "I reckon I'll just have to get the money some other way. I guess I'll have to take it out of your hide."

"Sir, I'll get your money as quick as I can. I'll see if there is any way I can get it sooner. I swear to you—I don't have nothing here."

Wilmer turned on his heels without another word. He stomped back to his truck.

Mark saw the other man in the truck watching him and waited until the truck pulled away and headed back toward the main road.

Krystal was pulling on her panties when Mark came in and pointed at her other clothes. "Let's get dressed and go down to Marietta. We'll get this deal going, and then we can reach out to Wilmer and pay him back."

"I figured you'd want me to stay and guard the house," Krystal said.

Mark shook his head. "No, him skulking around here makes me uneasy. We'll lock everything down and set this deal in motion. Even if Wilmer was to come back, he won't destroy our work. But if you were here alone, he might hurt you or have somebody do it for him."

Krystal suddenly looked scared. "Have you got a gun?"

Mark opened a drawer and pulled out a black pistol. It was boxy with things that protruded from the top. "What kind is it?" she asked.

He dropped it on a table. "It's like a toy. They're called airsoft guns and shoot little plastic pellets."

Krystal laughed. "If somebody comes here to do us harm, you might want to hide that."

"Why?"

"Cause all those corners sticking off that thing will make it hurt like hell when someone sticks it up your ass," Krystal replied.

She finished dressing and grabbed her puffy coat. "Let's go. The sooner we get this deal done, the sooner we can get Wilmer off our backs."

Mark looked all around as they walked outside, which made Krystal even more scared. They bundled into her Honda, jacked the heat up, and headed toward Marietta.

As they turned onto the pavement, Wilmer finished telling Roger what Mark Goodwin had said.

Roger was worried. "I guess he must have some cash stashed. But what if he told you the truth?"

Wilmer shouted, "He's a lying son of a bitch! He has money enough to be cooking meth I could smell it. I want my damned money!"

Roger remained silent and nodded.

Wilmer calmed down after he got his anger off his chest. "Firm hand, but I want them still working. Got it? No broken bones or house fires." Wilmer adjusted the heat as he drove. "Me and my wife are going to be camping on Lake Allatoona. Do you know how to get there?"

"Sweetwater? Is that what you're talking about?"

Wilmer nodded. "You can just tell the Ranger at the gate that you'll be visiting me. They don't ask for names."

Roger sat quietly. Then he said, "How soon do you want it done?"

"They have neighbors close by," Wilmer said. "I'm figuring y'all go in late Sunday night. Everything should be quiet. Get the cash, and then come back to the campground. I'll have the rest of your money."

Roger thought about what he needed to do. He didn't

want to split the money with Cochran, but he had a feeling this was a job for two people. Roger didn't like complicated situations. "I need the front money now."

Wilmer cut his eyes over. "You'll get it when you come to the campgrounds."

CHAPTER 8

THE BALL STARTS ROLLING DOWNHILL

SATURDAY, FEBRUARY 22, 2003
CANTON, GEORGIA

It was just a few minutes after midnight, and Mark Goodwin was back in the painter's mask. He was also freezing his ass off, he reflected. He was dressed in a couple of sweatshirts and two pairs of jeans. He had on rubber boots and rubber gloves, but the temperature had dropped enough that his hands and feet felt like big hunks of ice. When he could, he would stomp his feet and try to warm his hands under his armpits. He was happy that the wind had died down.

There wasn't any better choice though. He was busy gassing off the meth oil he had made. He needed to do it after the neighbors were in bed and not likely to notice the horrible rotten-egg smell of the acid as the meth processed. And he couldn't afford to waste any of the precious oil. Since Wilmer Westbrook came by the trailer, Mark knew his time was running out. He had already gassed off enough oil to be able to filter out three or four ounces of meth. He would just have to tough out the cold until he had at least enough salted out to make a pound of finished product.

Mark intentionally kept the back porch lights off and worked with a little battery-powered light he wore on his head. When he shook the gas can he had modified, the acid gas would bubble up through the meth oil. Shaking the gas can was the only way to get the hydrogen chloride to expand out of the can, down the hose he had fabricated, and then cause the reaction, which settled out the powder that was marketable. But the process took its own time, and the cold didn't help.

Krystal was inside, bundled up as well, looking out the windows to make sure the neighbors weren't roused by his work. She was closely watching the front of the house for a few minutes, then would move to one of the back windows. The inside of the trailer was blacked out so that her night vision wasn't impaired.

Mark had been at it well over an hour, and Krystal would tap on the windows occasionally to alert him to something going on in the neighborhood. Each time it had been a false alarm, but Mark wasn't taking any chances. He would extinguish the light and stand still, looking and listening.

He was intently working at the plastic tubs of oil, trying not to get his face directly over the container, when Krystal tapped on the window again. Mark decided this was the time to take a break. He guessed he could finish off enough to filter out a good solid pound before daylight. The filtering could be done inside the house and wasn't as dangerous for him or Krystal.

He opened the back door as quietly as he could and moved inside. He hugged Krystal tight, enjoying the warmth her body provided. She hugged him back.

"How much longer do you think?" Krystal asked.

Mark tried to focus on warming up. He thought it over,

and then said, "I'm guessing about a couple of more hours ought to get us over a pound. That'll get us enough to go down to Marietta and get paid. I promised him at least a pound."

"I thought you were figuring we could make more money off of this batch?" Krystal said.

Marked nodded. "I did think we could, but we needed to get some money in hand to pay off Will. I went along with the price, but he said if this round was fire, he would pay more for the next round."

Krystal nodded into his chest without looking up. "Are we going to cut the next batch?"

Mark laughed. "You're catching on. Yeah, we'll use those horse vitamins to cut it by about a quarter or a half. That'll give us more money out of the next batch. And it should put us in good shape until we can get more cooking materials. That seems to be getting harder and harder."

Krystal hugged him tight again when she felt him shivering. "I want a fur coat once we're rolling in the money from all this."

Mark tried to get his body under control. He knew he was working against a clock to get the gassing off done before the neighbors woke up. "We will be, Krystal. This will put us better than we've ever been. I've just got to grit my teeth and get out there and finish."

She nodded. "Can I do anything else to help you?"

"Tomorrow, I want to look for some food coloring."

Krystal didn't understand. "What?"

Mark smiled down at her. "I'm going to get some food coloring out of the kitchen when I get everything filtered out and dried. I got the idea to color the product and give it a name."

Krystal seemed confused. "What will that do?"

Mark laughed again. "Nothing. Except folks using this Red Thunder or Blue Lightning, or whatever we end up naming it, will be something people will come back asking for. Ol' boy will want more of that colored meth, and we'll be able to push the price up."

Krystal looked up at Mark. "You sure do know a lot about this business."

He shrugged. "I know I've got two more hours of freezing my ass off before we can move back in here and finish things off."

"Can we plug up the space heater for this last part?"

He shook his head. "I wish. We'll be filtering the dope out of acetone, which is very flammable. But that part won't take as long as this salting. Once we get all the stuff that'll burn outside, we can cut the heat on."

She spoke through chattering teeth. "Okay, baby. I know it's worse on you than it is on me."

Mark dreaded going back out for the next round, but he could see light at the end of the tunnel. He figured he would be able to finish the batch by daylight. About two more hours in the cold, then about another hour or so inside the house to filter out the powder from the acetone. They would give the meth a full day to dry. By Monday morning, the meth would be ready to package.

Mark rubbed his hands together and stepped outside.

Wilmer Westbrook finished hooking the little camper trailer to his truck. The sun was up and the air was warming. The weatherman on TV had forecast that warm air was moving up from the Gulf. He couldn't believe the temperature by the end of the day was predicted to be in the sixties. He planned for the foursome to sit outside around a campfire as long as they could.

He wore rough old work gloves to protect his hands as he tightened the hitch and hooked the safety chains in place. He was excited to get the trailer down by the lake where they could party without so many prying eyes this time of year. And he would have several people who could swear he was at the lake if Sturdevant made a mess of things and Mark called the cops.

Wilmer was thinking about the prospects for the next few evenings. He had known Melvin Foster since high school and they had enjoyed smoking weed and partying since then. Melvin hadn't gone far after school and ended up working as a local handyman. He did odd jobs around and earned enough to be able to smoke a little and hang out. His current girlfriend, Dolly Baker, was a different story. She was smart, had just finished college, and was looking for a place to settle. She was a knockout, and when Wilmer and Gail had hinted about some sexual hijinks, she had not shut them down. Just thinking about Dolly in the tight jeans she was in the last time they met caused Wilmer to get excited.

He finished hooking the trailer and used his truck to pull it out onto the driveway where they could load up their provisions. He opened the side door of the camper and let the cool, fresh air get inside. He took a moment to grab a fast-food bag that had been left on the floor and then turned to go inside.

Gail was busy packing up lunch meats and bread to eat and a small assortment of soft drinks and liquor. She had been excited to leave since they had gotten up this morning. She was rushing around the kitchen, packing things up like a madwoman. They planned to stay at the campground through Tuesday, but she was packing enough food for more than a week.

Wilmer came up behind his wife and kissed her on the neck. "Are you as excited as I am about getting down to the lake?"

She turned and kissed him on the lips. "I sure am. I've been watching Melvin, and he has one hell of a body. I can't wait to get him snuggled up in the camper."

"You sure are horny," Wilmer remarked.

She laughed. "Don't lie to me and tell me you haven't imagined getting Dolly naked. She is hot. And a little bit of meth will light her fire for sure." Wilmer had taken some meth from Mark over a year ago when he gave him his first loan.

Wilmer nodded. "It'll get the party started."

Gail turned back to her packing. "Tonight will be a good night!"

Wilmer started gathering supplies he thought they would want. He pulled out their box of toys and some lubricant as well as a roll of aluminum foil and put everything into one of the boxes Gail had started. He planned to use the foil and a butane lighter to hot rail the meth.

Gail tossed a package of plastic cups into another box she had started with tequila and bourbon. She threw in a saltshaker and a couple of fresh limes. Since the little trailer didn't have much in the way of heat, she topped the boxes off with warm blankets.

Wilmer came back into the room and dropped a couple of automatic pistols in the box with the alcohol. Gail looked puzzled. "What are those for?"

"In case I need to give one to your knucklehead cousin. He probably won't be able to get his hands on one."

Gail shrugged. "Are you going to have Benny watch the house?"

Benny McGee was Wilmer's half-brother and frequently

sat at their house when they were away. "Yeah, I think we should. These damned meth-heads we do business with would rob a dead man's body if they thought there might be a dime in the pockets."

Gail continued packing. "We don't want to come home to an empty house."

Wilmer walked over to the phone on the wall. He dialed Benny's number and waited for him to answer. After several rings, he heard a muffled "Hello?"

"Can you come over here and stay at the house while we're gone to the lake?"

Benny mumbled a response that Wilmer took to be in the affirmative.

"We're leaving in a couple of hours. Get your ass on over here as quick as you can."

Benny hung up the phone without responding.

Roger Sturdevant had dreaded this moment since he first realized he would need Lumpy to help him get Wilmer's money.

Roger had seen Lumpy Cochran respond violently to situations in prison. He was quick to anger and quick to strike out. And when he fought, he wanted to destroy his opponent. That wasn't unusual for anyone he had met in prison, but Lumpy seemed to carry things further. He needed Lumpy to be the strong and silent menace standing behind him while he explained the facts of life to the cooker.

Roger just couldn't figure out how he alone could manage to threaten this meth cook and not get blindsided by the man's girlfriend. His first hitch in prison had been for getting in a fight with his girlfriend. He wanted to change the TV channel, and she said she liked the show that was on. He figured he paid the rent and could watch what he wanted. When she got in his face, he hit her in the mouth and she went down. Roger had turned around and was adjusting the TV set when she hit him in the back of the head with a black cast-iron frying pan. He served nine months on a ten-year sentence. Since then, he hadn't liked the idea of anyone getting behind him. And he didn't enjoy fried foods as much.

Lumpy was sitting in the room, in the basement of Roger's parents' house, that they called their living room. The room was largely unfinished, but there was a TV near the outside wall. Lumpy was trying to find a movie to watch but seemed disappointed in what he saw as options.

"Roger, I sure do wish your folks would get a movie package we could watch down here. It'd be nice to have some skin movies. I know some of those pay channels have them at night."

Roger ignored him. "I need some help with a job."

Lumpy stopped turning the channels. "This job we got cleaning cars is about all I can stomach. I want something that will earn us some good money."

"The job I got lined up will give us some serious folding money."

Lumpy sat up. "What do I got to do? Have you got a stickup lined up?"

"I got a deal where we go collect a debt from this guy who is a meth cook. All we need to do is threaten him a little and then get his money. Should be pretty easy," Roger said.

"What does it pay?"

"I'll pay you seventy-five for your trouble. Just to stand around and look mean."

Lumpy was not convinced. "That ain't a lot of money for this kind of job."

"I'm only getting two hundred for the job," Roger said.

"Well, if this ol' boy is a big-time meth cook, I'll bet he's got more money than that around his house. And there's bound to be meth around. We should be able to move that stuff for a couple of bucks, too."

Roger nodded. "He won't be in a position to say anything."

"So, why are you doing me a favor? You afraid to do this yourself?"

Roger rubbed the back of his head. "He has a girlfriend who lives there. She might could try to jump me while I'm collecting the money. I just need you to cover my back."

"Is the plan to beat them down? Send a message kind of thing?" Lumpy rubbed the knuckles of his right hand. "I don't mind a little rough stuff. Maybe we can work his girl over, too."

"If they give up the money, then no. We just collect the debt. If they give us trouble, we are supposed to rough them up a little. But the man paying us wants them to still be able to cook meth. No serious beating."

He has a weird look in his eye, Roger thought.

Lumpy stood up. "Fucking his girl won't keep him from being able to cook meth. And them meth girls like to get it on. The ones I've been with like to get smacked around while you give it to them. I bet she might like for us to throw some her way."

"The man was real particular about not hurting these folks. He made a big deal of that," Roger said. "If we rough up the girl, it'll be to get them to talk, that's all."

Lumpy nodded. "Okay. But if he holds out, are you going to give the beatdown?"

Roger nodded. "I've done some beating when I was owed money. But the man says it won't be necessary."

Lumpy seemed disappointed as he turned back to the TV. "When do we do it?"

Roger didn't want to go into all the details. He figured the less Lumpy knew, the less chance he might try to double-cross him somehow. "They have neighbors close by. The guy that hired me wants us to go in late Sunday night. Everything should be quiet, and he says he has an alibi planned. We spend fifteen or twenty minutes in their trailer, get the cash, and then are back home in time to go to work on Monday."

Lumpy shrugged. "I guess it don't make no difference." Then he had a thought. "Did you get any money upfront?"

"We pick it up before we do the job. We're meeting them Sunday afternoon at the campgrounds down by the lake. He'll give us the front money, and then we'll go collect."

Lumpy flopped backward on the couch. "Shit, I sure could use a bottle of bourbon right about now."

"Don't worry. This job should be a piece of cake. Then we can splurge on a good bottle. I've never had any good whiskey."

Lumpy laughed. "I have. I spent some time up in Kentucky and Tennessee in my younger days. I even bar-tended for a couple of weeks at a honky-tonk that was near Fort Campbell. Them soldier boys would come in on payday with a pocket full of money and start drinking like they were dying of thirst. I sold them good bourbon until they were good and drunk, then I started pouring the rotgut. I learned a lot about bourbon and whiskey at that shithole. When we collect, I'll pick us up some good bourbon. Maybe we can pick up some ladies, too."

That thought got Roger's attention. He had no desire to force sex on the cook's woman, but he sure could stand to have some love from a willing partner. Roger hadn't been with a woman since before he went to prison. Most of his relationships had been problems, but just before his last stint in prison, he had hooked up with a woman who prostituted herself at a truck stop in Calhoun. She had sex with him and he helped her pay her bills. He had found that to be just right for him, no commitments. Getting tangled up with a woman had always been a problem.

Roger thought, *It sure would be nice to lay with a woman after so many years.* Then, without thinking, Roger rubbed the back of his head again.

"I'm gonna check with my old man and see if I can borrow enough money to put gas in my truck for Sunday," Roger said as he turned and started up the stairs.

Wilmer backed the little camper trailer into the lot the Park Ranger had assigned them. The spot was little more than a level area beside the one blacktop road around the park. He planned to leave the trailer hooked to the truck so they wouldn't have to worry about anchoring it down.

Gail was helping him park by criticizing how he was backing the truck, how he guided the trailer, and where he stopped. Wilmer ignored her and got the trailer in what he thought was the best spot.

Gail climbed down from the big truck and looked the trailer over to see if it was level. She shrugged, as if saying it would do. Wilmer lowered the legs that kept the camper stable and stood back to admire his work.

Wilmer opened the camper door and swung it wide. The camper would sleep four people, but they would need to know each other pretty well. *Fresh air would help the experience*, he thought.

Daniel Byrd stepped out of the shower when a loud bang went off. Without thinking Byrd crouched and grabbed his hip looking for the pistol, only to find his shampoo bottle, which had fallen from its shelf. His heart pounded, and when he looked down, his hands were shaking. Even though he denied it, after two years, Byrd was still suffering from the effects of seeing a Judge kill a Sheriff and then himself. Loud noises were the worst.

At least the dreams were coming less often. It had been over a month since he had jumped out of bed in a cold sweat from one of them. He had not discussed his problems with anyone for fear that he could get into some kind of trouble. And besides, he knew people who had been through worse experiences and still got through each day.

He shook off the shock and thought back to this evening. Although he had tried to call Rose a couple of times, leaving messages on her machine, he hadn't heard anything back. So when, last Friday, a Canton Police Officer Byrd had met for coffee a couple of times had asked if he wanted to go out with her and some friends, he said yes. Sure, it would be mostly cops, but he was excited to meet some new people. And Doc had agreed to catch any calls in his area for the night. Canton Police Officer Montana Worley had agreed to pick Byrd up and would be arriving soon.

Byrd grabbed a clean pair of jeans out of the closet and picked out a flannel shirt. Once he had his clothes on, he checked himself in the mirror. His hair was as long as it was when he was working drugs, and he thought about getting a cut. He would try to do that next week, he thought. He did note that his clothes seemed a size too large, probably due to his daunting work schedule.

He pulled a leather jacket on over his shirt and checked to make sure his handgun was covered. He was standing by the door looking in the mirror when he heard Montana knocking.

Byrd looked through the peephole, then swung the door open to let the willowy brunette Cop into his apartment.

She was dressed in jeans, a Western shirt, cowboy boots, and a leather jacket. She looked Byrd up and down. "We're going to a Western bar, so you need some cowboy boots," she remarked.

Byrd looked embarrassed. "I don't have any."

"Wha-a-at? What kind of cop doesn't have cowboy boots?"

Byrd shrugged again. "The kind who always wore deck shoes undercover."

It was her turn to shrug. "Okay, but you'll be the only one in this place without any."

"Where are we going?"

"A place called Buckboard in Smyrna. Ever heard of it?"

Byrd nodded. "Sure."

Montana nodded. "Good. A guy from Woodstock is playing there tonight—Mark Wills?"

Byrd shook his head. "What are some of his songs?"

"'Jacob's Ladder'? Or one of his new ones is 'Wish You Were Here.'"

"Oh yeah. I've heard both of those on the radio. He's from Woodstock?"

Montana nodded as she led Byrd outside. "He grew up in Blue Ridge, but he lives in Woodstock now."

"Wow! Do you know him personally?" Byrd said as he locked his door.

Byrd squinted as the setting sun seemed to burn his retina. He followed Montana down the steps and over to her little blue Nissan. "No, but he and his family do lots of charity events in the county."

She whipped the door open and flung herself into the driver's seat. Byrd was more cautious as he worked himself into the passenger seat. She fired up the car and started to back out of the parking space.

Byrd busied himself getting the seat adjusted. "Who else is coming tonight?"

She kept looking straight ahead, smiling. "Nobody."

"What happened?"

"Everybody flaked out at the last minute." Montana continued smiling. "If you don't want to go, you don't have to."

Byrd was suddenly flustered. "No. I mean, could we get something to eat first?"

"Not going straight for the alcohol?"

He shook his head. "I skipped lunch. If we're going to a bar, I'd like to have something on my stomach. It's been a while since I could go anywhere and have a drink. I'm glad to have a designated driver."

"Do you want to eat at a drive-through or sit-down?"

"What time does the show start?"

"Mark is on at seven," Montana said.

"We should probably do fast food. Where would you like to go?"

Montana slapped the steering wheel. "Damn!"

Byrd was startled. "What?"

"Where to eat is the hardest decision of the day!"

They both laughed, and Byrd started to relax. A little.

CHAPTER 9
EVERYBODY IS GETTING BUSY THIS SUNDAY

SUNDAY, FEBRUARY 23, 2003
CANTON, GEORGIA

It was just after midnight when Montana and Daniel pulled into the parking lot of his apartment complex. She swung her Nissan into a space and switched it off. She sat staring straight ahead. Byrd wasn't sure what to do.

After several seconds he said, "Do you want to come in?"

Montana smiled. "I thought you'd never ask."

They got out of the little car and walked across the parking lot to the stairs to Byrd's apartment. He fished his keys out of his pocket, noting that the temperature had warmed up significantly. *Georgia weather!* he thought.

He unlocked the door and held it open for Montana to come inside.

"What did you think of Mark?" she asked.

"He was good! And he had a good band with him. That's the most dancing I've ever done, I think."

She laughed. "Well, then it was worth all the damage you did to my toes."

He flushed. "Sorry."

She laughed. "I'm joking. Do you have any hard liquor here?"

"Sure," Byrd said as he moved over to the pantry. "What would you like?"

"Do you have any bourbon?"

He reached onto the shelf and found a bottle of Buffalo Trace. He turned it toward Montana. "Will this do?"

She nodded. "Showing off that big money the State pays you?"

He smiled, a little embarrassed. He had bought it for the night he and Rose would finally get back together. Since that possibility seemed dimmer every day, he decided to go ahead and crack open the bottle. He poured a couple of inches into an old-fashioned whiskey glass and passed it to her. She took a sip and winked.

"Worth every penny, but are you saving it for a rainy day?"

"Nope, just a good day." He poured himself a glass and took a long drink. He had only had a couple of vodka-rocks at the show and wasn't feeling buzzed. Montana had been careful to drink only water since a DUI charge could cost a cop their career.

When Montana saw him take a long drink, she finished hers off and extended the glass for another. He poured the golden liquid slowly, watching for her reaction. She let him pour the glass more than half full. When he stopped, she said, "I'm a glass-half-full kind of girl. So, don't let it get half empty."

He was confused. "Aren't you worried about driving home? I don't want to see you get in any trouble."

"Well, what can we do about that?"

"I don't mind getting you a taxi. How far away do you live?"

"I just live across town," she said as she moved closer. "But I was hoping we could hang out for a while and get to know each other." She put her arms around his neck, not spilling a drop of the bourbon.

Byrd flushed again. "Well, that works for me." He put his arms around her, and they kissed. He moved his hands down her back to her rear end.

"Whoa, wild man. This is our first date. I'm not that kind of girl."

Byrd took a step back. "Sorry, I didn't mean to be too pushy."

"Yeah, I'm not going to bed with you on the first date. I'm fine with sleeping on the couch."

"Nope, I've got a perfectly fine bed in the spare room." He changed the subject. "Where does the name come from? Montana?"

She laughed and shook her head. "I could tell you it's a family name. That there's this long story about my Mexican heritage. But that's a crock. My dad was assigned to an airbase in Montana when I was born."

"You're a military brat?"

"Yep. My sisters, Alabama and Virginia, are too."

"Really," Byrd seemed skeptical.

She laughed again, harder this time. "No, there's just me and my brother, Ronny." She slapped his leg. "But I had you going, didn't I?"

She took a gulp from the glass, sat it on his coffee table, and standing on her tiptoes, she grabbed his face with her hands. She kissed him and pulled him to her.

After a long kiss, they came up for a breath. Then he ran his hands up into her long dark brown hair and looked into her eyes. "Well, I have to say this is a good way to get to know each other," he said with a smile.

Krystal and Mark were still up at three in the morning.

They had finished off the last of the salting-out process and had taken a sheet from the bed and strained the meth till it was just slightly wet. It took both of them to hold the sheet up over a bucket and pour the salted-off meth into the middle of the bedclothes.

They were both nude since they had found the cold air made their skin itch less. The itching was a byproduct of the meth working its way out of their bodies, and the meth made their body temperatures rise uncomfortably high.

Mark would then wring the sheet around and force the remaining acetone from the mix and let it drop into the orange bucket. They had compressed and set aside just over two pounds by Mark's estimation.

When the last of the meth had been squeezed as dry as possible, Krystal took the wet sheet and threw it in the old washer in the hall of the trailer. Then she started cleaning up the mess they had made. She was not a particularly tidy homemaker, but the meth had given her the fidgets.

Mark sat down at the table and began the process of putting the finished work into ziplock bags and weighing it out. He was higher than he had been in a while, but the process of bagging the meth up helped him stay focused. He was feeling the need to scratch his whole body and so he twisted in the kitchen chair to try and control himself. He had seen Krystal squirming and knew she would soon be asking for sex.

Krystal finished up the cleaning and pulled a garbage bag into the living room. She was preparing to drag it out on the porch when Mark stopped her. "Hey, put something on. We don't need that son of a bitch next door paying us any more attention than necessary."

Mark knew she didn't mind giving the neighbor a show in the state she was in, but a nosy Mr. Grimes could be a problem right now. She grabbed a sundress and pulled it over her head. "Okay. You're right, he may still be up."

Mark nodded. "He works nights, and on his off days, he sits up watching TV till dawn. We don't need him sniffing around right now. And I mean that literally."

She laughed. "I must be immune to the smell now. I guess it would stink like hell if he got close to the house."

Mark went back to work without commenting. He was barely aware of the smell himself. But he knew it was there.

By six in the morning, he was finished with the packaging. Krystal helped him take the bundles and put them in a cardboard box. They stacked them as neatly as they could. The damp product didn't want to take any particular shape and tended to slide around. Once they had all the bags of product placed in the box, they looked down at all the time and exertion they had expended. They had put every ounce of effort they could muster into this cook, both Krystal and Mark working around the clock. The bags of wet, dirty tan meth, looking for all the world like moist playground sand, looked like money to them. Mark decided he would add the food coloring tomorrow.

Mark looked at the bags once more and then turned to Krystal. She was tweaking harder than usual. She was rubbing her neck and pulling at her hair. Krystal, true to her promise to her mother, had an eight-ball of meth she had cut out of the batch first. The eighth-ounce bag was smaller than a ping-pong ball, and she had twisted the cellophane bag closed. She grabbed the bag and stuck two fingers into the wet drug. Then she rammed a finger in her mouth, sucking it clean. Mark could see the surge hit her almost immediately. Her face and chest flushed with the increase in blood flow, and her eyes dilated.

Then, with a mischievous look, she stuck the other finger

into Mark's mouth. At once he tasted the bitter, sharp taste. He closed his eyes, and in seconds he felt the rush. He was aware of every nerve in his body. He made both hands into a fist and started hitting himself in the side of the head. He had the urge to pull his hair out by the roots, but he fought it off.

His eyes were still closed when he felt Krystal fondling his nipples. Suddenly he was overcome. He pulled Krystal around toward the couch, pawing at her breasts as they went. He was smothering her with kisses as they both lay down. She was literally clawing at his skin, and he saw that his chest was bleeding from one of her attacks. She growled deep in her chest and started to buck as though she wanted to throw him off. Mark knew they would be at it for a while.

Byrd heard Montana moving around but opted to lay in bed a while longer. He could hear her wandering around the kitchen searching for the materials to make coffee. Soon the kitchen was filled with the aroma of brewed coffee.

The coffee smell had been enough to rouse Byrd out of bed. He wandered into the living room in a wrinkled pair of pajamas he found crammed deep in a drawer. "Glad to see you found the coffee pot."

"Welcome back to the world. You seemed to crash pretty hard about two this morning."

Byrd rubbed his head. "I think the bourbon caught up with me. But I'm right as rain this morning." He poured a cup of black coffee and joined her at the table. He sat with his back to the wall, even in his own apartment. "You look pretty as a picture this morning."

"I appreciate the kind words, but I look like I haven't put on makeup and slept with my face on the pillow of a strange bed." She seemed to be comfortable with her appearance, something Byrd liked about her.

Byrd laughed. "Those strange beds are killers."

The night before, they had talked about their paths to getting into law enforcement. Byrd talked about the freedom he enjoyed as a GBI Agent and the complex cases he most enjoyed. Montana talked about the hurdles she faced to be accepted in a man's world. They talked about college and how they had grown from the experience. She had graduated from Kennesaw State, and her parents had supported her through college. Byrd had worked his way through North Georgia College by being a radio operator for the Georgia State Patrol.

When Byrd had mentioned the State Patrol, Montana had exclaimed, "You worked for God's Special Police?"

He was confused.

She laughed. "GSP. God's Special Police. All troopers are aloof and arrogant."

Byrd countered, "They just have a tough job to do. Around here there's plenty of help, but out in the country, they have bailed my ass out of trouble more than once. Out in the sticks, you have to be your own backup. I've worked in places where the locals can be as crooked as the crooks."

After he said it, he regretted it. He was feeling the bourbon. He agreed that cops in the rural parts of the state were paid less, were less educated, and might more often fall prey to crooks with bad intentions. After that, they had dropped the line of discussion, kissed on his couch for a little longer, and then gone to bed.

"Did you rest okay?" Byrd asked. He was careful where his eyes went as she sat in one of his dress shirts. He wasn't sure how much she had on underneath.

"I slept fine. Better than those old beds at the police academy."

"Which academy did you go through?" he asked. Georgia had several regional academies, in addition to the main facility in Forsyth.

"I went to GPSTC." She pronounced it "jip-stick." The Georgia Public Safety Training Center in Forsyth.

He laughed. "That's where GBI School is. We all hated that place. The dorms were Spartan, to say the least. And they use inmates to clean the rooms."

It was her turn to laugh. "Don't I know! I was getting out of the shower after PT and a convict came into my room."

"Damn! That would make me a little paranoid about being in my room alone."

She shook her head at the memory. "I screamed at him and he ran right out. It was our last week, and when I reported what happened, they moved the guy out of the prison there on campus. But I'm glad that part of my life is over. Now when I have to go to GPSTC, I rent a room out of my own pocket."

"The city won't pay for it? The GBI sure won't."

She leaned back in the chair. "I guess all governments are cheap."

Then she put her coffee cup down and stood. "I need to get home and changed."

He nodded. "Do you have to work today?"

It was her turn to nod. "I'm working a split watch today. I go on at noon and work till midnight."

"I didn't know Canton PD did a split shift."

"It's something my Sergeant is trying. It works out pretty well as far as your activity goes. But it's tough to get anything done on the days you have to work. You pretty much get up, get dressed, and go to work."

"Would you like for me to fix you any breakfast before you go?"

"Are you much of a cook?"

Byrd shrugged. "I went to a class where I learned how to cook meth."

Montana raised an eyebrow. "Coffee is good enough to keep me awake, Julia Child. I'll grab something on the way home."

"I understand," Byrd said. "But don't rush off."

She stood, leaned over, and kissed him. They both had coffee breath.

"I've got to go."

She went into the next room, dropping his shirt on the floor. She was wearing a black bra and panties. Byrd watched her pull on her jeans and shirt.

As she walked out, she said, "But we can get together again soon. Maybe we can do a date where we can spend some quiet time together. Have you heard of a movie called *Maid in Manhattan*? It came out before Christmas. It stars JLo." She hesitated. "That's Jennifer Lopez."

Byrd said. "I know who JLo is. I haven't seen that, but I'm always up for a movie."

Montana thought for a moment. "Or we could do dinner and some dancing. Can you slow dance better than you line dance?"

Byrd looked at his feet. "Everything is relative. I'm better at slow dancing than most other kinds. I just kind of rock back and forth and turn in a slow circle."

Montana frowned. "I guess I need to get some steel-toed evening shoes."

Wilmer Westbrook was not in a good mood when the sun hit him in the face. Melvin Foster and Dolly Baker had shown up late on Saturday afternoon and had immediately started up a fatty of primo West Coast weed. In no time, they were all high and drowsy. While they all ended up in their underwear, there were no sexual hijinks last night. He had floated the idea of a little meth shared around, but everyone was too mellow to want to get all spun up. The couples ended up sleeping on beds at opposite ends of the camper. This was their second time inviting a couple into the camper for some sexual exploration. The first time had been a bust, with awkward tension and then early departures.

Wilmer gave up on going back to sleep. He rolled out of the little bed and pulled on a pair of shorts and a T-shirt. Then he stumbled toward the kitchen area. He found breakfast supplies in the refrigerator and the cooler they had brought. He threw several strips of bacon on the tiny stove, and when he was finished, he used the grease to scramble eggs in the same skillet.

Gail followed him after a few minutes and began a pot of coffee. He noticed that Gail was only wearing a loose gown with nothing on underneath. He walked up behind her and put his hands on her breasts. He kissed her neck and nibbled her ear. He knew she loved to have her neck kissed in the morning. She leaned back into him and moaned.

When they heard movement in the other sleeping area, Gail moved away from Wilmer. Dolly and Melvin came out of the nook where they had slept. Dolly had on a robe and Melvin had pulled on a pair of his shorts. Wilmer watched Dolly stretch and wake up her body and realized she was naked under the robe. He saw that Gail was staring at Dolly, too.

Wilmer served up the eggs and bacon on paper plates and sat them on the table by the door. Dolly and Gail slid into a bench together, which left Wilmer sitting by Melvin. He poured up coffee for everyone and sat down across from Dolly. "Everybody sleep good last night?" Wilmer asked the table.

Dolly kept her eyes down and nibbled on the food, barely sipping the coffee. She seemed to want to say something, but was uncomfortable.

Gail leaned over near Dolly. "I slept great. The first night out in the camper is the best. What about you, Dolly?"

Dolly smiled and put her right hand in Gail's lap. "It was fun," Dolly said. "But today could be more fun." She laughed and looked up at Wilmer with a sly smile.

Wilmer smiled at Gail. "I might have told Dolly and Melvin that you had something that would spice up our time together. They're both interested."

Wilmer looked to Dolly, who was now slumped on the bench. He saw that her breasts were almost completely uncovered as the robe bunched up. Suddenly, Wilmer felt Dolly's bare foot in his crotch. She was wiggling her toes. He saw Gail's foot pushing into Melvin's groin in a similar manner. Melvin leaned his head back and seemingly enjoyed the massage. Wilmer decided that was the best course of action, too.

Dolly was slumped over next to Gail, and now everyone at the little table had their eyes closed. Dolly quietly said, "I hear around town that you might have some of the hottest meth in the country. I'm guessing that would help us all get in the mood, Will."

Wilmer laughed. "I might be able to come up with something. Is that something you and Melvin have done before?"

Melvin nodded without opening his eyes. "We use a little now and then. I never did a needle though."

Wilmer gave Dolly a pointed look. "How about you? How do you use it?"

Dolly opened her eyes to narrow slits and poked her tongue out. She ran her tongue slowly around her lips. "I put a little taste in my mouth. Usually with gum or something to take the bitter taste out."

Wilmer smiled. "Meth has a low melting point. I think it will do more for your coffee than cream."

Reluctantly, Wilmer let Dolly move her foot away from him and he stood and walked to a cabinet in the front of the camper. He took out a small bag of methamphetamine and walked back to the table, grabbing a measuring spoon from a drawer on his way. He sat at the table and measured out a small mound of the dirty-looking powder and dropped it into his coffee. He did the same for Gail. Then he turned to Melvin. "How much have you used before?"

Melvin looked uneasy. "I've used a little. I'm up for whatever."

With Melvin's assurance, Wilmer measured him a similar dose of the stimulant. Then he looked to Dolly. She simply nodded and motioned her right thumb up. "Make it a hot dose. That helps me get hot."

"You sure?" Wilmer asked.

"Damn sure. I used a little while I was working my way through college."

Wilmer was surprised. "What kind of job did you have that you could get high at work?"

"I worked at a club in Marietta. I started out serving drinks, but then I moved to stripping when I found out how much money you could make."

Gail was sipping her coffee, letting her stomach absorb the meth. "Did you turn tricks, too?"

Dolly shook her head. "No, I never did that. But I needed to be jazzed up to dance a whole shift. I started bumping a little at work. I had used cocaine, but it seemed like the coke would only get me pumped for one set. We danced a dozen sets a shift. I tried meth and it kept me going and got me all hot and bothered. I didn't turn tricks, but I was happy to rub myself all over these guys. And a few times I got so turned on that I masturbated on stage. Word got around that I was a hot number on stage and suddenly I was making lots of money. But every man in the place wanted a piece of me, and I got tired of being pawed and pinched."

"What's it like to undress in front of a room full of men?" Gail asked. Wilmer saw that Gail's eyes were looking at Dolly with a hunger he hadn't seen in a while.

"When I started dancing, I was scared to death. The other girls told me to relax and enjoy the feeling you got from having so many men watching and wanting you. And that was, for sure, a turn-on, but one of them gave me a taste of meth, and it took everything to another level. But, even though I was making more money than I ever had, I knew I couldn't keep tweaking. I saw what it was doing to some of the other girls."

Wilmer gave her a pinch more in her coffee. Once the meth had a moment to dissolve, she stared into Wilmer's eyes and drank the coffee down. Wilmer was not going to be outdone, so he drank his cup to the bottom. Then he stood and pulled off his shirt and pants. He held Dolly's eyes while he dropped his drawers on the floor. Wilmer started to feel the drugs storming through him. He could tell by the flush around her neck that the meth was taking effect on Dolly. Looking at Dolly, he said, "Anybody need a quick wash in the shower before we get this show on the road?"

Dolly stood and dropped her robe. She was tanned all over and lean like a tennis player.

Wilmer decided that his day was looking up.

CHAPTER 10

NOTHIN' SAYS LOVIN' LIKE SOMETHIN' MADE WITH PAINT THINNER

SUNDAY, FEBRUARY 23, 2003
CANTON, GEORGIA

Mark Goodwin needed something to take the edge off. The bottom, as meth users call it, can be harsh. The rush is gone. The energy and the intensity have passed. Mark felt like every nerve in his body was raw. He looked over at Krystal, who was laying on the floor of their bedroom where they had been when she passed out. They were both naked, and Mark was now aware of how cold the trailer was. He stood up and grabbed the pants he had dropped earlier and tugged them on.

He also realized how hungry he was. Mark couldn't recall how long it had been since he had eaten a real meal. He foraged in the cabinets in the kitchen, looking for something that would be palatable. All he found was canned soup. That would have to do. He also found a half-empty can of soda and finished it off. He realized he needed to hydrate after so many hours of working and then spending most of the night having sex.

While sipping the soda, he wished that he and Krystal could occasionally make love rather than the animal coupling that his work pulled them into. There was rarely a time of cuddling or romance, just the rough slamming together of bodies.

Mark couldn't smell the strong chemical smell that permeated the trailer, but he knew it was there. He heated some chicken noodle soup on the stovetop in a rough-looking pot and then poured it into a bowl. He sipped it from the bowl after he found they were out of crackers, all the while trying to be quiet and not wake Krystal.

He stood in the kitchen and looked at the boxes of product he had made with his own hands. He shook his head when he thought how much money the powdery rocket fuel would put in his pocket. He was finally going to be able to make a profit off his work. Mark hadn't really had a sense of accomplishment in his life, and this feeling was new to him. He wondered if this was what it was like to have a child.

Mark peeked out the window and saw Mr. Grimes, the man he had borrowed the truck from, working outside between their trailer and his. Mark noticed that he kept looking this way and seemed to be moving around with no defined objective. Then Mark heard Krystal stirring in the next room and went to check on her.

When he came into the bedroom, he understood why Mr. Grimes was wandering around outside. Krystal was standing by the window, naked as the day she was born, and massaging her breasts. She was acting as if she didn't know the old man was watching.

"You're putting on quite a show for our neighbor. You know you might make his heart quit."

Krystal laughed. "He'll die happy then. Why don't you

come over here and help me entertain him?" Her skin was flushed, and she ran her fingers into her hair, pulling and rubbing on her scalp.

"Aren't you sore from last night?"

She walked over to him and reached into the front of his pants. "Are you sore?"

He nodded. "Some. But I might be able to rise to the occasion."

She smiled a wicked smile and knelt in front of him. "This shit you made this time is crazy strong. I'm still itchy and horny. Your stuff just gets better and better."

He had to admit that he was feeling the meth again, with his pulse surging as he watched Krystal put on the show. Mark pushed his pants down and glanced over at Mr. Grimes as Krystal took him in her mouth.

Daniel Byrd was stepping out of the shower when the phone rang. He walked over to the bedside table, leaving wet footprints on the carpet.

"Hello," he said into the receiver.

"Danny, are you awake?" It was Doc Farmer.

"Yeah, Doc. What can I do for you?"

"I got a call on a shooting in Pickens. What in the hell anybody is doing shooting somebody this early in the morning is beyond me. I'm heading down that way, but I wanted to let you know."

"Doc, I'm up. I can handle it if you want."

"Did you do any good last night? I hope I didn't catch your call for nothing!"

"I spent the night hanging out with the girl I told you about from Canton PD."

"Damn. She spent the night?"

"Sort of. She slept here but stayed in my guest room."

"Good for her!" Doc remarked. "If you want to come on up here, we can knock this out pretty quick. A man shot another fellow breaking into his house. His neighbor came home drunker than hell and tried to get in the wrong house. The drunk is still alive, and there won't be a lot to this."

"I'll head that way. Should I meet you at the jail?"

"Sounds good." Then the line went dead.

Byrd pulled on khaki pants and a dress shirt as he went through his morning ritual. Then he was out the door and headed toward Jasper. Traffic was light on a Sunday with churches only just letting out.

Byrd covered the twenty miles as quickly as the traffic would allow and pulled up to the Pickens County Jail shortly after noon. The back parking lot was reserved for Deputies and staff, but Byrd's GBI Expedition was well known and he pulled into a space near the back door. In seconds he had pressed the button on the wall and the on-duty Jailer triggered the release for the door.

Byrd heard Doc call his name. "Danny! I'm up here in the control room."

Byrd followed the voice and came to the jail control room and dispatch center for the Pickens Sheriff's Office. A young woman was operating the radio and running the doors of the jail. Byrd knew her face, but couldn't recall her name. She smiled and he nodded back as he passed behind her to the jail office area. Byrd knew from experience there was another Jailer working in the back with the prisoners.

Byrd looked Farmer over and said, "Doc, did they get you out of church to come out on this?"

"The suit gave it away, huh? I think you really are a trained Investigator."

Byrd laughed. "I keep trying to prove myself to you."

Doc Farmer leaned on a worktable. He lowered his

voice so the Dispatcher couldn't hear. "So, this Canton cop might be a prospect for you?"

Byrd shrugged. "I enjoyed spending time with her. Maybe this will go somewhere."

"It must have *some* legs if she stayed up with you and talked that much. I'm guessing there was drinking involved."

"Maybe. But nothing out of the way."

Doc pushed the issue. "What do you call out of the way?"

Byrd wasn't going to give anything away. He decided to make the story sound wild and unbelievable, then maybe Doc would leave him alone. "Exchanging underwear. I did that with a girl once, but I couldn't get the little snaps on the thing to work."

Doc laughed again. "What kind of underwear did she have that uses snaps?"

Byrd was trying not to smile. "One of those things women wear that's kind of like a one-piece swimsuit."

Doc shook his head. "You got me."

The young Jailer stuck her head around the door and said, "It's called a teddy."

Byrd's face turned red. "I was just screwing with him! I don't make a habit of wearing women's underwear."

"I'm not judging you," she said as she returned to her seat.

"Well, I've been looking for a nickname for you," Doc said. "I think I just found one. Teddy!"

Byrd was wishing he hadn't come to help Doc. He was still flustered by the turn of events. "Whatever name you give me won't be as well-known as yours, Doc."

Doc was grinning, probably loving that Byrd was squirming. Byrd tried to get back on track. "Where is our victim?"

"He's over at the hospital. We probably ought to hurry.

They were patching him up but said he would be good to go when they finished up."

Byrd nodded. Happy to be talking about something other than his personal life. "Is he getting charged?"

Farmer shook his head. "The Sheriff just wants us to do a report. We can talk to the DA and charge him later if anything comes up. Or the homeowner for that matter. At face value, it looks like the guy was in his own home and the drunk broke in on him and his wife. But you have to follow up on all the leads."

"If he broke in on them," Byrd said, "then the property owner is on solid ground. Georgia law is firmly behind a homeowner in this situation. We just need to be sure the homeowner is giving us the facts. If somebody breaks down my door in the middle of the night, they are going to have a problem."

Doc nodded, and they started for Byrd's car. Byrd stopped in the parking lot.

"Doc," Byrd began, "how come you never seem down or depressed by what we see all the time? I just don't see how you do it."

Doc stopped and took the opportunity to light a cigarette. He took a deep draw and then let the smoke ease out through his nose. "Teddy, I go home at night and say a prayer for the souls of our victims. Then I do my best to put everything in God's hands."

Byrd shrugged and hung his head. "I guess I need to do that. But I sometimes wonder if we even make a difference."

Doc put his arm around Byrd's shoulder, careful to keep the smoke out of his face. "Son, we do more than we'll ever know. We impact lives every day. Sometimes we know it, and sometimes we don't."

Byrd met his eyes. "I wish I had your faith."

Doc chuckled and dropped the cigarette. He crushed it with his foot. "You have more faith than you know."

Doc turned back toward Byrd's car. Byrd preferred to drive, and Doc was fine with that. The two GBI men spent the rest of the afternoon interviewing the shooter, the man who was shot, the neighbors, and the hospital staff.

Roger pulled his truck up to the Ranger Station at Sweetwater Park. He had driven his old beater since he really had no other options. He knew the truck had Texas license plates that he hadn't bothered to replace. Roger had considered stealing plates for the truck, but he wasn't sure how quickly the tags might be reported. For that reason, he had waited until dark to venture out in it.

The old truck looked like hell, but it drove okay and started without complaint. He drove well under the speed limit all the way to the lake. Lumpy spent most of the drive squirming in the seat, unhappy with their slow progress.

"You're going to get us caught for going too slow. The law will think you're smoking weed. And you couldn't get a better ride for us to use? Shit, this thing stands out like a sore thumb."

Roger looked over at Lumpy. "We ain't got nothing else. And I damn sure don't plan to walk way up to where this cooker lives."

Lumpy slumped over against the passenger door and kept quiet.

Wilmer had told Roger the campground was closed from ten at night until eight in the morning. Campers had to check in and get an assigned campsite, but visitors just had to identify who they were there to see.

Roger pulled the old truck up to the window of the Ranger station, which was little more than a hut. A lady, dressed in a uniform far too close to a police uniform for Sturdevant's taste, leaned out and pointed at the sign on the window. The sign read NO NEW CAMPERS AFTER DUSK. She gave the two men a careful look over, then said in an official tone, "We don't allow any new campers this late. Too much risk setting up a site after dark."

Roger nodded his head. "Yes, ma'am. We ain't here to camp," Roger said, "I'm looking for Wilmer Westbrook. He has a camper trailer here."

The Ranger consulted her list and told Roger how to get to the lot where Wilmer should be. "The gates will be locked at ten sharp," the Ranger reminded them as she opened the gate.

Roger coasted the truck along the drive that offered access to the campsites and made their way around to the camper sitting just off the asphalt drive that circled the campground. When they saw a place to park near Westbrook's trailer, Roger pulled the old truck off the roadway so that his headlights illuminated the camper.

Before he had stopped the truck, Wilmer was coming out the aluminum door and walking toward them. They were surprised to see that he was shirtless in the still-winter evening. They saw his face was flushed and he looked like he had scratches on his arms.

When he got up to them, he stood at Roger's window. He looked Lumpy over. "Who is this?" Wilmer asked. His mouth was smiling, but his eyes were not.

Roger spoke up. "I did time with him back in Texas. I figured that two of us would be more likely to get your money than one."

Wilmer balked. "I ain't paying you any more than we agreed to. If you want him, you have to pay him out of what I told you."

Roger ignored him. "That's handled." Roger spoke very quietly, "I need a gun."

Wilmer leaned in and lowered his voice. "For what?"

"They're not going to take us seriously without one. It'll be just for show, but I need something to get the point across."

Westbrook thought it over for only a couple of seconds. Without commenting, he went to the cab of his truck, reached into the console, and took out a .380 Beretta and a small Smith and Wesson revolver. He looked the guns over like he was checking out a library book and handed them to Roger. "Just don't use these. Wave 'em around if you want to, but don't pull the trigger. Got it? You fuck this up, them guns might be traced back to me. I'm not sure how all that works, but I don't want that happening."

Roger kept his voice low. "I don't want any problems out of this either. But if you want your money, we are probably going to have to twist some arms. We don't want to find out this guy is an MMA fighter or something and we're standing there holding our dicks."

Wilmer grunted and turned back to the trailer.

"One hundred dollars," Roger said.

Wilmer stopped and turned back. He tried to give his best mean look, but Roger just waited.

Wilmer dug a hundred-dollar bill out of his jeans pocket and tossed it to Roger. Then, without any more talk, Wilmer strode to the camper door. He stood at the door for a moment, waved at Roger, and then stepped inside.

Roger took the guns and shoved them under his seat. *One crime at a time,* he thought. A convicted felon with a firearm was dead meat if the cops found the guns. He looked back at Wilmer, standing inside the door of the little camper, and hoped he wasn't getting into something he couldn't get out of.

"Are we only going to have them little guns to use?" Lumpy asked.

Roger motioned toward the guns Wilmer had given them. "We just got what we got."

Lumpy turned up his nose. "That ain't much in the way of a gun."

Roger shook his head. "It's enough to get us thrown back in prison. I want to get rid of them as quick as I can."

Lumpy pulled a bottle of bourbon from his front pocket. It was almost empty. "I'm pretty sure taking a drink will get us thrown back in prison, too."

Lumpy took a long drink, emptying the bottle. Roger ignored him.

Roger was serious when he told people he didn't want to go back inside, but he didn't have any skills that he felt could make him decent money. He didn't want to flip burgers and wasn't willing to do any serious labor. Running cars through the wash was bad enough. Roger hoped the cash infusion from tonight would change his prospects. He was ready to start fresh. Or as fresh as someone who had already served seven years in state prison over the last ten years could be.

Roger carefully navigated the truck back around past the Ranger Station and out of the park. As they rolled onto the main highway, he glanced at his watch, then over at Lumpy and said, "Let's get some food. We may not get a chance to get anything before daylight. Everything will close at ten."

Lumpy grunted. "A drive-through burger suits me."

Roger knew there were several options back in Canton, and he pointed the old truck in that direction. He hoped it wouldn't be a late night. Jimmy Lee would expect them at the car wash on time on Monday.

Wilmer Westbrook closed the camper door and locked it

from the inside. When he had gone outside, everyone was dozing from all the morning activities. He was surprised to see Gail was dressed and working in the kitchen. Dolly and Melvin were clothed as well. He tried to look as casual as possible. He said, "Sorry, but I had some business that had to be handled."

Gail perked up. She had renewed her high just a little while ago, and she was feeling the energy. "Was that my jailbird cousin, Roger?"

Wilmer cut his eyes toward her and frowned. "Melvin and Dolly don't care about that." His tone was sharp, but she was too high to care.

"He just got out of a prison in Texas and my brother gave him a job washing cars. Will has got him doing some bill collecting for us."

"Gail! We don't need to go into all this."

Gail stood her ground. She turned to face Wilmer and her face looked like a thunderstorm. "Don't you talk sharp to me! These folks are our friends." She turned to look at Melvin and Dolly, laying in the front bed with their legs hanging off the side. They were both still high enough to not really care what Gail or Wilmer said. But the shouting had gotten their attention.

Wilmer knew he was on dangerous ground. There was no alibi if every one of his witnesses figured out what was going on. He walked over to Gail and put his arms around her. "Sorry, baby. I'm just a little stressed."

He leaned down and kissed her on the mouth. He reached down and grabbed her butt. After a second, she relented and leaned into him. "I guess I talk too much," Gail whispered. "I shouldn't put our family business out there."

They kissed a little longer. Wilmer knew he would have to "bump" soon. That is, take another hit of meth. He wasn't feeling it anymore, and the stress of the business going on soon wasn't helping.

"Did you get a little more go-juice?" Wilmer asked her.

She nodded sheepishly. "Yeah. I figured we might want to have a little more fun now that it's dark outside."

Wilmer thought that might be a good way to get his mind off things. And to help the others forget what Gail had said. He looked to Dolly and Melvin. "You two want to get revved up again?"

They looked at each other, and then both nodded. Wilmer walked over to the refrigerator and took out a pitcher of sweet tea Gail had made for the weekend. He poured some into a tall glass. Then he took a smaller glass, ran water into it, and put it into the microwave. Once the water was hot, he added a sizeable chunk of meth and watched it dissolve. He poured the water into the tea and took a quick drink. Then he passed it around.

Dolly took a gulp, and then Melvin matched her. Gail only took a sip since she was feeling pretty good already. They all waited for the stimulant to kick in.

Gail lit a couple of candles and turned out the overhead lights. Dolly sat up on the bed. "Hey, Gail. Why don't you and Will put on a show for me and Melvin?"

Wilmer liked the idea. "Why don't we put on some music and Gail can do a little dance for us? Dolly can coach you along, honey."

Gail nodded. "I think that would be fun. Can you turn on something with a beat for us, Dolly?"

Dolly clapped with joy and stood to turn the radio to a station that played rock. She fiddled with the dial and soon found a station with the right kind of music. Then she climbed back onto the bed and sat with Melvin.

Gail looked around the smaller area she would be performing in. "We don't have a pole in here."

Dolly looked around the camper. Then she had a thought. "Do you have a folding chair anywhere?"

"Yeah," Wilmer said. "I'll get it." He reached under the bed they were in and pulled a metal folding chair out and sat it up.

Gail looked confused, then turned to Dolly. Dolly jumped up and grabbed the back of the chair, leaning into it with her butt sticking out. "Like this," Dolly said.

Gail tried leaning over the back of the chair. She started to sway with the beat of the rock music. The song was pounding inside the camper as Gail unbuttoned her blouse.

Dolly spoke up. "No, girl. The first song is all about moving your body around and shaking your ass. The second song, you start dropping the clothes down to your panties. It's the third song everyone is waiting for. You want to build up to getting naked. It makes the audience drool to see the goods."

Gail stopped working the buttons and began to fling her body around the chair. She would gyrate her hips and arch her back, then she would drop onto the chair and point her legs to the ceiling.

As directed, she worked her clothing off a song at a time. When she was down to her bra and panties, she was sweaty and panting. The little camper trailer was getting hot inside.

As the sun went down, Doc and Daniel finished photographing and measuring the area of the house where the shooting had happened. Doc had interviewed the shooter while Byrd talked to the neighbors. They would need to interview the man who was shot, but the Doctors told them he was too drunk to give a statement. They didn't argue with the emergency room staff, since they could talk to him later. Then they had given a call to District Attorney Mason. Once everyone was happy, Byrd and Doc headed for home.

Daniel Byrd pulled into a local hamburger place with a drive-through so he could get something to take home. When he turned the Expedition into the drive-through line, he pulled in behind an old white and green pickup truck. The truck had a green toolbox in the bed, and none of the wheels had hubcaps. The tailgate was rusted out along the bottom, and a chain hung down from the rear, almost touching the ground. He noted that the license plate was from Texas and wondered how the old truck had made the journey without breaking down.

He pulled up to the intercom to place his order then he was around the side of the building behind the truck again. Like most cops, he noted the plate numbers and searched his memory for any similar numbers. The tag was expired, but Byrd wasn't in the mood to deal with a minor traffic violation. He watched the driver lean out and take the food and two drinks. That was the first time Byrd noticed there were two people in the truck. The passenger must have been leaning against the door the whole time.

Byrd followed the old truck with his eyes as he eased to the pickup window to take its place and watched the truck turn south on the highway toward the high school. Byrd paid for his meal and drove the short distance to his apartment. The truck had caught his attention, but there were no real red flags. He tried to put it out of his mind, but the images kept nagging at him. Particularly the passenger leaning into the door to hide. Byrd had seen that trick before used by crooks to ambush a cop making a traffic stop.

He sat his food on the table and took his gun off for the night. Then he dialed the GBI Communications Center number. On the second ring, Sophia Romano answered the phone in the GBI Headquarters building in Atlanta. "GBI, Romano speaking. How may I help you?"

"Hey, Sophia. It's Danny Byrd. How are you doing?"

"Hey, Danny. I'm good. What about you?"

"Better than I deserve."

"I know that's right!"

"Do you have time to run a tag for me?"

She laughed. "I knew you didn't just call to talk. Lay it on me."

"Texas truck tag number sixty-six seventy-seven Queen Mary."

He could hear the keyboard clacking as she typed the number into the computer. They both waited in silence as the information was processed.

"Here we go," Sophia said. "Registered to Roger Sturdevant from Huntsville, Texas. It should be on a 1973 Ford pickup truck. Color is white and green. The response gives an address in Texas and a date of birth for Mr. Sturdevant."

Byrd was even more curious. "Huntsville is where the primary state prison for Texas is located. The two in that truck just didn't look right to me. The passenger was doing the felony lean, keeping over into the door, out of sight. Can you run a criminal history for me on Mr. Sturdevant?"

"Stand by." More clacking of the keyboard, a short wait, and then, "Roger Dale Sturdevant. White male. Has multiple arrests in both Georgia and Texas. Of all those, he served time in Georgia for domestic violence and in Texas for armed robbery. He was paroled in Texas, but he absconded. He has an active warrant for parole violations."

"Shit!" Byrd exclaimed. "I was behind him in a drive-thru line just a little while ago."

"What was he doing?"

"Getting a burger."

Sophia laughed. "I'm no Special Agent, but I don't think that was reason enough to stop him. And even if you had run the tag, there is no warrant attached to the tag return. It only comes up with the criminal history."

"Thanks, Sophia. I appreciate the help. And the kind words."

"No way you could have known. I can forward this to Intelligence and see if they can track him down in the morning."

"Thanks."

"That's what I'm here for. How are things with you?"

Byrd and Sophia had once had a brief, torrid relationship. Sophia broke things off when it became apparent that Byrd was more involved in his work than any relationship he might have. But there was still a connection.

Byrd hesitated. "Fine, I guess. I still have trouble going to sleep at night and probably drink more than I should. But I really do love working up here. I'm starting to fit in, I think."

Sophia was quiet for a second. "I know from talking to other Agents that you guys see some terrible things. I'm sure that takes a toll. But stop using alcohol as a crutch. You're better than that."

"Yeah, thanks," he sighed.

After several seconds of silence, Sophia said, "Come by here and see me next time you come to headquarters."

"I will. Thanks again." Byrd caught himself before he told her he loved her out of habit. That would have been messy. He hung up the phone and headed for the kitchen to mix a drink. Then Sophia's words echoed in his head. He put the glass he had chosen back in the cabinet and sat down to eat his burger.

CHAPTER 11

MONDAY, MONDAY

MONDAY, FEBRUARY 24, 2003
CANTON, GEORGIA
MIDNIGHT

Roger Sturdevant and Lumpy Cochran finished their burgers and rode north on the highway that would take them to Mark Goodwin's house. Roger wanted to wait as late as he could in case there were neighbors close by.

Lumpy seemed to be anxious, and fidgety. He watched for cop cars as they traveled. A storm front moving in made the night so dark that neither man could see much outside the reach of the worn-out headlights.

As the two got closer, Lumpy pulled the two guns from under the seat and looked them over by the dash lights. "Hey, put those away," Roger said. "Keep 'em under that seat till we get closer."

Lumpy didn't argue, but he was slower than Roger would have liked when he did put them away. Roger knew they were only a few minutes away from the row of trailers where Goodwin lived, but he still preferred to keep the guns under wraps.

There was a particularly tricky turn off the main road to the home. Concrete curbs on each side of the road were tall, and the curve was tight. Roger let the rear wheel of the old truck roll up onto the concrete, and for a second, he thought the Ford would turn over. As soon as he felt the tires leave the blacktop, he shut off his lights. He coasted along till he saw the row of house trailers up ahead.

Roger stopped the truck on the dirt path that led to Goodwin's trailer. He sat with the lights out. He looked at his watch and saw that it was five minutes past midnight. About the right time to knock on Goodwin's door.

It was then that Roger realized they had a problem. There were two trailers with lights on, and he wasn't sure which one Westbrook had shown him. He strained to get a better look at each of them, but they were too similar in the dark. He was sweating under his heavy coat. Roger knew that Lumpy was belittling him silently from the passenger seat.

There was an old truck parked in front of the first mobile home, and a Honda parked in front of the second one. Both looked like rattletraps. That fact didn't help him at all. Roger had assumed the meth cook would be the only one up this late. He shook his head. He hadn't counted on this.

Roger decided to try the first trailer house. He parked behind the other truck and shut his off. He got out and listened for a dog, a trick he had learned after being bitten once during a burglary. He stood quietly and could hear the TV on in the living room in front of him.

He walked back to his truck and told Lumpy to watch for him to signal. "If this is the right house, I'll give you the sign and you come on in."

Lumpy frowned. "You don't know which house it is?"

"I never seen it after dark. Now, if I wave, you come on up."

Lumpy nodded glumly.

Gingerly, Roger mounted the steps leading to the wooden stoop and front door of the old rusty home. Before he could get to the top of the steps, the front door flew open and he was bathed in light from the living room. An old man stuck a shotgun out the door at him.

"What the hell do you think you're doing?" the man said.

Roger almost fell over backward. He stumbled and then got hold of the wooden railing. He slowed his breathing and tried to sound calm, but his heart was pounding. "I'm looking for Goodwin. I thought this was his house."

The old man pointed the shotgun toward the ground. "You're at the wrong house, boy. That meth cooker lives next door. I would'a figured the stink would have helped you figure that out."

Roger sniffed the air, and then realized there was a strong chemical odor coming from the other trailer. He nodded, "Sorry, I do smell it now."

The man growled, "You tweakers have some late hours. Be careful roaming around this area after dark. You could get a load of buckshot." With that, he slammed the door.

Roger's hands were shaking when he got back in his truck. He climbed into the driver's seat and took a deep breath. Lumpy looked over at him and smirked. "You just got run off by an old man. Do you really think you can muscle this cook?"

Roger was angry, mostly at himself. He slammed both hands on the steering wheel. "He took me by surprise is all. I wasn't planning for that!"

Lumpy shook his head and spit out the open window. Lumpy turned back to face Roger. "Well," he said, "I hope you do better with the real deal. I'm going with you to the door this time."

Lumpy took the guns out from under the seat. He looked them over, chose the Beretta, and passed the revolver to Roger. Roger stuck the revolver in the front of his pants, and Lumpy did the same.

The two men looked grim as Roger backed the truck out and quickly pulled into the next driveway. Both men got out and waited for their eyes to adjust to the dark. They could hear voices from the trailer—a male voice and a female voice—but they couldn't make out any words. Roger sniffed the air and couldn't imagine how someone could live in the stench. The chemical smell was so strong in front of the house that he wanted to gag, but he knew Lumpy would have something to say about that.

After a few seconds, the men went up to the door of Goodwin's trailer. There was no stoop, just a rickety set of steps up to the aluminum door with the piano hinge. Roger looked around from a position to the left of the door on the ground. He raised his hand to knock. Before he could, Lumpy motioned for him to step to the side and took a big step forward. Lumpy kicked the front door with all his weight, his foot hitting near the bottom.

The door didn't open. Lumpy stood back and then made another attempt to kick the door in.

Roger saw Mark look out the little window in the trailer door, probably hearing the commotion. Not thinking there was any danger, Mark pushed the door open and stuck his head out.

Mark stood there in his jeans and a sweatshirt, confused about what all the banging was about. He was also barefoot and unarmed. Lumpy pushed him back inside with his left hand and drew the Beretta from his waist with his right. He shoved Mark onto the couch in the living room. Roger was standing at the door, taking everything in.

Suddenly, Mark's lady rushed in from the bedroom. She had been sleeping off her latest meth bump when she was wakened by the banging. She stumbled into the living room, trying to make sense of everything. She was wearing panties and an oversized sweatshirt. She saw what Lumpy was doing and jumped on his back. The woman wrapped her left arm around Lumpy's neck and used her right arm to pull the left arm back. She remembered the move from a self-defense class she had taken in high school. She was closing off Lumpy's oxygen supply and he was already getting light-headed. She held on tight as Lumpy tried to shake her off.

"Krystal," Mark shouted, "watch out! They've got guns!"

Roger, who had been watching from the door, stepped in and tried to pull Krystal off of Lumpy's back. Roger stuck the revolver down in his pants and tried to get a grip on the sweatshirt that Krystal wore. He felt the gun slide down his pants leg and hit the floor. Krystal swung her right elbow back and connected with Roger's head as Mark sprang from the couch and tried to wrench the gun from Lumpy's hand. Roger had taken a solid hit to the head, but he managed to yank down on the oversized sweatshirt. When Roger pulled with all his weight, he, Krystal, and Lumpy went down in a heap. As they fell over backward, the Beretta in Lumpy's hand discharged and the bullet narrowly missed Mark's head. The blast of heat burned Mark's cheek as he stumbled away from the gun.

The explosive sound of the pistol shot was over-whelming in the small space. Krystal rolled away from Lumpy and tried to run into the bedroom. Roger grabbed at her ankle, causing her to fall forward on her face.

Mark tried to kick Lumpy in the face while he was on the floor. Lumpy curled up so that the foot was deflected. Then Lumpy jumped to his feet and hit Mark with an open hand to the side of the head. The cupped hand landed just above Mark's ear and stunned him. Mark slumped over and crashed onto the couch. Lumpy climbed on Mark's back and quickly got his hands behind his back, just like the cops had done to him on several occasions. He sat on Mark's back with all his weight.

"Get that bitch before she gets to a phone!" Lumpy yelled at Roger.

Roger was on his feet and moving toward the bedroom when Krystal slammed the door in his face. Now, however, Roger knew he had to act quickly. The bedroom door was not solid, and Roger kicked it open with a single try.

Krystal was trying to bring a table lamp around and use it as a club when Roger knocked her onto the bed. Roger had little compunction about punching her in the face since she had nailed him. Krystal slumped to the floor, unconscious. "Damn, girl. Why do all you women try to hit me in the head?"

Roger called to Lumpy, "She's down for the count. Are you good with him?"

Lumpy called back. "We need something to tie them up. Can you help me with that?"

Roger reached down and grabbed Krystal's sweatshirt. He dragged her into the living room by the arm. "Watch her. I'll look in the kitchen."

As soon as he walked into the kitchen, Roger saw a roll of silver tape on the kitchen counter. He grabbed it and, as quickly as he could, he bound Krystal's wrists and ankles. He tossed the roll to Lumpy, who tied Mark in the same way.

Finally, the two men were able to take a deep breath. Lumpy looked over at Roger and said with a smirk, "That went well."

Roger wasn't in the mood. He reached up and checked his head for blood. When he didn't find any, he calmed down. He pulled Krystal into a kitchen chair and used more duct tape to bind her tightly to it. Then he helped Lumpy do the same thing with Mark. Mark struggled, but the two ex-cons were able to manhandle him into the hard-back wooden chair. When the two had him immobilized, Lumpy hit Mark as hard as he could with his closed fist. Mark slumped forward.

Roger looked around the room. "Do you see my gun?"

Lumpy shook his head. "You lost your gun?"

Roger got on his knees near the couch and found the revolver, then put it in his waistband. Then he glanced around the room and saw a phone mounted high on the wall and pulled the wire from the base. "I don't see an-other phone in this shithole."

Lumpy stood and looked around, too. "This place smells like cat piss. Did you see an animal?"

Roger shook his head. "You're smelling meth. They must have a bunch of it somewhere."

Lumpy walked over to Mark and started lightly slap-ping his face. "Wake up, buddy. We need to ask you some questions."

Mark moaned, and his eyes fluttered. He shook his head and then opened his eyes. "What the hell do you boys want?"

"Boys? How big are men where you come from?" Lumpy laughed at his own joke.

Mark was confused. "What do you mean?'

Lumpy grabbed the front of Mark's shirt and twisted the front so that it was pulled tight. Lumpy drew back his fist, but Roger grabbed his arm.

"Let him talk a little bit before you hit him anymore," Roger said.

Lumpy shrugged and stood up. "Whatever you say. It's your show."

Roger motioned for Lumpy to help, and the two dragged the chair Krystal was in into the kitchen. Roger wanted her out of the way. Then Roger had another thought. "Hey, go check and see if that old man is outside. He might have heard that shot."

Lumpy went into the bedroom and looked out the window. The lights were still on next door, but he didn't see anyone looking their way. "I don't think he heard anything."

Roger sat on the couch and faced Mark. "Well, then we don't have to rush. Now, Mark, it seems like you owe Mr. Westbrook some money. We're here to collect what you owe him. Let's make this easy. Just come up with the money you owe and we'll get out of here."

Mark shook his head, still groggy. "Boys . . . I mean men, I have got a whole shitload of work in that kitchen boxed up and ready to go to a middleman in Marietta. But it took every red cent I had to put together this cook. Does it look like I have a bunch of cash stashed?"

"Lumpy, take a look around and see if you can find a bunch of product," Roger said. Lumpy hesitated, but then he started searching.

Mark twisted around. "It's boxed up in the kitchen. In some pasteboard boxes beside the refrigerator."

Lumpy walked into the kitchen and found the cardboard boxes loaded with meth. He hefted a couple of the plastic bags. He found a bag about the size of a golf ball and put it in his pocket.

Krystal groaned and lifted her head. Lumpy walked over to her, smiling down at her. "You're a wildcat, girl. Are you like that in the sack? I bet you're a tasty thing."

She shook her head and turned away from him. Lumpy pulled at the top of her sweatshirt, which was stretched and twisted, and looked at her breasts. He leaned down and licked her face. He admired her for a moment more and then turned and walked back into the living room. "He ain't lying. He's got about a pound or two of fresh meth sitting out there in the kitchen."

Mark nodded vigorously. "I told you. I won't lie to you, gentlemen. I plan to move that powder tomorrow and pay Mr. Westbrook right away."

Lumpy slapped Mark. "I ain't buying that shit. You got some money stashed here. Now, where is it?"

Mark kept shaking his head. "I wish there was some. I'd sure give it to you. I don't want any more trouble. But we are flat broke till we move that meth. If y'all can wait just a day, we'll be flush. I can pay him off and make your payday better. I promise you."

Roger leaned over Mark. "You should have told Mr. Westbrook that before now. He thinks you're holding out on him. And I got no reason to doubt that. What guarantee do we have that you'll get any money tomorrow?"

Lumpy looked toward the kitchen. "I might be willing to take my part of the bill out of your woman in there."

Mark struggled, but the tape was tight. "She's got nothing to do with this. Leave her alone."

Lumpy pulled the bag of meth out of his pocket and sniffed the bag. "Is this nasty-looking shit worth that much money?"

Mark shrugged. "I make good stuff. People pay for it 'cause they can't find no better."

"What do you do with it? I ain't a junky, so I don't use no needle." Lumpy kept examining the bag.

Mark twisted his neck around and tried to look at Lumpy. "You can snort it or eat it."

Lumpy opened the bag and sniffed. He recoiled and looked to Roger. "Have you ever used any of this stuff?"

Roger nodded. "A little. I put it inside my lip like snuff."

Lumpy scowled, but he stuck a fingernail in the moist powder and took out a small dab. He closed his eyes and stuck his finger into his mouth and put the little bit of meth inside his lip.

Roger and Mark watched as Lumpy inhaled deeply and twitched. They could tell he was feeling the rush.

Roger thought about getting a taste for himself. Lumpy was breathing deeply and looking straight up.

Before Roger could react, Lumpy pushed the Beretta to Mark's left knee and pulled the trigger. Mark screamed loud once and then passed out.

Roger slapped at the gun. "What the fuck did you do that for? Huh?"

Lumpy just shrugged. "I think he's holding out on us. I aim to get the money that's here."

Mark began to moan, and his eyes fluttered again. Then the moans got increasingly louder. Lumpy took the tape and wound it around Mark's head, covering his mouth.

"There! You lying son of a bitch. Shut the fuck up." Lumpy slammed his fist into the wall. "FUCK!"

Mark's eyes were open now, and he was trying to breathe through his nose. His eyes were wild, and he continued to moan in spite of the tape.

Roger shook his head. "What a mess this has turned into."

Lumpy paced the floor. He shook the gun in the air. "This ain't my fault. He lied and is holding out on the money. It ain't on me."

"Lumpy, go check on the neighbors again. You better hope they didn't hear that shot."

As Lumpy checked outside, Roger was too focused on Mark and could only look on as Krystal ran past him, tape trailing from her arms and legs, headed for the door. She had her head down like a football player determined to get past a defender. Lumpy was faster than he looked, and he managed to grab Krystal by the hair as she swung the front door out. Her momentum carried them both onto the front steps.

Roger watched as they stumbled on the slick stairs. Lumpy tightened his grip on her hair. Krystal reached up with both hands, trying to work his hand loose. Lumpy held on tight. Before Roger could say anything, Lumpy brought the pistol up and shot her once in the back of the head. A mist of blood sprayed his face. Lumpy let her body fall to the ground and then swiped at the blood on his cheek. He stuck the bloody finger in his mouth and sucked it dry.

"What the hell are you doing?" Roger screamed.

Lumpy climbed back into the room and said, "She was going to run to the neighbors. That couldn't happen."

Roger threw up his hands. "Oh, my God. This is a death-penalty state! We are fucked. We need to get out of here."

Lumpy was twitching. He looked around wildly. "Should we load the meth up and take it to Westbrook?"

Roger was thinking about more important matters. "Wipe down anything you touched. We haven't left many fingerprints, but we should clean up all we can."

Lumpy pulled the end of his shirt out and started walking around the room, trying to clean door handles and smooth surfaces. He went from the front of the trailer to the back.

Roger rubbed off the front doorknob on both sides. Once he was satisfied, he turned to Lumpy. "Let's go."

Lumpy turned to Mark. His eyes were pleading, and he was shaking his head back and forth. Suddenly he vomited inside the tape over his mouth.

Roger held up his hand. "He don't know us. We ain't used no names. Leave him."

Without saying a word, Lumpy walked over and shot Mark between the eyes. A mist of blood covered Lumpy's arms and face.

Lumpy turned to Roger, his eyes black as night. Lumpy said, "No witnesses."

CHAPTER 12

NIGHT FLIGHT

MONDAY, FEBRUARY 24, 2003
CANTON, GEORGIA
12:30 A.M.

Sunday nights were usually quiet in the Cherokee County 911 Center. So far, this one hadn't been an exception. Bobby Kline had started with the center in 2001 as a springboard to a sworn law enforcement job with a badge and a gun. He would be twenty-one in July and hoped to be in a patrol car by the end of the year. But tonight, he was the designated Call-taker for any calls for emergency services in the county.

When he saw the light flashing on the phone console beside his elbow, he yawned and rubbed his face before punching the button that would answer the call.

"Cherokee 911. What is the nature of your emergency?"

"Can you hear me?" the voice on the phone asked. Kline noted it was a man calling. He sounded older.

"Yes, sir. I can hear you. What is the nature of your emergency?" *It's too late at night for prank calls*, he thought.

"I just heard the people next door shooting guns. I think y'all need to send Deputies out here." The man on the phone sounded concerned.

Kline waved his hand to get the attention of the Sheriff's

Office Dispatcher. She turned to see what was going on. Kline raised his right hand and made a gun with his fingers, then mimed shooting in the air. He began typing a summary of the call as he ran through the list of questions he needed answered.

Kline sat up in his chair. "What's your name?"

"Do I have to give it?"

"Sir, if the shooting involves your neighbor, the Deputies will want to talk to you." In the meantime, Kline checked the computer to see what the caller's address was.

The man responded reluctantly, "My name is Homer Grimes."

Kline asked for and got his address. He immediately sent the address and nature of the call to a Radio Operator who would dispatch Deputies to the house.

"How many shots did you hear?"

"At first, I weren't sure it was shots. My neighbor cooks meth and sometimes we'll hear a little boom. But tonight, these shit-birds came by my house asking about Mark and Krystal—that's my neighbors' names. Then I seen them boys go over to their house, and in a little while, I heard yelling, and it sounded like some shooting."

"But you're not sure they were shots?" Kline was typing the additional information to be forwarded to the Dispatcher across the room.

"Not at first," Grimes said. "But then we heard the door slam open and I know I heard a shot then."

Kline had taken enough calls to sense that this man was sincere. "We'll have people coming your way. Please tell the Deputy everything you've told me."

"Hang on, feller. Them boys in the truck are leaving over yonder. I can hear the truck cranking up."

Kline leaned forward in his seat. "Can you see the truck? Maybe get a tag number?"

Grimes was quiet for a moment. Then he came back on the line. "It's an older model Ford truck. I can't see well enough to see no tag."

"Mr. Grimes, can you please stay on the line until our Deputies are on the scene?"

Grimes grumbled a response and hung up the call.

Roger was shaking as he climbed into the seat of the truck. He had never felt such fear in his life. On the one hand, he was scared of spending the rest of his life in prison. On the other hand, he was scared of dying at the hands of Lumpy Cochran. Neither prospect seemed to be particularly good. When he left the trailer, he waited on Lumpy to get in, too. He thought for a minute that he should just drive off and leave him. He had a brief image of him standing in the driveway and firing shots at Roger as he hauled ass down the road.

Roger was driving faster than he should and his old truck wasn't up to the task. The steering wheel had lots of play in it, and the road was rough. He kept darting the truck from one side of the road to the other.

Lumpy was shaking for a different reason. The meth he had put in his mouth was making him feel wild and incredibly paranoid at the same time. He kept looking behind them as though he thought Mark and Krystal would come running after them.

They had made it to the paved road, and Roger was wrestling the steering wheel. The truck hit the concrete curb they had rolled over before. This time, with the higher speed, the truck leaped into the air for a moment and then skidded onto the road. Lumpy slid onto the floorboard and Roger was doing everything he could to get the truck under control. The truck slowed and Roger got it back onto the roadway.

Roger knew they were about three miles to the turn onto the state highway that would take them back to Canton. Roger slowed down and was planning to stay well under the speed limit when he felt the front wheels pulling to the right. At first, he wasn't sure what was going on. Then he heard the flap-flap-flap of a flat tire.

"Shit!" Roger exclaimed as he hit the steering wheel with both palms.

Lumpy was looking frantically out the back window. "What?"

"When I hit that curb, I must have busted the tire on the front. We got a flat."

Lumpy looked all around, his eyes wild.

"Spit out what's left of that meth, okay?"

Lumpy did as he was told.

Roger pulled off to the side of the road. He knew he had a good spare in the bed of the truck. He was hoping he could be as fast as a racing pit crew getting the old one off and the new tire on.

Roger got out and dragged the spare around to the front of the truck. He went back and got the jack and handle from behind the seat, ignoring Lumpy. Roger got the jack in position and began to pump the jack handle. His ears ringing from the shooting inside the house, he worked as quickly as he could, but he didn't have a light and the night was dark. He could smell the rain in the air.

Lumpy got out of the truck and started pacing back and forth nearby. Roger knew from his own experiences with meth that Lumpy could start seeing the shadow people at any moment. Roger was fumbling with the lug nuts of the truck when he heard the siren off in the distance.

Lumpy was frantic. "Do you hear that?"

Roger nodded. "I sure do. You need to get off the road and hide in the woods. You may have blood on you."

Lumpy went around in front of the truck and began to examine his clothes in the glow of the headlights. Roger grabbed his arm and pulled him away. "Get out of the light!"

As the siren got closer, Lumpy climbed the bank of dirt on the shoulder of the road and lay down among a stand of scrubby pine trees.

Roger got back down beside the wheel. He tried to get the wheel off the hub, but his hands were shaking so badly he couldn't manage to get the last nut off. He started crying for the first time since his first night in jail. He slumped over and sobbed.

The flashing blue and red lights came into sight, and Roger turned his back to the truck and sat on the hard ground. He watched as the patrol car went on by, never slowing.

After he had wiped his tears, Roger got the last lug nut off and took the flat off the truck. In less than a minute he had the spare tire mounted, lowered the truck, and tightened everything up.

Roger heard another siren in the distance. He threw the damaged tire into the bed of the truck and wiped himself off.

Lumpy called out to Roger, "Is that another cop coming?"

"It is!" Roger called.

Then Roger went around to the driver's seat, started the engine, and drove off as fast as he felt he could, without drawing the cop's attention. He hoped Lumpy was smart enough to stay in the woods for a while. He had pulled out onto the road as the second patrol car passed, siren wailing, and continued toward Goodwin's trailer.

Bobby Kline watched the expression on the Dispatcher's face as the first patrol cars arrived on the scene. She looked grim, and she was soon sending him a message.

Kline looked at the scene on his desk. He was shocked by what he read.

SIGNAL 50 X 2. BOTH SIGNAL 48. NO SUSPECTS ON SCENE. REQUEST CID AND 100 BE NOTIFIED.

In plain talk, the message was that two people had been shot and were dead. The Deputies on scene had requested that they notify the Criminal Investigations Division and the Sheriff, whose radio number was one hundred.

Kline dreaded calling the mercurial Sheriff. He took the coward's way out and called newly promoted Major Craig Weislowski first. The voice on the line, when the call was answered, was muffled and slurred. "Is this Major Weislowski?"

"Yeah, who is this?" the answer came back.

"Kline from the Dispatch Center. We have Deputies out at confirmed signals forty-eight and fifty with two victims."

"Shit! Any chance it's a murder-suicide?"

"I have only talked to the initial caller, but it sounds like a double murder. The caller heard the shots fired and then saw a truck leaving."

Weislowski was condescending. "I guess we should have you out there at the scene if you can call this a murder by what you heard on the phone. You could save the rest of us a lot of time."

Kline took a deep breath. "I need to let the Sheriff know."

"You do that! Better you than me."

When Weislowski hung up the phone, Kline said out loud, "Asshole!"

The Dispatcher heard him from across the room and nodded sympathetically. Kline dialed the number for Sheriff Albert Haggin.

The phone rang several times before a female voice answered. "What?"

"This is Kline in the 911 Center. Is the Sheriff in?"

Kline heard a muffled argument, and then Haggin came on the phone. Kline repeated what he had told Major Weislowski. Haggin listened and then said, "Fuck!" and hung up.

Kline shook his head. *What the hell kind of place am I working for?* he thought.

CHAPTER 13
THE HOT POTATO

MONDAY, FEBRUARY 24, 2003
CANTON, GEORGIA
2:00 A.M.

Sheriff Haggin rolled onto the little road that fronted the four trailers in a row. It didn't take a trained Investigator to recognize the home of interest was the second one in the row, with marked patrol cars and an ambulance littering the driveway. He found a spot to pull his sedan off the side of the path and got out, immediately noticing the strong chemical smell in the air.

His eyes were adjusting to the dark, so he took the opportunity to stand very still and breathe deeply. The chemical smell made him cough. He was scared but would do anything to hide it from his troops. Standing in the dark, he saw Craig Weislowski coming his way. That was good; he could get briefed away from everyone else. He leaned against his government car and waited on Weislowski.

"Sheriff, this is a mess. A man and a woman, each with gunshot wounds. Both shot at least once in the head."

"Any chance it was a murder-suicide?"

"The man was tortured before he was killed, and there are signs both had been tied up. So, the murder-suicide scenario doesn't seem likely. And there are about two pounds of meth boxed up in there. This house is probably a meth lab."

Haggin nodded. "That would explain the smell. It stinks to high heaven around here." Changing the subject Haggin asked, "What do we have on our suspects?"

Weislowski shook his head. "Not much."

Haggin felt a building rage. "What do I pay you for? We have all these people out here and you've got nothing?"

Weislowski held up his hands. "Calm down. We have just started processing the scene. I have one of the Detectives talking to the neighbor who called it in." Weislowski stepped closer. "And you're not going to want to hear this, but the mother of the female victim is sitting in her car over there. The neighbor called her. She says that the victims owed money to Wilmer Westbrook." He let that sink in.

Haggin hung his head. The Westbrook family were some of his biggest supporters. He held a campaign event in front of their store. Haggin stood shaking his head. "This is terrible. How is this going to look?"

Weislowski looked all around. "I think I have a way for you to go. Let's call in the GBI. We dump this on their laps and let them deal with the fallout if we don't have some-body in jail soon. And we keep our Detectives involved so we have an inside track on what's going on."

"How can we protect Westbrook?" Haggin asked.

Weislowski shook his head. "We can't. But we won't be able to anyway if it turns out he did this. We would end up having to arrest this guy and then the family would be all over you. This way, we can blame everything on the GBI."

Haggin nodded. "You're right. But make sure you have someone loyal to us working with the GBI Agents. I don't want any surprises. What happened to those two you were going to hire from Atlanta PD?"

"The county personnel office is giving me a hard time. We probably won't have them on the books until the middle of next month."

Haggin seemed resigned to calling the GBI in. "I guess we're stuck. Can you make the call?"

Weislowski shook his head. "By law the Sheriff or the District Attorney has to request the GBI, so it will have to come from you."

Haggin squinted at Weislowski. "You better be right about all this. We can't stand any bad publicity right now. Or the next couple of years, for that matter."

Weislowski nodded and went back toward the crime scene. Haggin sat down in this car. He would need to drive to a phone to call in the GBI. He had a mobile phone in his car, but the northern half of the county didn't yet have coverage. He started the car up and pulled away from the scene. Haggin was glad he didn't have to be in the little trailer with the bodies right now.

Daniel Byrd's phone rang next to his head. He had been in a deep sleep and the sound caused him to sit straight up. "Hello."

"Agent Byrd?"

He rolled over to look at the digital clock beside his bed. It was 2:15 a.m. "Yes. Who's this?"

"Operator Alford at the Headquarters Radio Room."

Byrd wiped his face and shook his head. "What's going on?"

"The Cherokee County Sheriff called and wants Agents out to a double homicide they have."

"Wow. I'm surprised they called."

Alford gave him the address. Byrd made notes of the time of the call, who called, and what he said. Then he noted the address. "Can you patch me through to Agent Farmer with Region Eight?"

Byrd waited for the call to go through, and then heard the clatter of the phone handset being picked up, dropped, and then retrieved.

A sleepy voice answered. "Hello?"

"Doc," Byrd said, "we have a double homicide in Cherokee County. Since they called us, I'm guessing it's a who-done-it. Do you mind coming out to give me a hand?"

"Sure, Teddy. I'll head your way. It'll probably take me an hour or so. I'll come as quick as I can."

"Doc, what did you call me?"

"Teddy. Or do you prefer Ted?" Byrd heard Doc laughing as he hung up the phone.

Byrd shook his head as he rolled out of bed. He rinsed off in the shower but didn't take time to shave. He grabbed the pants he had worn the previous day with all his keys and money still in the pockets, pulled them on along with a dress shirt, and tied his tie as he walked out the door.

Byrd made the drive with his blue lights on but there was so little traffic he didn't see the need to activate the siren. He followed the directions he had been given and was getting out of his truck at the scene by 2:45. He parked in the space behind the sedan he knew belonged to Sheriff Haggin. Stepping out of his car, he tugged on his suit coat and then pulled the overcoat on top. The temperature was above freezing, but the wind made it seem colder.

As he walked up to the trailer surrounded by crime scene tape, he activated his little handheld digital recorder. He would dictate his observations as he went through the site. When he came to the yellow tape, a uniformed Deputy put his hand out to stop him.

"What can I do for you?" he said with his hand held out, palm open.

"I'm with the GBI. Daniel Byrd," he said as he extended his credential case with the badge pinned on the back.

"I'll have to check with the Sheriff. I'm not supposed to let anybody in."

Byrd shrugged up his shoulders to keep warm. "I'll wait."

After the Deputy walked off to get him cleared, Byrd stood in the whipping wind. While he waited, Byrd began to describe the area. He had noted the temperature when he got out of the truck and he added that to his list of details. He noted which doors and windows were open and which lights were on at the time of his arrival. He knew that the first Officers on scene had probably opened doors and turned on lights, but he wanted a record of how things were when he got there.

When the Deputy came back, he lifted the tape and motioned Byrd in without comment. Byrd stuck his hands into his pockets to prevent him from casually touching anything at the scene, then strode across the yard and walked up to the front door.

He saw the first victim, a woman dressed in little more than a sweatshirt, laying on the ground. She faced her left, and her arms were spread wide. Her feet and legs were bare, and her hair looked wild. Byrd saw that a local Detective was taking photographs of her body with a cold detachment. He decided there was no need to duplicate the effort. He would get copies from the Sheriff's Office later. The Detective's camera looked much better than the State-issued one Byrd would have to use anyways.

He bent down, careful to keep his hands in his pockets, and examined as much as he could see of the female victim. Byrd noted the blood and brain matter in her hair. She had silver tape on her arms and legs, which appeared to have been torn. She was dressed in a sweatshirt and panties. He wondered if there were any other injuries on her front but knew he would have to wait on the Coroner to turn the body over. She looked young, but her skin had a slightly gray color that immediately told Byrd she was a meth user. He described the position, the clothing, and the appearance of the woman before he moved off to the door of the trailer.

When he got to the door, he noticed the smell coming from the trailer. Byrd had smelled it before. This house was a meth lab. The rising wind had kept him from smelling it sooner.

Byrd investigated the interior and dictated what he saw. The interior of the trailer was a bloody mess. The male victim lay on his back, taped to a chair that had fallen backward at some point. The male was much bloodier than the female, with a pool around his right leg and blood all over his face. He saw traces of vomit around the tape over his mouth.

Byrd was trying to decide about going into the house when he saw Sheriff Haggin come around the corner of the kitchen area. Haggin saw Byrd at the same time and waved Byrd over.

But Byrd stood his ground. "Sheriff, you might want to get your folks out of there and get some protective gear for them. I think you are all in the middle of a meth lab."

Haggin looked surprised. "Yeah, there are pounds of the stuff inside here. But we have to work this murder scene."

"The GBI has teams to mitigate clandestine labs. They work for our Drug Enforcement Unit. I can get some people up here in hazmat suits with breathing protection. It might be overkill, but I wouldn't want your people to have any ill effects."

Haggin was not convinced. "Nobody is having a problem. We need to process this scene so we can get these bodies out of here."

Byrd nodded. He knew he had to be diplomatic, or the Sheriff could send him packing. "I know Cherokee Fire has a good hazmat team. How about we get them up here? They can help the Coroner get the bodies taken care of and they can help your Detectives by airing out this trailer. Give them an hour or two and your folks should be able to finish without any need to get them decontaminated."

Haggin seemed to think it over. "Hey, Major Weislowski! Can you come here just a minute?" He turned to Byrd and said, "He is the Head of Investigations for my office. I'll let you guys work all this out. I'm going to my office to draft a press release."

Byrd winced. He tried to hide his concern. "I hope you can keep it simple for now."

"I know how to handle the press," Haggin said. Haggin took a last look over his shoulder at the girl lying on the ground and then walked to his car.

Major Weislowski joined them. "You must be Byrd. The Sheriff gave me your card the other day. Happy to have you helping out." Weislowski extended a rubber-gloved hand to Byrd. He realized at the last moment that he was wearing the gloves and pulled them off to shake hands.

Byrd repeated his concerns and offered the same solutions he had given Haggin. Weislowski seemed to have a better understanding of the potential risks of being inside the house where meth had been cooked.

"That's a good idea, to get the Fire Department up here. No need to risk one of my people over the killing of a couple of dopers," Weislowski said.

Weislowski motioned his people over and told them to

step outside. Then he walked with Byrd to the side of the trailer where the wind wouldn't hit them. "Thanks for coming out to help us. Right now, it looks like a couple of dopers got themselves killed."

Byrd responded in kind. "Happy to help. I have another Agent on the way, too. We usually work the western counties in our region."

Weislowski nodded. He seemed uncomfortable with what he was about to say. He cleared his throat and said, "The Sheriff wants me to work with you, if that's okay. He just wants to be sure he's up-to-date on where everything stands."

Byrd smiled. "I'll be happy to have someone who knows the county. I live here but I'm not that familiar with the back roads."

"Great. I'll grab my notepad and we can start talking to people. The girl's mother is here. She says she has some information that might help us."

Byrd looked down at the girl again. Weislowski may think these two were simply "dopers," but they were people, too. People with mothers and grandmothers, dreams and traditions. Now they were lying dead here. Byrd didn't judge their lives, but he was responsible for finding whoever took them.

Weislowski walked away to give instructions to one of the uniformed Deputies. Byrd turned the recorder off and waited. When Weislowski came back, he pointed to a beat-up minivan parked by the road. The lawmen walked over to the passenger door and Byrd tapped on the window. The man and woman inside the van, who were dozing, both jerked awake.

The woman in the passenger seat rolled her window down. She looked at Byrd and said, "Who are you?"

Byrd didn't bother to produce his badge. "My name's Daniel Byrd, I work for the GBI. This man with me is Major Weislowski of the Cherokee Sheriff's Office. We're here to investigate your daughter's death. May we sit in your car and talk with you?"

She hit the unlock button and waited for them to climb into the back seats. When they were settled, she said, "I know who did this. His name is Wilmer Westbrook."

Byrd was busy taking notes. He noted the date and time on his notepad and then activated the digital recorder. "Hang on a second. Let me get your name, date of birth, and home address. I need that for the report."

"I gave that to one of them Deputies over there," she said.

Byrd nodded. "I'm sure you did. But I need it for the GBI report. I hate to have you repeating all this, but you're probably going to have to repeat most everything you have told anyone tonight. I'm sorry."

She hung her head and sighed. "I know. I'm just so tired. I knew this day would come, but I hoped against hope that it never would." She swallowed hard and then continued. "My name is Ramona Clark. I used to be a Page. I'm Krystal's momma."

She gave Byrd her date of birth and home address. He took down her home phone number and determined she didn't have a cell phone or pager. She identified the driver of the van as her husband, Oliver. Oliver never spoke.

"Mrs. Clark, what can you tell us about tonight?"

She began to cry and moan softly. She wiped her tears and looked back at Byrd. "She was a good girl. She was the first one in our family to go all the way and graduate high school. She even thought about getting into a few beauty pageants, but she didn't have the money to buy good clothes. She was saving for one of them sparkly dresses and was working at a café. That's where she met that boy. She fell in with him and I knew she would end up dead one way or the other. Mark—that's her man's name—Mark Goodwin. Mark wasn't a bad feller. As far as I know, he never beat her or did anything to hurt her. Except he kept her on meth, and she was getting worse and worse on it. She kept picking at her pretty skin. Now she's got scabs all over her arms. I told her no one halfway decent would want a woman with scabs all over her arms, and the only way to get much of anywhere is to get a man to take you there. I guess it don't matter much now." Her eyes brimmed with tears before she quickly wiped them away. "She wasn't but twenty-two years old."

Byrd looked her in the eye. "I understand you may know who did this?" Byrd asked.

She nodded. "Yep. I know who did them in as good as I know my own name. It was Wilmer Westbrook. Mark owed him money that Wilmer put up for Mark to cook meth. He's come around their house a few times trying to collect. He's a mean son of a bitch. I'll guarantee that he did this."

Weislowski spoke up. "What does Wilmer drive, do you know?"

She nodded. "A new truck. A Dodge, I think."

Byrd looked over at Weislowski, who said, "The neighbor saw an old model truck leaving right after he heard shots."

Byrd turned back to Ramona. "Do you know anyone else who heard that Westbrook was threatening them?" Byrd asked.

"My word ain't good enough for you?" Ramona questioned, steely in her tone.

"Mrs. Clark, that's not the issue. We don't want this to

come down to your word against his. It's always better when we can have several people testify to something when things go to court." Byrd spoke in a level tone. He wanted Ramona to stay focused.

Ramona relented. "I'm not for sure, but I'll check with my kin folks. She may have told one of her cousins about Wilmer. She didn't have no brothers or sisters." Ramona lowered her voice. "I couldn't have no more kids after she was born. They did some damage to my plumbing. She was all I had."

Byrd nodded understandingly. He asked several more questions about Mark and Krystal's backgrounds. He got contact information for Mark's family, which Weislowski noted so that someone could contact them. When the interview was winding down, Byrd asked Ramona, "Do you know where we can find Wilmer?"

Weislowski spoke up again. "I have his address. His family is a big supporter of the Sheriff."

Ramona leaned over the seat to look back at Weislowski. "You better not cover this up. Tell your boss I'll go door to door to get him beat in the next election if I have to. I expect my girl to be treated like anybody else murdered in this county. It don't matter who the killer is friends with." She began crying again. She hung her head, and the tears dropped quietly on the floor of the van.

Byrd glanced at Weislowski. "I'll make sure this is handled. If he did this, I'll hand him the warrant myself."

Ramona took Byrd's offered business card. She wiped her face and asked, "Who will the property in the trailer belong to?"

"That's really a civil matter. But I'm sure your daughter's property will be turned over to you at some point."

Ramona sniffed and wiped her eyes again. "Krystal

had promised me a little of what was made. I was wondering if I could get it now."

Byrd frowned. "Some of the meth?"

Ramona nodded. "Just a little pinch. It would help me get through all this."

Byrd shook his head. "Everything inside there is evidence."

Ramona hung her head. "I guess it's wrong of me to ask, but I ain't got much of my daughter's things to remember her by. I guess, when this is over, I can get some of her clothes and such. But a little pick-me-up would help me right now."

Byrd tried, for a moment, to imagine the loss a parent must feel when a child dies first—and not from disease or an accident but at the hand of another person. Byrd felt the sadness wash over him but couldn't let his feelings affect his job.

They opened the van doors, and the cold air rushed in. Byrd wrapped himself in his overcoat as he stood up. Byrd pointed at the neighbor's house. "Have the neighbors been talked to?" Byrd asked.

Weislowski nodded. "One of the uniforms talked to him briefly. We may as well go talk to him while we are out here. He might tell us more than the other Deputy."

Byrd and Weislowski walked over to the stoop. The lights inside were on. Byrd took the lead, walked to the door, and knocked. When he saw a face looking out through the window in the door, Byrd extended his badge.

When they were inside the living room and seated on a worn-down couch, Byrd asked the neighbor, who identified himself as Homer Grimes, to tell them what had happened the night before. Grimes told them what he had seen, heard, and imagined in the last few hours. Byrd duly took note of what Grimes said. Grimes told them about the smells next door, the times he had seen the neighbors having sex or walking around inside and outside in little or no clothes. He would have told them about the moving truck that had skinned the bark off one of his trees when they moved in two years ago if Byrd had not cut him off.

"Do you know Wilmer Westbrook?" Byrd asked.

"No," Grimes responded.

"Have you seen a new model truck around?" Byrd pressed.

"The one them two killer boys came in weren't new. I can tell you that for a fact."

"Tell me about that truck then," Byrd said.

Grimes pointed at the gravel drive. "It was an old white truck with some green around the middle. Had a toolbox on the back. They parked right out there and come up here bold as brass."

"Would you recognize who was in the truck?"

Grimes shook his head and spat on the floor. "Nope. Them meth heads are all alike to me. They was two of them though. One was skinny and about my height. The other one stayed in the truck."

"Was there anything else you can tell us about the truck? What kind of tag was on it?"

Grimes shrugged. "I couldn't see much else. The tag weren't local, but I don't know what state it was." He thought about it more and then continued. "I do remember that there was a chain hanging down from the back of the truck."

Byrd's blood ran cold. "Was it a Texas tag?"

Grimes shook his head again. "I can't say. It was too dark."

Byrd considered stopping the interview to put a look-out for the Texas truck to officers in the area. He decided he needed more information to confirm it was the truck he had seen earlier. But his gut told him it was.

Byrd came back to his earlier question. "But have you seen a fairly new truck over at Goodwin's?"

Grimes gave it some thought. "Yeah. There is a man who come over there a couple of times. He left mad most of the time. Yelling over his shoulder and such." Grimes snapped his fingers. "By gum, I seen him sitting in front of my house last week. Him and another man was sitting in the road, looking over Mark's house. Is he one of them?"

Byrd looked over at Weislowski, whose gaze was on his hands.

"Thanks, Mr. Grimes. I appreciate your help tonight." Byrd and Weislowski stood and headed outside.

Byrd waited until they were away from the house. He turned to Weislowski. "Looks like this Westbrook is a better suspect than I thought."

Weislowski nodded without comment. Byrd guessed Weislowski knew his recorder was still on.

The two men got out to the line of cars parked near the crime scene. Byrd pointed to his Expedition. "Hop in. I'll drive."

Weislowski hesitated. "I don't mind driving."

"We may end up chasing these folks all over Georgia before the day is over. I've got radio contact with departments all over the state in my truck. And I have my gear in there."

Weislowski was hesitant and stood for a moment weighing his choices. Weislowski relented. "Give me a minute to get my cell phone out of my car and I'll hop in with you."

Weislowski jogged to his car while Byrd warmed up the GBI truck.

CHAPTER 14
ON THE TRACK

MONDAY, FEBRUARY 24, 2003
CANTON, GEORGIA
4:00 A.M.

Byrd was driving toward Canton with Weislowski seated silently by his side. The police radio—usually quiet at this time of day when police calls for service were at their lowest ebb—suddenly came alive.

"Thirty-four to Eighty-nine."

Byrd brought the microphone to his mouth. "Eighty-nine. Go ahead, Doc."

"Teddy, where do you want to meet up?"

"I'll meet you at GSP. We're on the way back from the scene to Canton. That'll be on our way."

"Who is we?"

"I have Major Weislowski with Cherokee riding with me. He's their head of CID."

"All right. I'm south of Ball Ground. I'll be with you in about ten minutes."

Weislowski looked at Byrd. "Who was that, and why did he call you Teddy?"

Byrd blushed. He was happy he was in the dark truck. "That's Doc Farmer. One of the Agents in my office. And Teddy is a nickname. Just like Doc is Jackson Farmer. I guess it's a rite of passage in our office."

Weislowski mumbled something Byrd couldn't understand. Then he pulled out the cell phone he had stuck in his pocket, dialed a number, and waited for the phone to connect.

The call connected and Weislowski spoke into the phone. "Sheriff, can you hear me?"

Byrd could hear a voice on the other end. Weislowski raised his voice. "I'm in the car with the GBI man, Byrd. We are going to try to find Wilmer Westbrook."

Byrd could hear the Sheriff respond but couldn't make out the words. After the phone was silent, Weislowski said, "I'll keep you posted."

Byrd swung the Expedition into the driveway of the State Patrol Post and pulled around to the back. He saw Doc's Crown Victoria parked under the carport area and Doc stood in the back, smoking a cigarette.

When Byrd dropped to the ground from the tall GBI truck, Doc met him at the door. "Son, we're keeping some terrible hours this week. I sure do hope it gets better!"

Weislowski came around to their side of the truck. Byrd inclined his head toward the Major. "Doc, this is Craig Weislowski. He is the Major over Cherokee's CID."

The two men shook hands. "Nice to meet you, Major," Doc said.

Weislowski nodded. "Same here. We appreciate you guys pitching in to help. Our experience level is pretty low in the CID right now."

Doc nodded. "It's tough all over trying to find people. We work fourteen counties up here in North Georgia, and almost every agency struggles to keep good people."

Weislowski grinned. "Either one of you boys looking for a job? We can put you right to work."

Doc laughed. "I have too much time in with the State to start over. About all we do have is a good retirement."

Byrd had other things on his mind. He knew the Patrol Post would have a pot of coffee on. As a haven for any State Officer, the GSP Posts were open all night. Radio Operators who manned the Posts knew coffee was a priority. He motioned for Doc and Craig to follow, and he led the way into the kitchen of the brick building.

Byrd found ceramic cups in the cupboard and sat them on the table. Then he poured black coffee all around. The men dropped their heavy coats on the chairs around the table, and then they sat down for a moment to savor the strong, hot coffee.

After a long gulp of coffee, Doc looked at Byrd and asked, "What do you need me to do, son?"

Byrd thought about it for a couple of seconds. Then he turned to Weislowski. "Craig, who was the detective working the scene up there? Doc can give him a hand."

Weislowski nodded. "That's a good idea. His name is Ronny Beavers. He could use help. And the Fire Department should be on scene by now."

Doc frowned. "Fire Department? Did the place burn?"

Byrd shook his head. "Worse, I guess. It's a meth lab. But there wasn't an active cook. I think the Fire Department will probably just use their fans to get some clean air into it and then you should be able to do your work."

Doc finished off his coffee and took out his notepad. "Give me the address."

Byrd did. Then Weislowski added some landmarks to make the place easier to find. Doc stood up and headed out the door. He stopped for a moment, looked back, and asked, "Where are you boys headed?"

"Everybody is pointing the finger at a local man named Wilmer Westbrook," Weislowski said. "He lives a few miles from here, right outside of town. Figured we should pay him a visit pretty soon."

Byrd nodded. He remembered the phrase the instructors at the GBI Academy would scream at the new Agents and repeated, "Wakey-wakey! Rise and shine!"

Doc groaned. "If I never hear that again in my life, I'll be just fine."

Byrd finished his coffee and put the mug in the sink. Weislowski followed suit, then held up his hand. "We should get some uniform support before we go to Westbrook's house. I don't want to take a bullet and have him claim he thought we were burglars."

Byrd liked the idea. "I don't have a problem with that."

Weislowski had another thought. "Should we go ahead and get a search warrant?"

Byrd thought about that option. "I think our probable cause is thin. Do you know anything that would corroborate Krystal's mom's information?"

Weislowski thought about the question. "Not really."

Byrd mulled over the options. He looked out the window for a moment and wondered what the best course of action was. He didn't want to lose a murder case over not having sufficient probable cause for a warrant. On the other hand, he didn't want to lose the murder weapon.

"Could you get a couple of uniforms to back us up? That way, if we find something, we can run into town and get a warrant while the Deputies hold the scene."

"Good idea," Weislowski said. He pulled out his cell phone and called Dispatch. He soon had two Deputies on the way to the Post for a quick briefing.

Wilmer Westbrook was tossing and turning in the tight space he had to sleep in. He had expected the two knuckleheads he had sent to get his money to be back long before now.

He and the others had partied until almost two, smoking some more of the weed Melvin had brought along. Wilmer hadn't initiated any sex play this evening, but he hoped that tomorrow morning they could try another round before they left for home. Gail was snoring and motionless beside him. He could hear Dolly and Melvin rustling around, but they seemed to be in a deep sleep as well.

Wilmer rolled off the bed and looked out the door. His heart almost stopped when he saw Roger Sturdevant standing outside the door looking back at him. Wilmer stumbled back and grabbed the table by the door for support. Once he had gotten over the shock, he pulled on a shirt and stepped outside.

Wilmer was freezing in the predawn hours, when the temperature was the coldest. "Where the hell have you been? Did you get my money?"

Roger shook his head and moaned. "Not a dime of it."

Wilmer was confused. "How did you get in here? You didn't try to get in the gate, did you? The Rangers would notice that."

"I parked outside and walked in."

Wilmer frowned. "That's good. Well, if you don't produce, I'll be damned if I'll pay you anything. As a matter of fact, I want the money I gave you back."

The night was dark, but there was a streetlight several lots away from where the two men stood. Wilmer suddenly realized that Roger was crying. Wilmer's heart sank.

"What happened? What did y'all do?"

Roger just shook his head. He moaned again. "It was awful. Lumpy went crazy."

Wilmer dropped to his knees. "Damn it!" he yelled, pounding the ground with his fist. "I knew this was going to get fucked up."

Roger fell to his knees beside him. "It wasn't my fault. Lumpy done it all!"

"How bad are they hurt? Can Mark still cook, or did you have to break him up?"

Roger moaned again. "He ain't broke."

Wilmer felt a surge of relief. "Okay, is he mad at me? Is that it?"

Roger shook his head and began to shake as he cried harder. "He's dead. Lumpy shot him dead."

Wilmer shook his head. *That's not what Roger just said,* he thought. *I misheard him.*

"What did you just say?" Wilmer asked. He was praying for a different answer.

"Lumpy shot him and his woman. They're all dead. He just shot them!"

Wilmer's heart was racing again. Adrenaline and meth surged through his veins. His hands were shaking, and he felt like he would vomit. He tried to stand up, but his knees wouldn't cooperate.

"Where are my guns? You didn't leave them at the house, did you?" Wilmer's mind was racing, trying to think of all the ways he might get caught.

Roger shook his head. "I got the Smith on me. Lumpy still has the automatic." Roger reached for the revolver tucked in his pants, and for the first time, he realized that it was gone. "Shit! I lost the gun in the dark, sometime after I got out of the truck."

"Here in the park?"

Roger nodded.

"Are you sure?"

"Yes," Roger said. "I stuck it in my pants when I got out of the truck just a minute ago. But I didn't shoot it. It won't be traced back to anything."

Wilmer thought that over. "You didn't use it at all?"

"No. I didn't pull the trigger once. I wish I had used it to kill Lumpy before he shot them other people, though."

Wilmer rocked back and forth. "Shit! I ought to kill you right now! You brought that other fucker into this. Damn you!"

Roger started to sob. He was talking, but Wilmer couldn't understand the words. Roger fell over on the ground and lay there. For a moment, Wilmer wished he had a gun. He wanted to put Roger out of his misery.

"Then where is Lumpy? Did you kill him?"

"Hell no! I was afraid he would kill me, so I dumped him on the side of the road. I left him."

Wilmer hit the ground with his fist. "Shit! Does he know who I am? Did you tell him my name?"

Roger shook his head. "He was here with me that one time. I never said your name, and there ain't no reason for him to know who you are."

Wilmer exhaled and put a hand on Roger's shoulder. "That's good."

"For you!" Roger shouted.

"Calm down. What are you going to do from here? Do you have a plan?"

Roger did calm down. The human contact had helped. "I have to get some cash. I want to get out of here. I'm going back to my momma and daddy's house to get my stuff, then I'm going to get on the road. Back to Texas or maybe even Mexico."

Wilmer saw some hope. "Are you sure Lumpy doesn't know my name?"

Roger thought about that. "No, I don't think so. It was never said to him."

Wilmer suddenly realized how cold it was. He wrapped

his arms around himself. He was thinking about his options. He turned back to Roger. "I don't have any cash here, but if you go to your folk's house, I'll meet you at noon at the gas station just off the interstate in Holly Springs. The one by the grocery store. I'll bring you enough money to get you out of the country. Okay?"

Roger stood and brushed himself off. "Yeah. I can do that."

Wilmer stood, too. "Just get the hell out of here and don't ever come back."

Roger mumbled and walked away, back toward his truck.

Wilmer stumbled as he made his way back to the camper door. His bare feet were freezing, and he was shaking from the cold. At least, he assumed it was from the cold.

He opened the door of the camper and climbed in. He had trouble seeing in the darkness, but he sensed someone moving near him. He felt someone lean into him and whisper in his ear. "You ready for some more action?" It was Dolly.

She reached down and massaged his groin. Wilmer was in no mood for sex. He pushed her hand away and sat on the corner of the bed. He shook his head. Just a few hours ago he would have given anything for time in Dolly's arms. Now he just wished he could go back in time a few days. He wished with all his heart that he could just fix this mess. He hung his head, and the tears started to fall. Not a single tear for Mark and Krystal, just tears for what he was afraid would happen to him.

CHAPTER 15

PROPER PRIOR PLANNING PREVENTS PISS POOR PERFORMANCE

MONDAY, FEBRUARY 24, 2003
CANTON, GEORGIA
6:00 A.M.

Lumpy walked along the shoulder of the highway. He had no idea where he was or how to get back to Roger's parents' house. After all the law cars had passed, he had hustled along the quiet road back in the direction they came in from.

The meth had made his heart pound so hard he wasn't sure, at first, that Roger had gone off and left him. He was having trouble with his vision, and he heard voices calling to him. He knew the meth was messing with his head, especially when he heard cars approaching that turned out not to be there.

He continued to hide off the shoulder of the roadway when he heard a car. Under other circumstances, he would put out his left thumb, hoping for a ride. But he couldn't see well enough to know which cars were the cops.

He stumbled along, hoping he would see a country store with a pay phone. He had no idea what his chances of finding one were.

Lumpy ended up walking for, what seemed to him, hours when he finally came to a country store with a pay phone. He fished in his pocket and pulled out some change. He thought about who he could call, then remembered a cousin who lived in Ball Ground. He dug in his wallet and found the crumpled piece of paper he kept important phone numbers written on. He ran his finger up and down the list until he found a number he thought would work. Jimmy Lee Cochran was the name, although Lumpy doubted he would recognize the face.

His cousin answered the phone after several rings. "This better be good!"

"Don't hang up. This is your cousin, Ricky Cochran. Everybody calls me Lumpy."

There was silence on the line. Lumpy was terrified Jimmy Lee would hang up on him. He couldn't think of anyone else who might help him. "I'll give you a hundred dollars cash if you'll come pick me up right now."

"What if I don't want your money?"

"I've also got about an eight ball of meth I'll give you."

Again, the line was quiet. After several seconds Jimmy Lee came back on the line. "Where you at?"

Lumpy described the business as best he could. When he finished, Jimmy Lee said, "I know where it's at. Be looking for a red Corvette."

The line went dead, and Lumpy slumped beside the phone booth. He felt a sense of relief for the first time in over an hour. He stretched out his legs and tried to relax, but his heart was pounding from the meth still hanging around in his body. He pulled his legs up to his chest and waited for Jimmy Lee.

Byrd led the two Cherokee Deputy Sheriffs out of the

State Patrol Post parking lot and onto the main highway. The short procession wound through downtown Canton and ended up at a modest house just outside the city limits.

Byrd had turned onto the side street where the Westbrook house was located and was surprised it was the first house on the left. The house was brick and sat back off the road. Byrd pulled his GBI vehicle into the driveway while the two marked patrol cars parked on the shoulder of the road in front of the home.

Byrd grabbed his aluminum flashlight from the door pocket and held it with his left hand. He tucked his notepad under the same arm to ensure that his right hand was free to access his gun.

The two uniformed Deputies both got out of their cars and stood together at the end of the driveway as Byrd and Weislowski made their way to the front door of the house. Byrd was surprised to hear the TV in the living room turned up loud and saw lights on in several rooms. He looked to Weislowski, who shrugged. Byrd stepped to the left of the door, and Weislowski stood to the right. Byrd used the metal flashlight to bang on the front door.

Weislowski saw the man first. He ducked back from the door and pointed at the front window of the house. "I see somebody moving around in there." Weislowski shouted at the door, "Sheriff's Office! Come to the door, please!"

After a few seconds, the door opened a crack. A rush of marijuana smoke came out, preceding a single bloodshot eye peering from the gloom of the foyer. Byrd turned his flashlight toward the person at the door and saw whoever it was recoil backward and cover their eyes.

Weislowski used his toe to push the door open. "Are you okay? Can we get you some medical attention?"

With Byrd's light, they could see a small, chubby man

dressed in sweatpants and a sweatshirt. Byrd spoke loudly, "Are you Wilmer Westbrook?"

The man held both hands out and shook his head. "You got the wrong guy. Will ain't here. I'm house-sitting for him. He has a lot of guns and valuables that he has me keep safe for him."

Weislowski laughed. "And you do that by smoking weed and watching late-night TV?"

The man became defensive. "Who said I was smoking weed? I wasn't doing nothing wrong."

Byrd stepped into the foyer. "We're looking for Westbrook. Who are you?"

The man continued to hold his hands out. "I'm telling you, whatever Will did ain't got nothing to do with me."

Byrd nodded and took on a soothing tone. "And we know that. We're not here for you. We just want to talk to Wilmer."

"Him and his wife are at the lake. Took his camper down the other day. Been there ever since."

"Which lake?" Byrd asked.

"Allatoona. Sweetwater Campground. He has a big new Dodge truck that he pulls this white and blue trailer with."

Byrd tried again. "What did you say your name is?"

The man hung his head. "I'm Will's half-brother. My name is Benny McGee."

Byrd wrote the name down. "And when was the last time you saw Wilmer?"

The man turned and led the men into the living room. "When they left a couple of days ago," Benny said.

Byrd took a more conversational tone. "Is Wilmer still doing business with Mark Goodwin?"

Benny snorted. "Last I heard, Will said that Mark had

fucked him out of a bunch of money he was owed. I hear Mark's one of the best meth cooks in this part of the country. Not that I would know anything about that kind of business."

"Was Wilmer in that business?" Byrd asked.

Benny looked at his feet. "I don't know much about his business. I just heard Will bitchin' that Mark had took advantage of him and wasn't paying as fast as Will thought he should be."

Byrd glanced at Weislowski. "When is Wilmer supposed to be back?"

Benny looked back up. "Tonight, sometime. Why are you guys looking for him?"

"There was an incident at Mark Goodwin's house early this morning," Weislowski offered. "Do you know anything about it?"

Benny's eyes narrowed. "What do I get if I tell you what I heard?"

Weislowski stepped closer to Benny. "Maybe no charges for the weed we smell in this house. We are in a hurry and don't want to waste time on a misdemeanor case. But I guess we could if you forced our hand."

Byrd's digital recorder was running when Benny said, "He tried to hire one of his wife's cousins who works at the car wash. He wanted Mark beat up over the money he owed."

Weislowski pushed him to give more information. "What's his name? We can't help you if you don't help us."

Benny squinted. "Roger Sturdevant. He just got out of jail in Texas."

Byrd hung his head. "Shit! I saw his truck last night in Canton."

Weislowski turned to him. "What time?"

Byrd tried to remember a time frame. "It must have been between nine and ten. The burger place near my apartment was still open."

Weislowski shook Benny's hand. "Thanks! And get rid of the weed before we come back with a search warrant."

Benny McGee's head bobbed up and down. "Did Sturdevant hurt Mark bad? To have all these laws at my door, he must have busted him up bad."

Weislowski turned back to address McGee. "Bad enough. Mark and Krystal are dead."

Benny just stood there. With his mouth open.

Byrd tucked his notepad under his arm. "I guess we're headed to Sweetwater."

Doc pulled his GBI car off the little road near the Goodwin trailer. He grabbed his overcoat out of the back seat, threw it on over his suit, and made his way to the crime scene tape and the Deputy who was guarding it. He badged the Deputy and walked toward the door.

Doc saw the woman, Krystal, and stopped for a moment. He knelt beside her body and took a look. He pulled a set of rubber gloves from his suit pocket and touched the back of her head where the apparent injury was. He could see that the bullet had entered the back of her head and hadn't exited unless it had come out through her open mouth. He looked her over from head to foot, using his flashlight. When he had seen what he could, he took a moment to say a silent prayer for her soul.

Standing, he shook his head at the waste of a life, then walked up to the trailer door. An orange ventilation fan furnished by the Fire Department was pulling the chemically smelling air out and allowing fresh air in. A Deputy in plain clothes stood near the door and was busy looking the living room over with his own flashlight.

"Excuse me," Doc said to the Detective. The man turned to the sound of the voice and stopped in his tracks. Doc was surprised that the Detective looked barely old enough to drive a car, much less be a Detective on a homicide scene.

The younger man stuck out his hand. "Hey, you must be with the GBI. I'm Ronny Beavers."

Doc shook his hand. "I'm Jackson Farmer, but most people call me Doc."

"Be careful coming up those stairs, Doc. They're not much. Please come on in and tell me what you see. This is my first homicide, and I've just been looking at everything I can till the Fire Department is finished."

Doc sniffed the air and frowned. "It doesn't smell as bad in here as some meth houses I have been in."

Ronny nodded. "The Fire Department has done a good job of getting this thing aired out. We should be able to start processing the bodies soon."

Doc stepped over to where Mark Goodwin lay on his back, his sightless eyes staring at the ceiling. Doc squatted beside Mark and looked his body over. He saw the vomit, which had overrun the tape around his mouth. He examined the bullet hole in his forehead. This bullet looked like it was also still somewhere in the head. Doc thought that it was probably a .380 or .38 caliber. No less deadly, but certainly less damage to the body. Again, he said a quick prayer for the soul of the victim. Doc couldn't help the feeling of sadness that went with his job.

Doc stood and looked around the room. Ronny pointed into the kitchen. "The meth this guy made is boxed up in the kitchen."

Doc stuck his head around and looked into the kitchen, but his focus was on the living room. He knew no one would be charged with the drugs. At least no one from this house.

Ronny took off his gloves and threw them in a pile. He flexed his hands and let the skin breathe. "Do you know Dan Byrd?"

Doc nodded. "Yep. He's the Case Agent on this. I'm just helping him out."

Ronny nodded. "Is he a pretty good guy?"

Doc was wondering where the question came from. "He's one of the best. Why do you ask? Wasn't he here earlier?"

Ronny looked sheepish. "He went out with my sister last night. Or the night before. I'm not sure what day we're in."

Doc helped Ronny out. "It's Monday morning."

Ronny laughed at himself. "I'm pretty new to all this, so I guess I'm just trying to process everything."

"I'm not new to this, and I still have to work to process everything. People aren't meant to die like this." Doc changed the subject. "So, your sister went out with Danny?"

Ronny blushed. "Please don't tell him I was checking on him. She's my older sister and I worry about her. She got divorced from a real jerk last year, and she has dated several people since then but nothing serious. But she talked about Dan and seems really interested in him."

All the pieces fell into place. "She's a cop with Canton PD?"

Ronny nodded. "Yep. Several of us were going out, and then she called me and said she wanted to go out with Dan alone. I haven't heard how things went."

Doc laughed. "Me neither, but I sure would like to know. Danny needs somebody to go out with. He works too much."

Ronny chuckled. "That sounds like sis. She works as much as she can and stashes the overtime money away."

Doc turned back to Mark, bringing the conversation back to the case. "What have you been able to tell about the scene here so far?"

"It looks like, to me, that she"—he pointed toward Krystal—"got loose and made a break for it. I don't know if it was before or after Mark here got it."

Doc nodded. "With her body out in the cold, and his inside this trailer, even though it's colder than a well-digger's ass in here, it will be hard for the Medical Examiner to tell who went first."

Ronny stroked his chin. "If I were guessing, I would say they were both tied up, and she broke loose."

Doc nodded again. "I can't argue with that logic."

Ronny continued. "I think someone was trying to get Mark to tell them something. The meth was pretty much in the open, but they wanted something from Mark. That's why they shot him in the knee."

Doc looked at Mark closer. "I missed the capping."

Ronny looked puzzled.

Doc said, "Shooting in the kneecap. It's a way to get people to talk. It's supposed to be very painful."

Ronny knelt beside Mark again, looking at the pain etched on his face. He turned back to look up at Doc. "I sure do wish he could tell us what happened."

Doc smiled at the young Detective. "He will. We just have to listen to what he is saying."

Wilmer's hand shook as he made a pot of coffee. Daylight was over an hour away, and the overcast skies meant it would be dark for a couple of hours more. No one else seemed to be stirring. After trying to pour coffee into a cup and sloshing it all over the counter, he sat in the dark kitchen and tried to focus.

Wilmer tried to think of any way the murder of Krystal and Mark could point back at him. The only people who knew for sure that he had anything to do with the chain of events that led to their death would be Roger and Lumpy. He entertained the idea of shooting both of them himself but immediately dismissed it, knowing he didn't have the backbone to do it. He knew his best bet would be for Roger to make it to Mexico.

He found that rocking in his seat helped a little. He looked outside and wished he could turn the clock back. As he rocked back and forth, he heard Dolly come out into the center of the camper.

She leaned down and whispered in his ear. "You got any more of that rocket fuel? We could get down here on the floor and have a good time, and the others could just keep on sleeping."

Wilmer was in no mood. He turned up to look at Dolly. "We've used it all up. I'm tapped out."

She grumbled. "Shit. That's a bummer."

She turned around and walked back to her bed. In just a few minutes Wilmer could hear her snoring.

Lumpy was not surprised that the Corvette his stupid cousin drove was a '70s model with as much body filler as paint. He pulled up in a cloud of exhaust smoke and bathed Lumpy in his headlights.

Lumpy dropped onto the seat and slammed the door. "Hey," Jimmy Lee said. "Careful slamming that door."

Lumpy tried to remember how many bullets he had left in the Berretta. He didn't want to use his last round to kill Jimmy Lee. Instead, he leaned back in the seat and closed his eyes. "Where are we headed?"

"I'm taking you to my house. I've got to be at my job in an hour. When I get off, I'll take you wherever you need to go. And I'll be gettin' that crank from you."

Lumpy laughed. "I've heard that shit called everything from work to rocket fuel to crank in the last couple of days. I hadn't never tried it before today, but I can sure tell you that none of them names do it justice. It'll sure take the top of your head off."

Jimmy Lee mumbled something in the dark. Lumpy didn't care what he said. He didn't care what his *name* was. He just needed a place to crash for a little while, and then a car to get the hell out of Dodge.

He rode in silence until Jimmy Lee turned the car into a driveway. The house looked like it was just a basement. As they pulled the raggedy car up near the door, Lumpy got a good look at Jimmy Lee, who was a big dumb lug as far as he could see.

Jimmy Lee got out of the car, ignoring Lumpy, and headed to the windowless door of the basement/house. Lumpy followed behind, making sure the pistol was still in the waist of his pants. He walked into his cousin's home, which was as junky as his car. There was a car engine in the living room. The furniture was worn and had stuffing coming out of holes in the fabric. Lumpy sat down on the dirty couch and put his feet up on the engine.

"Who the fuck is this?" A woman's voice rang out.

Lumpy's cousin responded. "He is supposedly my cousin. He's just staying here till I get back from work. He's paying me to give him a ride so he can get out of town. Which I'm gonna do as soon as I can."

"Well, I ain't cooking for his ass. I guess he can just sit in here till you get back."

Lumpy's cousin walked to the door. "That's fine. Just

leave him alone. When I get back, I'll take him to where he wants to go."

"How much is he paying?"

"It don't matter," the cousin said as he walked out and slammed the door.

The woman came into the light, and Lumpy could see that she was about forty, with thinning hair pulled back in a bun. She was dressed in jeans and a flannel shirt and had a cigarette clamped in her mouth. She looked Lumpy over and then went to the refrigerator, where she pulled out a beer.

She popped the top and took a long drink. Then she turned back to Lumpy. "How much are you paying him?"

Lumpy smiled. "Not how much. More like what."

She frowned. "What does that mean?"

He reached in his pocket and pulled out the ball of methamphetamine.

She licked her lips. "Is that what I think it is?"

"Depends on what you think it is."

"Crank?"

Lumpy nodded. She couldn't take her eyes off the drugs.

"You want some?" he asked.

"It's been a while since I've had any of that. Is it rocket fuel?"

"I got nothing to compare it to. But it was stronger than anything I've ever had."

She kept staring at the dirty tan ball in Lumpy's hand. "What do you want for it? Nobody gives up dope for nothing."

Lumpy patted the seat beside him. "I am just wanting something I haven't had in a while. I haven't been with a woman in over four years. My cousin won't even notice if you was to give me a little while he's at work."

She looked at Lumpy and then back at the golf ball of meth. She turned around and left the room. Lumpy hoped she wouldn't tell Jimmy Lee about what he had said. He was pushing the ball back into his pocket when she came back into the room with a syringe.

"Whoa! I don't use a needle." Lumpy was holding up both hands.

"You won't use anything else once you try this." She pulled off her flannel shirt and dropped her pants on the floor. In her panties and bra, she sat on the couch beside him and used a rubber hose, which had been crammed between the cushions, to tie off his right arm. He was scared, but he let her proceed.

She took a pinch out of the plastic bag and then used a lighter to heat the meth in a spoon. When she saw that the meth had melted to a liquid, she stuck the needle into the spoon and sucked the meth up, taking a good-sized pull. She leaned over and found a vein in her left thigh. She put the needle into her leg, and Lumpy thought she must have gone right into the vein because he watched as her eyes fluttered and her face turned red as a beet. She took several deep breaths and then opened her eyes to look at Lumpy. "You ever done it while you was doing meth?"

He shook his head.

"It may hurt some, but it's gonna hurt *so good.*" She took the same needle, which now had some of her blood in it, and stuck it into Lumpy's right arm. He knew immediately that she was in a vein. He tasted the meth in his mouth and felt it surging through his body. For a second, he was short of breath and thought he might be having a heart attack.

He reached up and began to pound on the side of his head. He felt like his skin was on fire and the room was brighter than any place he had ever seen. This was more intense than the little bit of meth he had put inside his lip.

He felt her pulling his pants off and lifted his hips to help her out. Then he felt her mouth on his groin. Suddenly, he ejaculated. He mumbled, "Sorry, but it's been a while."

She spit on the floor and laughed. "Don't worry. Before I'm done, you're gonna be spitting dust out of that thing."

He realized that his erection hadn't faded. In fact, his penis seemed harder than before. He pulled his shirt over his head and stuck the little pistol down into the couch. Lumpy closed his eyes tight, arched his back, and dug his heels into the floor.

She climbed on top and started riding him like a wild stallion. Lumpy hoped that he would live through this as his heart pounded in his chest. *But*, he thought, *if you gotta go, you gotta go.*

Daniel Byrd led the parade into the campground. When they got to the locked gate, he and the two patrol cars parked. One of the Deputies said that Dispatch could call the Ranger and get her to open the gate. Weislowski told him to do that, and then they waited.

The Ranger came out of a cottage behind them, her uniform looking fresh and neat, and walked to the gatehouse. When she got near, Byrd intercepted her. He showed her his identification. "We are here to locate Wilmer Westbrook. He is supposed to be in a camper parked here."

She nodded without comment and unlocked the gatehouse. Byrd followed her in, and she pulled out the log book of campers. She ran down the list and found the information on Westbrook's campsite and a description of his camper and the truck that pulled it. Byrd copied everything down.

As an afterthought, Byrd asked if she had seen a green and white truck in the campground in the last couple of days. She nodded and pulled out a second book and found the list of visitors from the day before. Byrd looked over her shoulder as she ran her finger down the page. He saw her finger stop. His pulse quickened when he saw the notation. In precise handwriting, someone had recorded the Texas tag in the visitor's log: "6677QM." She pointed it out to Byrd, who carefully recorded the time that the truck had come and gone.

"Thanks," Byrd said as she closed the book.

She looked Byrd in the eye. "Is there going to be any trouble?"

Byrd thought about that for a moment. "Not if he doesn't make any."

She walked over to the phone on the wall of the little hut. "I guess I need to call my boss."

"Wait till we see what happens. A few minutes won't change anything, and there may not be anything to report." Byrd walked back outside. He saw that Major Craig Weislowski was closing his cell phone.

"Reporting in?" Byrd asked.

"Yep. He keeps me on a short leash."

Byrd called the two uniformed Deputies over. He gathered them around a map of the park on the wall. He pointed to a campsite displayed on the wall. "He is in lot fourteen in a camper pulled by a big Dodge truck. There are only a couple of more lots that are occupied, so he should be easy to spot."

"Where do you want us to go?" Weislowski asked.

Byrd thought it over. "If the trailer is backed in, we'll clear the truck and then circle the trailer. The trailer only has one door, so I'll go to the door and one of you"—he pointed to one of the uniformed Deputies—"go to the back. Just in case. Major, if you'll cover the right-hand side and you"—he pointed at the other Deputy— "cover the left-hand side."

Byrd looked up at the sky. The sun would be up soon, but there was a heavy overcast. Almost as soon as Byrd looked upward, a gentle rain started to fall.

The Cherokee lawmen nodded and climbed back in their cars. Weislowski and Byrd climbed into the Expedition. Byrd let the truck idle along as he slowly followed the blacktop path around the campground. When they could see the big Dodge truck, he stopped. All the men climbed out.

The rain was falling harder, and Byrd turned up the collar of his overcoat. He gently pushed the driver's door closed and then reached behind the driver's seat to pull his Remington 870, a short-barreled shotgun, out. He moved the breach as quietly as he could to load a round in the chamber.

He raised the dark gray shotgun and walked up to the side of the truck. There was enough ambient light to see there was no one inside. The group of men fanned out around the camper. Byrd waited until he could see that the others were in position and then he used the butt of the gun to bang on the door.

"Sheriff's Office! Come out with your hands up. In the camper! Come out now!" Byrd moved behind a pine tree and used it to brace himself as he aimed the shotgun at the door.

Suddenly the rain turned into a downpour. Byrd and the other Officers were getting soaked. The door of the camper opened, and Wilmer Westbrook stuck his head out. He looked shocked and exhausted at the same time. He stared at Byrd, with the shotgun pointed at his head.

"In the trailer! You need to step out. Are you Wilmer Westbrook?" Byrd saw movement. He shouted. "Hands up! Step outside! Now!"

Wilmer nodded dumbly and stepped out into the rain. Byrd raised the barrel of the shotgun as Westbrook held his hands high. Byrd stepped up to Wilmer and grabbed his left bicep, holding him until one of the uniforms placed him in handcuffs.

Byrd turned to the camper and shouted again. "Inside the camper! Come out now with your hands up!"

Wilmer leaned toward him and said, "They're all asleep. There ain't no guns in there if that's what you're worried about."

Byrd took a chance and peeked into the camper. He led the way with the barrel of his shotgun. He didn't see anyone moving around. He turned to Weislowski. "This rain is so loud; they may not be able to hear us. I'm going to go in and roust them out."

Byrd stepped up into the camper. He pointed his shotgun toward the floor, and rainwater poured out of the barrel. He thought about the damage to the gun that might have occurred if he had discharged it with the barrel full of water. And then he briefly thought about the damage to him.

Byrd found a woman sleeping in her nook and shook her awake. She was only wearing panties, so he told her to grab some clothes and step outside. The woman was pulling on a shirt when Byrd heard movement on the other end of the camper. Byrd had to divide his attention between the two ends of the camper until she pulled on jeans. He pointed her out the door and then went to the back of the camper, where he found another man and woman.

"This thing is like a clown car. We keep finding people," Byrd said. He got the second couple dressed and ushered them outside.

Soon everyone was seated inside one of the cars. Byrd gathered driver's license information from each of the people in the camper and then separated them. Gail was alone with one Deputy; Dolly and Melvin were in the other patrol car. Byrd loaded Wilmer into the back of his Expedition and turned up the heat.

Byrd sat inside for a moment to warm himself. When the rain seemed to be tapering off, he looked at Weislowski. "I'm going to put a padlock on the door so we can come back later with a search warrant for the camper."

Weislowski nodded. "Do you have one with you?"

"I have one in my crime scene kit. It should be fine for the time being."

Byrd dropped down from the driver's seat and walked around back. He opened the back hatch and took the heavy-duty padlock from his crime scene kit. Then he walked up to the front of the camper and used the existing hasp to lock the camper from the outside.

The rain had become a drizzle, and Byrd stood for a moment looking around at the campsite. He rubbed his face and started back to his truck when he stepped on something. He looked down to see a Smith and Wesson revolver laying in the mud near the camper door.

He looked at Wilmer through the front windshield of the GBI truck and smiled. Byrd returned to the back of the truck, opened the crime scene kit, and retrieved a paper bag. By the time he got back to the gun, the rain had stopped.

Byrd looked up at the sky. He smiled and said, "Well, I guess this is the pot of gold. And I didn't see the rainbow."

He held the gun up so Weislowski and Westbrook could see it. Weislowski clapped his hands together. Byrd knew that Westbrook couldn't clap his hands, but he didn't think he would be in the mood to.

Sheriff Albert Haggin had gotten the call from Craig Weislowski as he sat in his kitchen nursing a cup of coffee. Once his Major had briefed him, he couldn't wait to get off the phone. He placed a call to a Reporter who worked for Atlanta's most prominent TV station. After a brief conversation, the Reporter told the Sheriff they wanted to do a live report from the Sheriff's Office for the noon news show. That made his day.

His men would get credit for an arrest on a horrible murder in less than twelve hours. Which meant that he would get credit. He called the barber he used and woke him up.

"I need a trim as quick as you can get to your shop. And a shave, too."

The mumbled reply was in the affirmative. Haggin dropped the phone into the cradle, and it immediately rang again. He considered ignoring it, but then reconsidered. *It could be Weislowski with more information.*

"Sheriff Haggin," he said into the device.

"Sheriff, this is Hoyt Westbrook. We need to talk. What is all this nonsense about my son being under investigation."

Haggin swallowed hard. "Hoyt, I'm afraid it is worse than that. He's under arrest."

"For what?!"

Haggin hesitated. "He'll be charged with murder."

"In spite of everything my family has done for you?"

Haggin softened his delivery. "I'm afraid so."

"Nothing you can do?"

"Nothing."

The line went silent, then he heard the click of the line going dead.

By God, I guess he knows who the Sheriff is now, Haggin thought.

CHAPTER 16

THE FIRST DOMINO FALLS

MONDAY, FEBRUARY 24, 2003
CANTON, GEORGIA
8:00 A.M.

The Coroner had insisted on waiting for the Fire Department to give the all-clear before he came into the home. He looked the trailer over and then gave Doc and Ronny approval to move the bodies.

Once that formality was out of the way, Doc helped Ronny move Krystal over onto a body bag. They checked her clothes for any personal property and then examined her closely for other injuries. The Medical Examiner would do this job, too, but it would be important to the investigation for them to know as much as they could right now. More photos were taken of the front of her body. By the time they were ready to load her in a body bag, Krystal was already stiff, and the process of getting her into a bag was difficult. Once the body bag was zipped up and ready to go, they motioned over to the ambulance crew who were waiting for the two victims.

The man and woman from the Fire Department loaded Krystal's mortal remains onto a stretcher and moved her to the waiting ambulance.

Once the body was out of the way, Doc began to examine

the ground where she had lain. He used his flashlight, sweeping it back and forth, to look for any evidence that they may have missed earlier. It was the reflection of metal that caught his attention. He stopped moving the light and called to Ronny, "Get your camera. I think we have a cartridge casing."

Ronny rushed back inside, grabbed his camera, and joined Doc. When he saw the metal protruding from the ground, he pointed the camera at the object and took several pictures. Then he laid a ruler from his pocket beside the metal object. After all this was done, the two swept the dirt back from the metal with their gloved hands. They had uncovered a brass cartridge casing, ejected from a semiautomatic pistol.

"Yep," Doc said. "Looks like it might be from a .380."

Ronny examined the stamping on the brass casing. "You got it right. And it looks like it's fresh. Not much weather damage."

Doc helped Ronny secure the evidence in a bag, mark it for later use in court, and then prepare an evidence receipt. Lastly, they put the bag with the other items of evidence they had already bagged and tagged.

Doc looked at Ronny. "Did you see any casings inside?"

"No, but I haven't gotten down on the floor. There could be some under the couch or one of the chairs."

The two men moved back into the trailer. They were just in time to avoid a rain shower that blew up, the sound of the rain on the metal roof soothing, even in the odd circumstances.

The men got down on the floor and shined lights around, but no metal objects caught their attention. Ronny stood up with his hands on his hips. "There has to be more cartridge casings here. We know there should be at least two more."

Doc inclined his head toward Mark's body. "They could be under him."

Ronny nodded. "We might as well move him. We've got more than enough photos. Do we need to get him out before we move the chair?"

Doc shook his head. "Let's dust this tape for prints before we touch it. But we should be able to sit the chair up without damaging anything."

They grabbed the back of the chair and, working together, got it back on its legs. Once the chair was out of the way, they saw the one ejected cartridge casing pushed into the cheap carpet.

"Bingo!" Ronny said. "We have one right here. I guess we might as well move all the furniture. Right now, we don't have any way of knowing how many shots were fired. But we know there is at least one more."

Doc got on his knees beside the chair. He grabbed his crime scene kit and pulled out a fingerprint brush and some black powder. Ronny got on his knees beside him and held a light on the silver tape. Doc developed several fingerprints and used clear tape to capture them. He prepared several cards with nice, clear fingerprint impressions. Doc stood up and looked the cards over.

"Ronny, my boy, I think we have some solid gold here. We have at least two people who did the deed. Which would have been my guess anyway."

Ronny looked at the cards but couldn't see what Doc was talking about. "I see all the prints, but how can you tell how many people there were?"

Doc held the cards up and pointed to one of the cards. "See this print? By the size of it, it is most likely a thumbprint."

Ronny nodded. "Yeah. I see what you mean."

Doc shuffled the cards and found two more. "These are thumbs, too. Different thumbs. So we have two people or a killer with three thumbs."

Ronny looked at the cards and laughed. "You sure do know what you're doing. I'm learning a lot this morning."

Doc packaged the fingerprints he had lifted and labeled them with the time and date of recovery. Every detail of the scene would have to be recorded and cataloged in meticulous detail.

Doc sealed the evidence bag with the cards and put them away. Then he turned to Ronny and said, "I'm going outside for a smoke. Give me about five minutes, and I'll be ready to go. Looks like we still have some work to do."

Ronny nodded. "I don't smoke. But I do drink coffee. Do you want some? I'm going to send one of the uniforms."

"You bet. Coffee and cigarettes are the breakfast of champions."

Roger pulled his truck around behind his parents' house. He wanted it to be out of sight. He knew both his parents were at work, so he wouldn't have to deal with that.

Roger climbed out and looked in the bed of the truck at the flat tire. He thought about getting it repaired, but he felt like he should just stay out of sight until he met Wilmer and got some cash.

Roger sat down on the back steps of his parent's home, dropped his face into his hands, and cried again. After a few minutes, he finally got his emotions under control and stood up. Roger slowly made his way inside and found a big plastic trash bag. He went back to his room and started packing his clothes into the bag although he didn't have much to pack.

When Roger had the bag packed, he slung it over his shoulder and walked back to his truck. He threw the bag on the passenger seat and looked around the yard. He half expected to see Lumpy coming for him.

Roger thought he should nap, but he doubted sleep would come easily. He went inside and dug through his parents' refrigerator, where he found meat and bread to make a sandwich.

Roger didn't worry about making a mess. He knew he would be long gone when his parents got home from work.

Wilmer Westbrook was quiet on the ride in the GBI car. He hadn't asked what he was charged with, and the two Investigators hadn't offered any information. Weislowski and Byrd had agreed before they left the lake to give Westbrook the silent treatment.

Byrd pulled into a space in front of the Cherokee County Adult Detention Center, the new name for what used to be known as the county jail. Byrd and Weislowski dropped out of the tall SUV. Weislowski had ridden in the back seat, and he yanked the passenger door open, unfastened the seat belt, and pulled Wilmer Westbrook out by his arm. With his hands cuffed behind his back, he put up no resistance. Weislowski motioned for Westbrook to follow the concrete path toward the front of the jail, and the three men made their way inside.

Weislowski nodded at the Deputy sitting at the front desk and then led Westbrook into a hallway. The hall was painted pale green, tiled in an off-white cheap floor tile, and smelled of disinfectant. The men turned down a second hall and pushed open doors marked "CRIMINAL INVESTIGATIONS."

Weislowski called a Deputy to babysit Westbrook, then

called the book-in desk on speakerphone and discovered that county Detectives were bringing Westbrook's wife and the other two from the camper up to the interview room on the top floor. He motioned Byrd outside, and once away from Westbrook, he asked, "Who do you want to talk to first?"

Byrd thought about the options. "It seems like Foster and his girlfriend have the most to gain by talking to us. I say we put them in separate rooms and see what they have to say."

Weislowski laughed. "My Detectives are falling all over themselves to get a chance to talk to the one named Dolly."

Byrd nodded. "I bet, but they need to talk to us first."

Weislowski looked around. "We can use the jail interview room, I guess. It has a video recording setup. There's really nowhere else to talk to them in private."

Byrd nodded. Then he took out his notebook and looked for his notes from last night. "Before we start, we need to get a lookout to everyone in the area for the pickup truck that was at the campgrounds."

He used the notes he had made to write out a quick description and passed it to Weislowski. "Having a tag number, we should be able to pick him up soon."

Weislowski nodded and picked up one of the phones on the desks in the Detective's Office. He dialed the 911 center and read off the description. As Weislowski read, Byrd spoke up. "Have them add that the truck has a chain hanging off the back end."

Weislowski frowned. "I forgot you saw the truck before the murders."

Melvin and Dolly were honest with the Investigators but offered little to add to the puzzle. After they had been assured that the officers didn't plan on charging them with the drugs in the little camper, the couple seemed to relax. Dolly could offer nothing to the Investigators. Melvin told them the only thing that was of interest, which was the late-night visitor to the campsite. But he hadn't seen who the visitor was, whether it was one person or two, or even if it was a man or a woman.

Gail Westbrook wasn't much more help. She seemed honestly surprised at the early-morning ride to the Cherokee County Adult Detention Center. Byrd thought she was evasive when he asked what the two couples had been up to in the campground, but otherwise, she talked about their marriage and financial situation in a candid manner, they concluded.

Weislowski had listened to her patiently, and both men took detailed notes as the interview continued. The room was graveyard quiet when Weislowski leaned toward Gail and asked, "Do you know Mark Goodwin and Krystal Page?"

Gail sat back, as if she had been pushed back into the metal chair she was sitting on. Her face was pale, and Byrd noticed that her hands were shaking. Byrd leaned in, too. "We understand that they owe your husband some money."

Gail had trouble getting the words out. "I don't get involved in his business."

"Right," Weislowski said. "You two have never talked about Mark and Krystal?"

Gail shook her head. "Why are you asking about them?"

Byrd took a couple of seconds before he spoke up. "They were murdered late last night or early this morning. Mark was tortured, it appears, and they were both shot to death."

Gail nodded and then hung her head. She moaned once and then threw up on the floor. Byrd avoided getting vomit on his shoes, but Weislowski's shoes were coated. Weislowski jumped up and grabbed a couple of paper towels from a drawer. "Shit," he said. "These are new shoes, dammit!"

Gail tried to apologize, but her stomach heaved again.

Byrd grabbed a trash can and put it under her face as she sat doubled over.

"Are you going to be okay, Gail?" Byrd asked.

Gail moaned and shook her head.

Weislowski left the interview room to clean his shoes. Byrd looked down at Gail as she slumped in the chair. "I'm going to give you some time to think," Byrd said as he put a foot up on the other chair in the room. "You need to decide if you're going to be a witness or a suspect."

Gail held up her hand. "Wait. I'll tell you what I know if it means I can walk on this."

Byrd pulled a chair up next to her and took a seat. "I can't cut that kind of deal. The only one who can do that is the DA." Byrd leaned toward her. "But the only way you're going to walk is by giving a full statement. No bullshit. I'll make a call right now."

Gail wiped traces of vomit from her chin. "Make the call."

Byrd made the call to the District Attorney, and they agreed to send an Assistant DA to help out with Gail. Once that was handled, Byrd called his office in Gainesville to give them an update.

He heard the upbeat voice of the Office Administrative Assistant. "GBI, Stevens. How can I help you?"

"Hey, Machelle. This is Danny Byrd. Can I speak to Will or Tina, please?"

"Sure. Will is out, but Tina is in her office. Hang on. I'll get her for you."

Seconds later, Assistant Special Agent in Charge Christina "Tina" Blackwell came on the line. "Do you have that murder wrapped up?"

"We have one in custody. He is going to be the one who hired the killing done."

"I know," Blackwell said.

Byrd was confused. "How do you know? Did Doc call you?"

"No, Headquarters called. The Atlanta TV stations called them. They had word the Sheriff over there is holding a press conference at noon to announce that you have one in custody for the murders. Did you not know that?"

Byrd wasn't happy. "Shit, no! Did he release any names?"

"Our understanding is that he plans to give up names and mug shots."

"Dammit! Wait! You said names. Plural?"

"Is that a problem?" she asked. He could hear the concern in her voice.

"Right now, we only have one in custody. We think we know who the other two are. They'll be the actual shooters. But we don't want them on the run if they aren't already. No one outside the Sheriff's Office knows we have names for them."

Tina understood. "I'll call the Sheriff and see if he'll hold off. But you have one in custody for the murder who wasn't the shooter? He set it up or what?"

"It looks like he paid these two clowns to kill this couple. But he hasn't been charged with the murders. I plan to take warrants as soon as we get a break here, but he is just now officially being detained for investigation."

"Try to get the warrants before noon."

"Great!"

He heard the sympathy in Tina's voice. "Life in the fast lane, buddy."

They kept Westbrook in handcuffs and pushed him into a hardback metal chair. The table he was sitting beside was screwed into the floor. He was wet and still in his street clothes. One of the jailers brought a rough wool blanket and wrapped Westbrook in it. He looked like he had just rolled out of bed.

Byrd threw his overcoat on one of the other chairs and then sat opposite Westbrook. He knew Weislowski had activated the video recorder and was watching from the room next door.

Byrd dropped his notepad on the table, making a sharp noise. Wilmer recoiled and looked away. Byrd pulled a small, printed card from his credential case and laid it on the table by his padfolio. Then he held the identification out for Wilmer to see.

"Wilmer, my name is Daniel Byrd. I'm a Special Agent with the Georgia Bureau of Investigation."

Westbrook nodded without speaking.

Byrd picked up the card on the table and read the Miranda warning printed on it word for word. He watched Westbrook over the top of the card. When he finished reading, he asked the mandatory questions. "Do you understand these rights as I have read them to you?"

Westbrook shrugged. "I guess."

Byrd waited.

"Yeah, I understand. But I don't know why I'm here."

"We'll get to that in a minute. How far did you go in school?"

Westbrook kept his head down. "I finished high school."

"And you speak English? That is your first language?"

Westbrook smiled at the question. "It's my only language."

Byrd noted all the answers on his pad. Then he laid his

pen down and looked Westbrook in the eye. "Wilmer, do you know why you're here?"

Westbrook turned to the wall. "All I know is that this is bullshit. And I'm wet and cold."

Byrd stood up. "Not as cold as Mark and Krystal are right now." He moved over near Westbrook. "You know why you're here. And you know that rooms with bars are going to be your home for the foreseeable future. The best thing you can do is tell the story to me right now, before we get someone else's version. Maybe you have a better reason than what we've been told."

"I don't know what you've been told. I've got nothing to say."

Byrd pulled the evidence bag with the revolver he had found outside the camper from his coat pocket and dropped it on the table with a bang, pushing it toward the middle. "We found this outside the camper you were in. I'm guessing it will be the gun used to kill Mark and Krystal."

Westbrook stared at the gun for several seconds before he spoke. His voice was hoarse when he said, "I want a lawyer."

Byrd slammed both hands on the table. He picked up the gun and his other property, then stepped to the door. Before he walked out, leaving Westbrook alone in the room, Byrd turned and said, "Get a good one. You're going to need it."

The Assistant District Attorney who came to talk to Gail was brisk. When the ADA came out, she pointed at Gail and said, "If her story stays the same, she is good to go. I told her to be absolutely honest with y'all. We can't compel her to testify against her husband, so everything is up to her."

Byrd nodded. As the ADA walked away, he signaled Weislowski to turn the video camera back on. Weislowski stayed in the equipment room, and Byrd rejoined Gail.

She sat back, relaxed for the first time since the group of men came to their camper. "I told that asshole not to hurt them," she said with feeling.

"Which asshole?"

"My husband. He was all worried that he would look like a pussy if Mark wasn't paying him like he agreed. So he hired a guy who works for my brother to do the dirty work. He should have known the guy he hired was a loser!"

As the story spilled out, Gail got angrier at her husband. When she finished, Byrd went back over some of the details with her. At last, Byrd asked her the question that was most important.

"Who was with Roger Sturdevant?"

Gail seemed surprised when he mentioned the name. "I should have known this master plan was shit! I guess that's how you came to us so quickly."

Byrd stayed on point. "What is the other guy's name?"

Gail shook her head. "The only other guy I know who has anything to do with Roger is some asshole he lives with in his parents' basement. I don't know his name, but he was paroled with Roger back in Texas. My brother can tell you his name. Both of them worked at his car wash. I can call him right now and get whatever he has on both of them."

Byrd stood up. "Let's go to a phone. I want you to call him and get the other guy's information for me. Tell him a Deputy will be coming to pick up copies of all the paperwork he has on them. But I need the partner's information as soon as possible."

Gail sighed. "I'm doing everything I can for you. You better come through with your side of the deal."

"We are legally obligated as long as you help us out. And you're doing that. Just don't let us catch you in a lie. That'll ruin everything."

She nodded, and then went to find a phone.

CHAPTER 17

THE HEAT IS ON

MONDAY, FEBRUARY 24, 2003
CANTON, GEORGIA
11:00 A.M.

Doc Farmer and Ronny Beavers walked into the Cherokee Investigator's office. They looked exhausted because they were. Doc dropped into an empty office chair and put his feet up. Ronny found his own desk and did the same. Byrd walked back into the office, throwing his padfolio on the floor.

"That's not a good sign," Doc said with a frown.

Byrd shrugged. "Nothing bad. But Westbrook didn't give it up. The others are clueless, except maybe Westbrook's wife."

Byrd sat in a chair near Doc. "What did y'all figure out?"

Doc thought about it. "Looks like they were killed with a .380. We found four cartridge casings. After examining the bodies, there are probably two slugs each in the two victims, both in the head. There is probably one more in the ground under the trailer. I'm figuring that the shot to the knee went through the floor and ended up buried."

Byrd nodded. "The DA will want us to find it if we can."

Doc rubbed his face with both hands. "Yep, but we were in no shape to be crawling under that trailer until we got some rest. And it is damned cold out there."

"No rest for the wicked, I'm afraid. We have an idea of what happened, and we think the two shooters are still in the wind."

Doc nodded. "What can we do to help?"

Byrd looked at the ceiling. "Doc, the whole thing was over a drug debt. Or a debt for drugs."

Doc looked confused. Ronny moved his chair over so he could hear the story.

"Our two victims are involved in cooking meth on a regular basis. We have their moneyman in custody, Wilmer Westbrook."

Ronny whistled low. "That family is one of the Sheriff's main contributors. How did that go over?"

Byrd nodded toward the door. "I expect that's where your Major is right now."

"What else do you know?" Doc asked.

"We know that one of the shooters is a guy named Roger Sturdevant. He has parole warrants out of Texas for failure to appear. He's driving a truck with Texas tags, at least the last time it was seen. We have a good description of it."

"Did one of the neighbors get a good look at it?" Ronny asked.

"Yep. One got a pretty good look at it, and then I saw it last night on my way home. I thought the two clowns in it looked suspicious, so I checked out the tag."

Doc sat up. "Are you sure it's the same truck?"

"Yep. They visited Westbrook at the campground where he was spending the night. I figure that was his alibi. But the Ranger at the gate jotted down the license plate."

Doc leaned in. "So, we're pretty sure that the guy who owns the truck is one of our late-night visitors?"

Byrd nodded. "I have a call in now to Intelligence. I'm

hoping we can show the neighbor Sturdevant's mug shots from when he was in Texas. But according to the computer, he bought the truck about two months ago. Right after he got out of prison."

Ronny stood up. "Is there any way to figure out who the other guy is?"

Byrd smiled. "His name is Ricky Cochran. His street name is "Lumpy." He's done time for several charges in Texas. He and Sturdevant got paroled the same day. Sounds like he came here with Sturdevant when Roger came back to his parents' house."

Ronny was shocked. "How did you figure that out?"

Byrd smiled broadly. "Wilmer's wife gave him up. Sturdevant and Cochran worked for Westbrook's brother-in-law at a car wash here in town. Major Weislowski sent a deputy over to pick up any paperwork the brother has on the two. In the meantime, we are hoping to have mug shots of both of them in just a little while."

Doc nodded slowly. "Good work."

Byrd shrugged. "I have to go get warrants for this crowd as soon as I can."

"What's the rush? Can't we just get the warrants after we have everyone in pocket? You know once you take warrants, the media will get ahold of the names."

Byrd lowered his voice. "The Sheriff is holding a press conference at noon. I'm worried he'll give up all the suspect's names."

Doc's eyebrows shot up. "You think he'd do that?"

Byrd looked grim. "I think he'd do anything to get on the evening news."

Doc nodded. "Yeah, you better get to a Judge."

"I plan to run to the courthouse and get warrants as soon as I can. In the meantime, I want a lookout for Sturdevant's truck. He has a parole violation out of Texas. We can arrest him for that," Byrd said.

Doc looked around the office. "Well, I can run out and get us some food. We all need something on our stomachs. This thing could last for a few days."

Byrd nodded. "Get me something healthy."

Doc laughed. "Healthy fries and a healthy burger. Got it."

Byrd looked around for Doc's partner. "Where did the Detective from Cherokee go?"

Doc looked around. "Probably the restroom. It's right down the hall. What do you need?"

"Can you get him to contact Probation in Texas?" Byrd asked.

Doc laughed again. "Why don't you ask him? His name is Ronny Beavers. You need to get to know him anyway."

"Is he good?"

Doc nodded. "He is. And he has a sister who works for Canton PD. Matter of fact, he said you went out with her the other night."

Byrd nodded. "I guess I do need to meet him."

Byrd went out in the hall, looking for Detective Beavers. He saw the man talking in the hall with DNR Ranger Willie Nelson. But when the two men saw Byrd, they broke up the huddle. Willie waved but continued on his way out of the building.

Byrd acted as if he had no idea what the two were up to. Beavers stuck out his hand. "I'm Detective Beavers. I've heard a lot about you. It's nice to finally meet you."

The two men shook hands. "You, too. I had no idea Montana had family in law enforcement."

Beavers laughed. "She doesn't like people around here to

know about her younger brother. She wants to make it on her own. And she seems to be doing a great job. I wouldn't be surprised if she became head of the FBI one day."

Byrd nodded. "She'll go a long way, that's for sure."

"Maybe you can use your pull and get her a job with the GBI."

"She can do that without my help," Byrd said. "But the GBI is a good place for a woman wanting to excel in law enforcement. They have a higher percentage of female Agents than just about anybody else in the country. My Assistant Special Agent in Charge is a woman. She does a damned good job, and I expect her to be a boss in our headquarters any day now."

"Well, thanks for the kind words about my sis," Ronny said. "Was there something I could do for you? You looked like you were a man with a mission."

Byrd told Detective Beavers what he needed. Ronny Beavers came back into the investigations office thirty minutes later. He was holding photos of Roger Sturdevant and Lumpy Cochran. Byrd was impressed.

As he sorted through the photos and information Detective Beavers had gotten, he wondered how much about the investigation was being fed to Willie for use in his campaign. Byrd had no intentions of getting mixed up in those politics.

Bobby Kline had stayed over after his shift ended. He knew the 911 center would be hopping and wanted to be a part of the unfolding events. When the information came in on the wanted pickup, he helped spread the word. All the Dispatchers at Cherokee 911 had already put the description of the man and the truck out on all the local police channels.

Kline noticed that the routine radio calls suddenly stopped. He knew every officer in the area was finding a place to park and look for the truck.

CHAPTER 18
STOP AND GO

Daniel Byrd met Craig Weislowski in the hall.

"Come on," Byrd said as he grabbed the Major by the forearm. "We need to get to the courthouse and swear out warrants for these people."

Weislowski resisted. "We can arrest any one of them based on the probable cause we have. We're just adding a step where it isn't needed."

Byrd turned back to Weislowski. "You want to have this discussion in the hallway?" Both men saw people coming and going in the busy hall but the gauntlet had been thrown. "When we have a warrant in hand, we are on a stronger footing. We need every advantage."

Weislowski frowned and put his hands on his hips. His voice was raised when he asked, "What the hell difference does it make?"

A couple of people now stood around them in the hall. "I want to have an arrest warrant in hand signed by a Judge," Byrd explained. "There's no question about probable cause when you have a warrant in hand."

A man standing near them leaned in. "Why is that so important?" he asked.

Byrd turned, face red, and shouted, "In case we have to kill one of them! Does that make sense?"

The man nodded and took out a notepad and started to flip the pages, looking for a clean sheet.

"Who the hell are you?" Byrd asked.

The man looked up, surprised at the question. "I work for the local paper here."

Byrd shook his head. How could he have been so careless? He grabbed Weislowski's arm and pushed him toward the door. "Let's go. We don't have time to argue."

Montana Worley took pride in being a woman in what was still a man's world. Senior cops looked down on her and wondered behind her back if such a "young little thing" could pull her weight. She had fought big men and gotten them in custody. Along the way, she had endured black eyes and torn muscles in her shoulder. But she wasn't a quitter—that was one thing, with all the self-doubt she pushed down every time she put on the uniform, she was certain of.

Montana Worley drove the Canton Police patrol car onto the shoulder of the interstate. The black truck was marked with silver letters, but she had learned that it didn't stand out too bad if she could find some shade. She figured anyone running for Texas would have to come down Interstate 575 to get started.

She knew she would probably get a call for service as soon as she put the police vehicle in park. That would be her luck. But, like every other cop who had heard the Dispatchers broadcast the information on the wanted truck, she wanted desperately to be the one who saw it first. That would really prove that she was up to the job. Maybe those old, has-been cops would respect her then.

She rolled the marked truck under an overpass and concentrated on the interstate highway behind her. The radio was quiet for a change, she thought, as she settled in.

Roger Sturdevant started his old truck and backed out of his parents' driveway. He looked all around, expecting the law to come out of the woods after him. He wanted the money Wilmer had promised him, and he wanted to see Georgia in his rearview mirror. He looked at the watch he wore and decided he would have plenty of time to get to the gas station where they were to meet. He couldn't manage to sleep, but he sure could use something to eat. He drove the truck at a moderate pace, watching for any kind of law enforcement parked near the road.

When he came into the City of Canton, he looked for a fast-food place. He saw a burger place coming up on the right and signaled to turn into the driveway. He was slowing to make the turn when he saw the police car in the corner of the lot. Roger quickly turned off the signal and continued down the street. He decided he would continue farther south and look for something.

Roger was focused on the rearview mirror when he looked over and saw that he was passing in front of the Georgia State Patrol barracks. His mouth was dry, and he had trouble swallowing. He continued past the State Patrol Post and crossed a river bridge. When he saw signs pointing left toward Interstate 575, he took that turn, hoping to blend in with the other traffic.

When Montana Worley saw the truck drive past, she couldn't believe it was the one from the lookout. It was an older model Ford pickup truck, a single cab. It was a faded white with a green stripe around it. There was a matching green toolbox in the bed. She saw the Texas plates, but still thought it was a coincidence. She grabbed the notepad she had written the license plate number on and verified it. Then she saw the chain hanging down from underneath the truck.

Her pulse pounded as she pulled her Tahoe into drive. The old truck was indicating that it would be taking the next exit. She accelerated to catch up to it. The police truck's powerful engine helped her close the gap quickly.

She could see the driver twisting around in the seat and looking back at her. She activated her dash camera as she followed the old truck around the interstate ramp. She was watching closely to see if there was a second person in the truck, but so far, she hadn't seen any indication there was.

Montana was at the extreme edge of the city and wondered where the closest backup was. She could keep following the truck till someone caught up with them. Then the driver signaled a turn into the gas station.

She knew her Sergeant would chew her out for making the stop alone, but she felt like she needed to act. She grabbed the radio mic from the dash as she turned on her blue lights.

The Judge seemed shocked at the details, Byrd thought, as he folded the arrest warrants and put them into the inside pocket of his jacket. He and Craig Weislowski were walking out of the Cherokee County Courthouse.

As soon as they walked outside, the wind made them cringe. The cold air was returning with a vengeance. They both pulled their outerwear closer and hunched over as they made for Byrd's truck.

Byrd climbed up, switched the truck on, and immediately turned up the heater. As he twisted the knob on the dash, the radio came alive.

"Three Forty-five to Cherokee. I am behind the Signal 50 suspect with the Texas license plates." Byrd's pulse quickened. The voice was Montana Worley.

He pulled the truck into reverse as he listened intently for a location.

"Say your location, Three Forty-five," came the Dispatcher's terse response.

"Say where you are," Byrd said out loud.

"We are pulling into the gas station on Marietta Highway near exit fourteen off the interstate."

Byrd buckled his seatbelt as he pulled the Expedition into drive and turned on his lights and siren. He saw Weislowski buckling his seatbelt. "Pull it tight," Byrd said.

Weislowski's eyes were wide. "I don't have my ballistic vest!"

Byrd shrugged. "Mine's in the back under my evidence kit." He squealed out of the courthouse parking lot. "That makes us even. I doubt that Sturdevant has a vest, either."

Byrd swung the big truck around and pointed toward North Street. Instead of turning right onto the one-way street, he shot across a parking lot and turned onto Main Street.

Weislowski's eyes got big. "This is a one-way street!" he shouted above the siren.

Byrd was grim. "I'm only going one way," he said as he dodged a minivan coming toward him. Byrd was able to use the gear lever to slow the truck down as he dodged oncoming traffic. He narrowly missed a blue sedan driven by a local lawyer as he swung the truck onto a two-lane street.

Byrd looked toward Weislowski and saw that he had his eyes closed. Byrd punched the gas pedal as the truck rocketed down the street. At the first intersection, he slowed to make sure he could get through and then shot the GBI vehicle across the gap. He passed a car, and then the big truck bounced across railroad tracks.

He would have to make a left turn and then negotiate the route to the interstate. Then he would be one exit from the traffic stop. Byrd listened intently as other officers came on the radio to say they were running to back Montana up, but none were close to her.

Byrd made the left turn onto Hickory Flat Highway much faster than the truck was designed for. He felt the left rear wheel lift up, and the truck fishtailed as he fought to keep control. As he got the truck back under control, the speedometer was creeping toward eighty miles an hour. Byrd was leaning forward in his seat with anticipation. He barely slowed as he swung the truck onto the interstate ramp and pushed the accelerator to the floor.

The engine roared, and the piercing rhythm of the siren made the radio harder to hear, but Byrd knew they were close. He charged down the interstate highway and stood on the brake pedal as they slid on the wet pavement at the top of the exit ramp. He took his foot off the brake as he guided the truck up to the gas station. He could see the Canton Police Tahoe near the pumps.

Byrd skidded to a halt and was on the ground before the truck was still. He could smell the brakes as he rounded the front of the Expedition. In one motion he pulled his coat back and pulled out his pistol. He was on autopilot, his years of training kicking in, as he ran toward the police Tahoe. He slowed as he saw Sturdevant spread-eagle on the cement near the gas pumps. Montana had one knee in the center of his back, her gun to the back of his head, as she expertly frisked him.

Byrd realized he had been holding his breath. He

exhaled and walked over to where the suspect lay. Byrd looked back to see Weislowski still in the GBI truck but shrugged and concentrated on the work at hand.

Montana swiftly pulled Sturdevant's hands behind his back and handcuffed him. Byrd reached down, grabbed an elbow, and helped her get the suspect to his feet. She smiled, looked at Byrd, and said, "My first murder arrest."

Sturdevant looked tired and oddly relieved. He hung his head as the Officer took him toward her back seat.

Byrd was relieved, too. He helped Sturdevant into the back seat of the police vehicle, then turned back to Montana. "Well, that's quite a catch you made, that's for sure."

Byrd looked over at his Expedition. "Do you have room for two? I don't think my copilot will want to ride back with me."

Montana looked over at the truck. Weislowski was still hanging onto the passenger-side grab handle.

She smiled up at Byrd. "From the smell of those brakes, it might be a good idea! Were you worried about me?"

Byrd flushed. "Just doing my job, ma'am."

She leaned over and whispered, "Thanks! I don't think I've ever been as scared in my life."

Byrd looked toward his truck and whispered back, "I don't think Major Weislowski has either."

Montana made to get in her patrol car. Byrd said, "I'll follow you to the jail. Tell the folks at Intake what you have him for, and someone will be down to get him for an interview in a few minutes."

The Cherokee Adult Detention Center was on the same exit where Sturdevant had been stopped. Weislowski rode the short distance to the jail with Byrd as they followed the marked Canton PD vehicle. As soon as Byrd pulled into a parking space, Weislowski jumped from the truck and stomped toward the jail. After a couple of steps, he turned and said to Byrd, "I'm never riding with you again. Ever!"

Byrd simply nodded.

CHAPTER 19
A HELL OF A RIDE

MONDAY, FEBRUARY 24, 2003
CANTON, GEORGIA
3:00 P.M.

Lumpy Cochran had spent most of the morning and afternoon with Jimmy Lee's wife. He was surprised at the tattoos all over her back. Some of them looked like they had been done in prison, he thought. She was at least forty years old and looked like she had worked hard all her life. *But*, Lumpy thought, *she is here, and she has a pulse.*

They had copulated throughout the morning, and then Lumpy was suddenly very tired. He pulled on his pants, tucked the pistol in his pocket, and curled up on the couch for a nap. He turned the volume down on the TV and it wasn't long before he was snoring loudly and tossing around.

Lumpy was still out when Jimmy Lee came in from work. He slammed the door hard as he came in, waking Lumpy up. When Lumpy sat up, he thought Jimmy Lee looked angry.

"Did you have something to do with those killings this morning? Everybody at work was talking about it," Jimmy Lee asked.

Lumpy ignored him. "If you'll give me a ride, I'll get out of your hair."

When Jimmy Lee's wife came in, matters got worse. She was dressed in shorts and a bra. The cousin looked at Lumpy suspiciously. "Have you been doin' my wife?"

The wife, fearing that things were not going well, turned and left the room. Jimmy Lee yelled after her, "Did you hear on the news if there is any kind of reward for them killers?" She didn't answer.

Lumpy ignored him again, standing and straightening his pants. "Has your 'vette got any gas in it?"

"Hell yes. And I need some cash to go with that bit of meth you offered." Jimmy Lee stood in the middle of the floor with his fists on his hips. "And if there is a reward for you, I ain't taken you nowhere."

Jimmy Lee turned the TV to a news channel. "I'll bet money you're wanted."

Lumpy just laughed and reached in his pocket. The gun came up, and he pulled the trigger. "Will you bet your life?"

The first shot hit Jimmy Lee in the stomach. Lumpy shot twice more, missing both times.

Jimmy Lee fell to the ground and held onto his abdomen tightly. His wife came in at a run but stopped short when she saw Lumpy with the gun in his hand.

Lumpy's cousin moaned from the floor, reaching for the TV stand. "You son of a bitch. You won't take my car!"

Lumpy saw the old Western-style revolver behind the TV before Jimmy Lee could get his hands on it. Lumpy grabbed the gun with his left hand, then pointed a gun at both of them.

Lumpy spat at his cousin. "Hell, you should be thankin' me for only taking your car and not takin' your life."

The wife sidestepped away from Lumpy and tried to sneak out of the room.

Lumpy motioned for her to move over by her husband.

"I sure would have liked one more ride," Lumpy said. "But I've got to get out of here. I hear Texas calling me! So, I need you to reach in your man's pocket and get me his car keys."

She shook her head at first. "He'd rather know you was riding me than riding in his car."

"I guess he'll sure be pissed when I've done both!" Lumpy pointed the gun at her gut. "If you don't do it for me, I guess I'll kill the both of you and dig out the keys myself."

She quickly kneeled down and got the keys. She tossed them to Lumpy, who smiled at her and turned for the door.

She looked up at him from her spot on the floor. "Any chance I can get one more taste of that rocket juice?"

Lumpy shrugged. "Why not."

Her husband lay on the floor moaning. His eyes fluttered, but he didn't say anything.

She grabbed the needle, heated up the meth, and tied off her arm. She shot herself up and then stood in the middle of the floor as the rush hit her. She tensed up and then relaxed again. Then she held the needle up toward Lumpy. He nodded.

She tied off Lumpy's arm and worked the needle into him. He stood still with both guns hanging by his side. The needle stung like hell, but soon he was feeling the rush that was the precursor of the power that would overcome him. He leaned down and kissed her for the first time. When he ran his tongue in her mouth, he realized how many teeth she was missing.

He left her standing in the middle of the living room and scrambled into the red Corvette. He fired it up and revved the engine before he backed out of the driveway and drove away.

She turned to check on Jimmy Lee and then stopped in her tracks. A mug shot of Lumpy was on the TV screen with the words "Double Murder Suspect." The sound was off, but she saw Lumpy's picture clearly and then saw a trailer with crime scene tape around it.

As soon as she was sure the taillights of her husband's worn-out car were moving away, she left Jimmy Lee lying on the floor. She ignored his moans as she ran to the neighbors to call 911. She hoped there was a reward.

Roger Sturdevant sat in the interview room, wringing his hands. Byrd and Weislowski watched on the video monitor as he alternated between slumping over and sitting upright. Byrd watched for a few minutes, then motioned to Weislowski. "Let's go give him a chance to get this off his chest."

Sturdevant seemed relieved when Byrd and Weislowski came into the room. The men sat at the table bolted to the floor and watched Sturdevant. At last, Byrd leaned forward, touching Roger's outstretched hands, and said, "Roger, you are done. The question is, do you take the fall for everything, or do you tell us what happened? Either way, we have enough evidence to fry your ass."

Roger nodded. He laid his cuffed hands on the table palms up. "I'll tell you everything I know. Which ain't much. I fell in with the wrong crowd, which is what has always got me in trouble. I just end up in the wrong place at the wrong time."

Byrd sat back from Roger and shook his head. "Before you go too far in the wrong direction, I want you to know that we know everything. Wilmer Westbrook is in jail here, and he spilled his guts." Byrd was bluffing.

Roger sighed. "I figured that blowhard would give us

up! But you gentlemen should know that Lumpy is the one who pulled the trigger. I didn't shoot nobody."

Byrd leaned forward. "What gun were you carrying?"

Sturdevant shook his head. "I didn't have no gun."

"Roger, lying to me is not the way to go."

Sturdevant sighed and slumped in the chair. "I had this revolver, like a little cop gun."

"Was it a Smith and Wesson?"

Sturdevant nodded vigorously. "Yeah, a Smith and Wesson. That's what it was."

Byrd smiled. "See, that wasn't so hard."

Sturdevant smiled, too. "I'm ready to get this off my chest."

Sturdevant held nothing back, at least nothing he could remember. His version of events made him seem like an innocent bystander in the chain of events. He was talking faster than Byrd could take notes, and he had to slow him down more than once. Byrd had already gotten the highlights, including that Lumpy was on foot and in the area of the murders.

Weislowski went outside and called the dispatch center. He made sure that every Officer in the area was looking for Lumpy Cochran. Deputies were soon crisscrossing the area.

Sturdevant's truck had been brought into a closed lot behind the Sheriff's Office. Doc and Ronny placed evidence tape around the doors so that they couldn't be opened without breaking the seal. They dusted the outside for fingerprints, but the results were all smudges or partials. Nothing that would be useable.

Once the truck had been sealed and the outside processed, the men made arrangements for the truck to be carried by wrecker to the GBI Crime Lab in Atlanta. They would get a Deputy to follow the tow truck down to maintain the chain of custody. Everything had to be done with the ultimate prosecution in mind.

Once the truck was tended to, Doc and Ronny resumed cataloging the piles of evidence they had recovered in and around the trailer, so that it could also be carried to the State Crime Lab.

When Doc and Ronny finished their work, they made their way back up to the Detective's Office. As they were pushing the door of the Detective's Office open, Ronny's cell phone rang. "Detective Beavers?"

Ronny listened, then said, "Thanks!"

When they came through the door, Daniel Byrd and Craig Weislowski were huddled over a desk, looking at a map. Ronny stood in the door. "Cochran is on the run in an old-model red Corvette. We just got a 911 call."

"How long ago?" Byrd asked.

Ronny shrugged. "Probably five minutes ago."

Byrd looked at his watch. "Are we sure it's Cochran?"

Ronny nodded and frowned. "We need to get someone to the caller's house. Cochran shot her husband, who is also Cochran's cousin, and then stole his car."

Byrd shook his head. "I hope he doesn't know how hot he is right now. Maybe we can grab him on a traffic stop before he finds out we know his name."

Doc stopped short at the door. He had seen the TV on the wall. The volume was down, but he saw the mug shots of Roger Sturdevant and Lumpy Cochran underneath a banner proclaiming MURDER SUSPECTS. "Can someone turn the volume up on the TV?" Doc said.

Weislowski looked up with surprise and then found the remote. The video had switched to a close-up of Sheriff Haggin. "If you see these men," Haggin said to the camera, "please don't try to approach them alone. They are armed and dangerous."

Byrd frowned and looked to Weislowski. "What the fuck is he up to?" Byrd asked.

"I can't control him. He's my boss. Everybody has a boss," Weislowski said.

Montana stood at attention in the roll-call room of the Canton Police Department as her Sergeant yelled at her. He had gotten so angry at one point that he was spitting, she noticed. She knew he was only worried for her safety and would have given the same chewing out to a male officer. When he was finished, she thanked him for his concern and promised to do better.

His tone softened. "All right, get the hell out of here and go look for the other man. Dispatch just put out a lookout on a worn-out, old-model red Corvette."

She turned and bounced out of the room toward her patrol vehicle. She turned back long enough to shout, "Thanks, Sarge!"

Montana found her same spot on the interstate. She knew that the odds were against lightning striking again, but she began her vigil anyway. Late-afternoon traffic was rushing by with people on their way to work an evening shift in the city. She put the radio microphone in her lap, anticipating the need to call something in. Then she hung the mic back up in frustration. She was convinced there was no way on Earth the other suspect would come by her hiding place.

Suddenly she saw the old model Corvette coming toward her in the flow of traffic. It was close behind a tractor-trailer truck, and so she had a hard time seeing the license plate. She dropped her Tahoe into gear and merged into the motorists shuffling to get to work.

She pulled the radio mic off the hook and held it. She was reluctant to call on the radio until she was sure it was the right car. But her training got the better of her. "Three Forty-five to Cherokee. I am trying to catch up with an old-model red Corvette. We are southbound on I-575 nearing exit fourteen. One occupant."

The radio came alive. "Cherokee to Three Forty-five. Keep us advised of your position."

Before she could acknowledge the Dispatcher, one of her fellow Officers, Jeff Milligan, came on the radio. "Cherokee, I'm about four cars behind her. I saw the Corvette as it came into the city. Let Holly Springs know we are coming toward their city."

The tension was obvious in the Dispatcher's voice as she acknowledged the information. "Cherokee to all units. 10-3, 10-33." In other words, stop transmitting, emergency traffic.

Montana had been able to maneuver behind the Corvette, and her heart pounded as she saw the license plate matched the car in the lookout. "Three Forty-five to Cherokee. I have verified the plate is a match for the lookout."

Byrd rolled the Expedition out of the parking lot at the jail and headed toward the house where Lumpy's cousin lived. He was signaling a turn onto the interstate to head north when the radio came alive with the traffic on the Canton Police channel.

He, like Montana, figured that the Corvette was going to be a false alarm. Then he heard her confirm the license plate over the radio. His heart raced as he checked his rearview mirror before crossing three lanes of traffic, to a chorus of honking horns, to get in the parade of cops. Just in case.

Montana was in full felony mode. She waited as the second Canton Officer, Milligan, pulled in behind her. Once she saw an area with room for them to get out of the roadway, she turned on her blue lights. She was tense, expecting the driver to run in the hotrod he had stolen. When she saw the driver signal that he was stopping, she began to doubt herself.

Maybe this doesn't have anything to do with the murders. Maybe they got it wrong, she thought. But that didn't keep her from being cautious.

The driver pulled over on the roadside and sat with his hands on the steering wheel. She dropped to the ground behind the door of her patrol vehicle and waited as Milligan joined her.

Montana called for the driver to step out of the car. They waited for the man to comply. When the driver sat in the car, staring into the side mirror, she called out again. "Driver, step out of the car with your hands in the air."

The driver of the car continued to sit with his hands on the steering wheel, not moving. He made no attempt to get out of the driver's seat. Montana looked back at Jeff, who shrugged. After several seconds with no change, Montana drew her Glock and said, "Cover me. I'm going to move up to the back of the car where he can hear me."

Milligan raised his gun. The traffic continued to whiz past the officers as they concentrated on the stone-faced driver.

Montana crouched slightly, keeping her weight on the balls of her feet, as she moved up closer to the red sports car. She stopped midstride as the door suddenly swung open. She knew she was caught between her patrol car and the bad guy's vehicle. Not where she wanted to be by a long shot.

She saw the driver roll out of the car door and stretch out on the ground with his hands pointed at her. Her first thought was that he was suffering a medical emergency, something she had encountered several times in the past. It was this moment of hesitation, her shift of focus, that every cop dreads—a situation that is rapidly evolving, uncertain, and potentially lethal.

She heard the "pop" and saw the flash before she saw the gun. Suddenly she was hit in the chest with what felt like a sledgehammer. Then quickly, she was hit again. She felt herself falling and couldn't control it.

Montana knew her life depended on getting out of the line of fire. Her vest had taken the two rounds, but she couldn't count on being so lucky next time. She used her heels to push herself toward the side of the road. She was breathing hard as she pushed up to her knees and turned toward the red car. From her position, she still couldn't see the gunman.

Montana could see that Milligan had brought his gun up as a third shot shattered the glass in the window by his head. This time the noise was much louder. The next shot hit Milligan in his right arm, causing him to drop his service weapon on the ground.

Milligan ducked behind the protection of the door as she heard the engine of the sports car rev. Montana got to her feet, crouched behind the car, and made sure her shots wouldn't hit a passing car. The effort to get to her feet had caused black spots to float in her vision. Montana put one hand across her chest and started shooting as fast as she could pull the trigger. The pounding of her pistol in her hand was oddly comforting. It reminded her she was still in the fight.

She saw the back glass shatter, but the car accelerated away.

Byrd was traveling with the flow of traffic. He could see the two police cars with their lights flashing about a mile ahead of him. He could see the lights of a Holly Springs police car coming up from behind and overtaking him.

He anticipated bringing Lumpy in and was working on an interview strategy when he thought something seemed wrong up ahead. It looked like Montana had stumbled and was worried she might fall into traffic. As that thought formed, he saw the window of her police car shatter. He had no doubt what was happening. He saw a man who had been laying on the ground get to his feet beside the sports car and jump into the driver's seat.

"Cherokee, shots fired. Officers down. Shots fired." It was Montana screaming into her walkie-talkie.

"Cherokee, Holly Springs Seven Fifty-four is on the scene. The shooter is fleeing. I am stopping to help the Officers. Have Woodstock units be on the lookout. The subject is armed with a Signal 69 handgun!" The Hollys Springs Officer did his best to give a description of the car as it pulled away from him.

Byrd was passing Montana's police Tahoe when he saw the marked Holly Springs car stop in the lane of traffic beside the other Canton car. In moments the interstate highway would be total gridlock. He could see Montana standing up, and the male officer was bleeding from his right arm.

Without hesitation, he turned on his lights and siren and forced his way past the scene. The big truck fishtailed as he ran into the grassy median to stay in the hunt. He could see the suspect's car belching black smoke as it roared ahead of him.

Byrd felt compelled to divide his attention between the rearview mirror and the car in front of him. He was aware that the responding cops would offer more first aid than he could muster. He stood up on the gas pedal as the traffic slowly parted for him. He darted around cars too slow to get out of the way and found he was closing on the Corvette as it swerved across traffic to make the next exit.

"Cherokee," the Holly Springs Officer was back on the radio, "one Officer is hit in the arm. The other was struck in the vest. I need a Signal Four for both. Notify the ER that injured Officers will be coming."

Byrd exhaled as he shot the big truck off the interstate and tried to get behind the fleeing car. Byrd's pulse was pounding, and his ears were ringing as the adrenaline coursed through his system. He took the exit far too fast, even for him, and drifted into oncoming traffic, missing a collision by inches. He made the turn and dodged afternoon traffic as they shot through downtown Woodstock.

He was able to get the radio microphone in his hand as he avoided a delivery truck. "Eighty-nine to Nine Hundred. I'm 10-80 with a homicide suspect."

Sophia Romano was sitting at the radio console in GBI Headquarters, newly arrived for her evening shift. She was looking over the daily logs of calls to the communications center for the state agency. She was absorbed in her work when she heard Daniel Byrd calling.

An experienced Radio Operator knows immediately when something critical is going on, not by the words spoken but by the tone of the caller's voice. And the wail of the siren in the background reinforced the crucial nature of the call.

She swiveled to the microphone and responded, "GBI Atlanta to all units, 10-3, 10-33, 10-80 in progress. Eighty-nine, say your location." Even as she spoke, Sophia was busy typing the flash teletype that would let agencies in the area know the situation. *To North Metro, GBI Agent in pursuit of homicide suspect.* She typed.

"Nine Hundred, we are traveling eastbound on Town Lake Parkway off of Interstate 575. Suspect vehicle is an old-model red Corvette with Georgia plates. Suspect is armed with a handgun and just shot two Officers."

"I'm clear, Eighty-nine. Do you have any other units with you?"

The response was not what she hoped to hear. "Nope."

Sophia slammed her hands on the desk. *Damn you, you stupid son of a bitch!* she thought. Into the radio, she said, "I'll get GSP and Cherokee rolling units your way."

"Thanks. I'll keep you up to date."

She completed the teletype as she dialed the GSP Communications Center.

Lumpy had been shocked when the window behind his head shattered. He heard a sound like someone pounding on the side of the car, and he realized it was the sound of bullets striking the fiberglass body. He also knew one of the bullets the woman cop fired had hit its mark—his left shoulder burned like fire. He had no choice but to use his damaged wing to negotiate the traffic as he dodged left and right. Jimmy Lee's worthless car didn't have power steering, and it was taking both hands to wrestle the 'vette.

Lumpy knew he had to find a place to hide and do it quickly. He saw a gas station coming up on his right and thought he could blend in with all the other cars there. Then he saw the big white Expedition coming up behind him with blue lights flashing all over it.

What a shitty day I'm having, he thought.

Byrd had never been as determined to catch someone

in his life. He was gripping the steering wheel with both hands but had to take one hand off occasionally to change the sound of the siren or to downshift the transmission. The yelp sound was best for intersections, while the wail tended to work better on long stretches of highway.

He used the transmission to regulate his speed, to keep from burning up his brakes. The Expedition was big, but it had plenty of acceleration. Right now, Byrd needed everything the truck had.

He could hear the report of his pursuit going out on the State Patrol radio channel and the local agency channels. He knew that help would not be close since every officer in the area had responded to the officer's shot.

Thankfully, the red sports car was apparently not in good mechanical condition, and Byrd was able to keep him in sight. They had run through several traffic lights, turned onto secondary roads, and swerved through one parking lot.

The red car swerved through a lane of traffic onto East Cherokee Drive. When Byrd took the turn, he shifted the roaring truck down to second gear. When he did, the engine whined, and the tachometer needle shot around the face. Once the Expedition lurched onto the new road, he shifted back up, and the big truck surged forward like a rocket.

Byrd updated Sophia by radio. "Nine Hundred, the suspect has turned onto East Cherokee Drive and is continuing to head east."

He smiled at Sophia's calm voice on the radio. "Eighty-nine, GSP Canton and GSP Marietta are responding units. Keep me updated."

Lumpy was in a lot of pain. His shoulder continued to burn like fire, and he was having to use every bit of strength he had to guide the old car. He had no idea where he was but knew the sun was behind him. He was pushing the old car hard, and the interior was beginning to smell like burning oil. On the last hard turn, he had pushed the brake pedal almost to the floor and had barely slowed the Corvette.

He stood on the gas pedal and passed a car on the shoulder. Then he looked back and saw the cop in the SUV. Lumpy had hoped he could shake him. Now he saw the blue lights getting closer.

He decided to take the next right-hand turn.

The Corvette belched smoke, on the verge of being totally obscured by it. The car's pace had slowed. Byrd was able to close the gap and was right behind Cochran as he continued to run.

Fearing a repeat of the roll out the door with guns blazing, Byrd kept his car to the right-hand side of the red sports car as it coughed its way onto a small country lane. When the car slowed to a crawl, Byrd saw the door crack. He pushed the gas and hit the back of the sports car as hard as he could. He was rewarded with a sound like an explosion. The fiberglass car splintered in a thousand pieces as the SUV rode up into the sports car's haunches.

The Corvette sat so low that the big truck rode well into the trunk, ripping out the fuel tank as it went. The car spun around, and Lumpy was thrown to the ground.

Byrd backed the truck away from the wreckage, relieved that the airbags hadn't deployed. He drove the truck around the remains of the sports car and chased Lumpy as he ran away from the road toward a pine thicket. Byrd tried to cut off his path to the woods but was too slow. Lumpy ran across a small grassed area and into the tree line.

Byrd hit the curb hard and bounced the truck toward Lumpy. When he realized he would not be able to block the killer's path, he slammed the Expedition into park and dropped to the ground.

Byrd was running seconds behind him. "Stop, you son of a bitch!" Condensation swirled around Byrd's mouth as he shouted. Byrd was watching for movement in the stand of pine trees. They were just tall enough to hide Lumpy as he ran, but the movement of the treetops was a dead give-away.

Byrd worked his way around the small pine trees and came into a less densely grown area. He was looking for signs of Cochran's path when the shot sounded. He heard the slug *thwack* into the tree near his head. He noted that the gunshots sounded much heavier than the .380 he expected.

He dived to the ground as he heard Lumpy move on the dry leaves. Byrd brought his gun up and fired three quick shots in the direction of the sounds.

"Nine Hundred to Eighty-nine. Say your location." This was the third time she had made the call in the last ten seconds. The radio was silent.

She turned her attention to the phone. A State Patrol Radio Operator was listening on the other end. "My Agent is not answering. How far away are your Troopers?"

"They are less than five minutes out from his last location. There are Deputies and City Police in the area, too."

Five minutes is a long time, Sophia thought. "Thanks. Stay on the line, and I'll let you know if I can raise him."

She shook her head and stared at the radio console, willing Byrd to respond. "Nine Hundred to Eighty-nine. Say your location."

Sophia closed her eyes for a moment. *Damn it, Danny,* she thought. *Why the hell can't you wait for help?*

Sophia turned her attention back to the phone. "Can you get a chopper on the way?"

The GSP Operator was ahead of the game. "I have one that should be about two minutes out from the last location."

Sophia nodded to herself. "Thanks."

Lumpy was a raw bundle of nerves. The meth had helped him work out a plan to shoot the two cops trying to arrest him. But his heart was pounding in his chest, and he seemed to be looking through a tunnel. He had no peripheral vision at all, and his ears sounded like he was in a roaring ocean. Then he saw the movement in the corner of his limited vision. He had heard of the shadow people, the imaginary figures meth causes you to see indistinctly but look so real he wanted to shoot at them.

Then he saw the cop who was chasing him. He figured he was a cop, the way he drove, but he hadn't seen a badge. Lumpy fired a single shot from the cowboy gun he had stolen from his cousin, then he dropped to the ground and rolled into a sitting position beside an oak tree. The burning in his arm wasn't bothering him as much but there was blood dripping from the sleeve of his jacket. He thought it seemed like a lot of blood.

The cop shot back at him, and he heard the bullets whiz by his head. He was so high that they didn't register. "Are you a cop?" Lumpy shouted.

He heard a muffled response. The cop was shouting, "No! I'm a very aggressive used-car salesman. Your Corvette is ruined!"

What an asshole, Lumpy thought.

Lumpy checked his guns. The cowboy gun held three more live rounds, and the .380 was empty. He had used the little semi-automatic pistol on the woman cop but had jumped to the big revolver when it ran dry. The big gun had taken down the other uniformed cop with just two shots. He figured he had enough left for the guy in the woods with him.

Lumpy moved to the left, hoping to flank the suited cop. He heard the GBI Agent shout, "For the record, you're under arrest for murder and aggravated assault on a police officer."

"Lawman!" Lumpy shouted. "You're by yourself. I kill you and I can get back to Texas."

The cop shouted back, "Maybe. But I won't make it easy for you."

"That woman cop made it easy. Maybe you're easier than you think!"

Byrd flung his overcoat behind him as he worked his way around the woods. He could taste the anger, bitter in his mouth, as he looked for a route to Cochran. He had an idea where the voice was coming from, but he couldn't make out any movement. He was struggling to keep his breathing under control as he crouched near an old pine tree that towered over him. He feared the condensing breath would give away his location.

Byrd checked his back pocket for his single extra magazine and was reassured when he found it. He put his feet down carefully as he moved deeper into the forest.

Bam!

Aw, fuck! Byrd thought.

He lunged forward and found a big tree to get behind. The bullet sounded like a bee buzzing past him. He hadn't heard the bullet strike near him, but that was a small consolation.

Then Byrd saw Lumpy crouching near a tree about a dozen yards ahead. Lumpy stood and moved toward the next big tree. Byrd held his breath as he aimed his issued Glock. Byrd didn't hear his gun discharge, but he felt it buck in his hand. For a second, he wasn't sure the pistol was working.

Lumpy stumbled, but then he turned and fired at Byrd. Byrd heard the bullet whiz past again, but he was locked onto his target. Byrd fired twice more in rapid succession. Lumpy spun in the air and fell on his back.

Lumpy felt the shots burn into his right side. They came so fast that Lumpy wasn't sure how many times he was hit. He turned in what seemed like slow motion. He had no sense of falling but knew when he hit the ground. The rain had made the ground soft, and he felt like he had landed on a mattress.

He lay there looking up at the dull February, Georgia sky. He couldn't seem to catch his breath, and he felt cold and wet all over. Cochran's ears were ringing from all the shooting, and his legs felt numb. But he could see the cop in the suit coming toward him. All he could think about was shooting the gun in his right hand one more time.

He tried to sit up but could only get onto his left elbow. He was having trouble focusing on the man coming toward him.

Byrd held his pistol out in front of him and advanced on Lumpy as the fugitive tried to sit up. Lumpy managed to shift onto his left elbow and swing the big gun to point at Byrd.

Byrd fired. Again, he didn't hear his gun discharge, but he heard the distinctive sound of the lead projectile slapping into Cochran's chest. Lumpy rolled to his back. He shot the big revolver up in the air and then dropped it beside him.

Byrd shuffled nearer to Lumpy and saw him trying to get up. Lumpy rolled his head up and pointed the revolver toward Byrd.

Byrd ignored the gun pointed toward him. Before Lumpy could take his shot, Byrd pointed his weapon. Then, deliberately, he shot Lumpy in the face. Byrd stood over him as he watched the light go out of the killer's eyes. *Wherever you're going*, Byrd thought, *it was my pleasure to send you there.*

Byrd sat on the ground, as his knees gave way. He heard a helicopter hovering over his car a few yards away.

He could hear sirens in the distance but didn't have the strength in his legs to walk out of the woods right now. He looked at the killer laying in front of him and felt a wave of sadness. He could already smell death in the air.

Sophia heard the GSP Operator come back on the phone line. "We think our Aviation unit has your Agent's car spotted. Is it a white SUV?"

Sophia was holding her breath. "Yes, that's him!"

"The Trooper says both cars have been in a crash. The Pilot doesn't see anyone moving around, but they plan to orbit the area. Do you have any physical description of your Agent or the suspect?"

Sophia thought about that. "The suspect, no, I don't have a description. But the Agent will be wearing a dark suit. He always wears a dark suit."

"I'll pass that on. The Pilot says it looks like your Agent

hit the suspect's car. He says he can see where the SUV ran up into the edge of the woods near the Corvette."

Sophia let out a deep breath. "That sounds like him."

"I'm giving the location to Cherokee 911, and I have a Trooper just coming on the scene. I'll let you know what he says once he gives me a status."

The call disconnected, and Sophia slumped in her chair, her heart pounding in her chest. She realized she still had another seven hours in her shift.

CHAPTER 20

THE CAVALRY IS COMING

MONDAY, FEBRUARY 24, 2003
CANTON, GEORGIA
5:00 P.M.

A bugle charge in the cavalry was to signal the troops but also let those under siege know help was on the way. To Byrd, the sound of sirens could be compared to the cavalry coming.

Byrd could hear sirens from every direction. He tried to stand up, but his legs were still not cooperating. He settled for dragging himself to the base of an oak tree and propping himself up. The wet pine straw soaked his pants, but he didn't care.

Some of the sirens continued past him, but he could hear others as the cars screeched to a stop. He pulled his badge and ID from his shirt pocket and prepared to hold them up to any Officers arriving.

Byrd heard crashing footsteps behind him as Officers searched the woods. Byrd raised his voice. "I'm over here!"

As a Trooper walked up, he radioed, "One Ninety to Canton. I have the GBI Agent in sight."

Byrd leaned over, happy to see a familiar face—Frank White.

As Trooper Frank White walked, he leaned down to his radio microphone. "Canton, roll an ambulance."

"10-4, One Ninety. Should they come 10-18?"

Trooper White approached Byrd and looked at him. "Danny, are you sure you're okay?" he asked. Glancing around, the Trooper saw the body of Lumpy Cochran.

Byrd nodded. "Just a little overwhelmed. I'm not hit, near as I can tell."

White turned back to his radio. "10-4, Canton. And make that two ambulances."

"Frank, you might as well tell them to roll the Coroner. And can you have your Radio Operator let GBI Headquarters know that we'll need an OIS team up here?" The GBI Officer Involved Shooting team would need to be sent to investigate the death of the suspect.

White kneeled down beside Byrd. The seasoned Trooper knew, when the adrenaline is pumping, officers don't realize they've been hit. "Are you sure you're not hurt? Shot anywhere?"

Byrd laughed. "No. I don't know how the hell he missed me, but I think I'm okay. I'm just having trouble getting my feet under me."

White reached down and helped Byrd get to his feet. Byrd wobbled like an infant learning to walk. But he kept himself upright, and with White's help, he started walking out of the woods.

Just in case, Byrd felt his clothes, and White helped him by running his hands up and down Byrd's back and front. The big Trooper checked his hands and didn't see any blood.

They continued out of the woods until they reached White's patrol car. White opened the driver's door of his shiny blue and gray patrol car and guided Byrd into the seat. "Sit here and try to relax."

Byrd nodded. "I need to use your radio."

White squatted by the car. "Sure, whatever you need."

"GBI Eighty-nine to Canton," Byrd spoke into the radio microphone.

The response was quick and professional. "GBI Eighty-nine."

"Canton, can you let GBI Headquarters know that I have been involved in a shooting and need a team to our location? Also, I need Region Eight's SAC notified. And can you raise GBI Thirty-four?"

"GBI Eighty-nine, GBI Thirty-four is en route to your location. He advised me to let GBI Headquarters know, and I have your SAC by public service. GBI Eighteen wants to know if you are 10-4?"

Byrd leaned over in the seat as he spoke. "Tell Eighteen I am okay. We have one suspect on scene who is 10-42. We probably need some support over here."

It took a moment this time for the Radio Operator for the State Patrol to respond. "GBI Eighteen says that he has Agents on the way, and a team from GBI Atlanta will be coming to work the shooting."

Byrd slumped back. "Thanks, Canton."

Byrd was sitting with his eyes closed as he heard someone walk up to the GSP car. Doc Farmer leaned into the patrol car. "Teddy, you look like death warmed over."

Byrd didn't bother to open his eyes. "I feel like it, Doc. And when are you going to quit calling me that?"

"Teddy? I guess I'll only call you that till one of us is dead."

Byrd groaned. The sounds of more sirens covered his mumbled response.

Doc squatted beside the GSP unit. "Son, you just about got your ass killed. Are you sure you're not hit?"

"I'm not hit. Just an adrenaline dump, I guess."

Doc nodded. "Do I need to call your mom and dad? Or anybody else, for that matter?"

"No, I'll call my mom and dad from the hospital. I don't know of anyone else who might need notifying." He thought for a moment. "Can you call the GBI Radio Room and let Sophia know I'm fine? She's going to be mad as hell at me!"

Doc laughed. "You got that right. She must have called for you a hundred times on the radio. Is she the one you had the thing with?"

Byrd was sheepish. "A thing?"

"You don't have to answer that." Doc backed away from the car door.

He saw a Cherokee County ambulance roll onto the scene. "I think your ride is here."

Trooper White helped Byrd climb out of the car. "Looks like the Ditch-Doctors are here to take you to the emergency room. Are you ready?"

Byrd stood on shaky legs. "Yeah, let's get out of here."

Trooper White nodded. "I'll stay here and protect the crime scene."

Cherokee EMTs helped him onto a gurney and then worked to get his vital signs. One of the technicians attached a blood pressure cuff and listened for his heart. The other counted his pulse and then rechecked him for signs of bleeding.

Byrd closed his eyes again and accepted the ride. As he was loaded into the ambulance, Doc leaned down and said, "I'll follow you to the ER, son."

Byrd opened his eyes long enough to say, "Thanks, Doc."

"Hang in there. I talked to Will on the radio. He's about

thirty minutes out. And he said the Director is on the way here."

"Did he say anything to you?" Byrd asked.

Doc shrugged. He leaned down and whispered his answer. "Sounds like he's pissed that you went off on your own again."

Byrd leaned back. He heard one of the EMTs tell the other the patient's blood pressure was going up.

GBI Director Buster Hicks came into the hospital emergency room at a near run. He had parked out in the visitor's lot, not wanting to clog the emergency area with another police car. He made his way to the front desk wearing the charcoal gray fedora that was becoming his trademark.

The clerk on duty at the front desk recognized him from TV. "Sir," she said, "your people are in Room Sixteen. I'll buzz you in."

He paused at her desk. "How about the Police Officers? How are they doing?"

She blushed. "Technically, I can't tell you. But their Chief is in the hallway. He's in uniform, so he should be easy to pick out."

He waved the problem aside. "Yes, ma'am. You do what your policy says."

Hicks pulled a GBI lapel pin from his pocket. It was a simple design with the State seal and the letters "GBI" at the top. He handed it to her. "Thanks for your help. And your kindness."

He walked briskly through the automated doors and looked for Room Sixteen. He saw a group of people standing near the door that would take him to his Agent and spotted Sheriff Haggin and SAC Will Carver. The others were unfamiliar faces.

Hicks stopped at the group, extending a hand to Carver and then to the Sheriff. Then he turned to the other two men. "I'm Buster Hicks."

One man spoke first and extended his hand. "Major Craig Weislowski."

The other man was older and looked vaguely familiar. He extended his hand. "Director, I don't think we've ever been introduced. I'm Jackson Farmer. I work in Region Eight."

Hicks took off his hat and turned to Farmer. "I understand you were a big part of the team that solved this case. I just want you to know how much I respect your work. I have heard nothing but good things from Will about you."

Doc's face reddened. He could only mumble "Thanks," before Sheriff Haggin spoke up.

"Director, I want you to know that we stand with your man 100 percent on this shooting. I haven't said anything to the media about the GBI being involved. I just wanted to keep your agency's name out of all this."

Hicks put his hat back on and turned to face the Sheriff. "Sheriff, you have to get reelected every four years. I understand you do things to help that along." Hicks took a step closer and lowered his voice. "But don't ever say that your grandstanding is to protect the GBI. If we do our job well, you can take the credit. If we don't do it well, we will face the consequences. Do I make myself clear?"

Haggin took a step back. "I get where you're coming from."

Without responding to the Sheriff, Hicks pushed into the examining room. He saw Byrd on the examining table. Hicks stopped near the door. A Doctor was checking his pulse, and a Nurse in scrubs was busy recording his vital signs.

Byrd propped up on his elbows. "Director, we're going to have to stop meeting like this."

Hicks chuckled. "I'm glad to see you aren't hurt."

"Nope. These folks have loaded me up with enough dope to take the pain away into next year."

Hicks nodded. "I'm not staying in here then. I don't want you to say anything about the shooting. I just wanted you to know that I'm here if you need anything."

Hicks was turning to leave when the GBI Case Agent from Atlanta came into the examining room. The Agent paused to acknowledge Hicks before asking Byrd, "Are you sure you're not hit anywhere?"

Byrd shook his head. "I don't think so. Why does everybody keep asking me that?"

Doctor Gomez, Hicks noted from her name tag, shook her head. "I told you we had done X-rays of every inch of his body."

Byrd sat up. "Every inch."

Doctor Gomez frowned. "Lay back down and give it a rest." She turned to the Agent from headquarters. "Why is this an issue?"

"When we went over his clothes, we found two bullet holes in his jacket."

Gomez turned back to Byrd. "He's one lucky man."

Byrd slumped back and said, "Cochran tried his best. But I told him I wasn't easy."

Doctor Gomez laughed. "That's not what the ER Nurses are saying about you." The Doctor and the Agent talked to each other out of Byrd's hearing and left the room.

Byrd propped up on his elbows and looked around. When he landed on Hicks standing near the door, he asked, "Sir, can you find out how Montana is? She is one of the Canton PD Officers. These folks" —he nodded toward the Nurse—"won't tell me anything about her."

The Nurse gave him a dirty look. "There is a thing called HIPAA. I keep reminding you about that."

Hicks turned to the Nurse. "We fully understand your dilemma." Hicks then said to Byrd, "Let me see what I can find out."

Hicks peeked out the door and saw a man wearing a Canton Police uniform and a second man in a sports coat. The uniformed man was wearing three stars on his collar. Hicks went up to him. "Chief?"

The man held out his hand. "Director, I doubt you remember me, but I saw you speak last year at the Chief's Conference. I'm Rob VanDower. And this is Ronny Beavers. He is the brother of one of our wounded Officers. He works at the Cherokee SO."

Hicks shook hands with both men warmly. "Good to meet you. And thanks for your help."

Beavers mumbled his apologies and went to check on his sibling.

"We owe you, Director. Your man put down a killer. He did everyone a favor. That took some balls, I must say. Chasing him into the woods alone. Damn ballsy move."

Hicks raised his eyebrows. He hadn't heard any details about the incident. He coughed. "Well, our friend Agent Byrd can be impetuous."

The Chief noted Hick's response and smiled. "I see that you have some issues to talk to your man about, too. I have a female Officer who did a damned good job today, but she rushed into bad situations twice. Once she was alone, and the second time she was lucky to have backup. It certainly wasn't because she had preplanned anything."

"I'm guessing that Officer is why I came out here in the hall. Danny wants to know how she is doing."

The Chief looked serious. "She and her partner are both

lucky. Milligan, the senior Officer out there, was hit in the forearm. Thank God the bullet didn't hit any bone. There is some muscle damage that the Doctors say they can repair. Worley has a couple of cracked ribs. Her vest took both rounds. She'll probably be released pretty soon."

Hicks exhaled. "They are both lucky. That situation could have been much worse."

The Chief hung his head. "We are all blessed. We got a bunch of killers off the street, and the cost to law enforcement could have been much worse."

Buster Hicks touched Rob VanDower's forearm, leaned his head forward, and closed his eyes. After a moment of hesitation, VanDower bowed his head, too.

When Hicks looked back up, his voice was hoarse. "Chief, if the GBI can do anything for you or your agency, please call me at any time." Hicks wrote his cell phone number on the back of his business card and passed it to the Chief.

"Bless you, sir," VanDower said and then turned away.

Hicks returned to Byrd's room to find Will Carver with him. Carver looked startled to see Hicks back in the room.

Hicks stopped in his tracks. "Am I interrupting?"

Carver stepped back from the table Byrd lay on. "No, sir. I was trying to give our problem child here some fatherly advice. But he's too stoned to take it all in."

Hicks stepped closer to Carver. "I hear he went off on his own."

Carver frowned. "I'm beginning to wonder if he has a death wish. He ran this suspect into the woods and shot it out with him alone."

Carver looked over his shoulder and saw that Byrd was out. "I'll have to say that what he did was what needed to be done. But, damn, he is reckless."

Hicks looked thoughtful. "Have you read his personnel file?"

Carver shook his head. "Just the evaluations that came from his former supervisors. I never read his background package."

"I have," Hicks said. "When he was nineteen, he was diagnosed with a kidney disease. Doctors told him he would most likely only live ten years. There was no real treatment. They experimented with lots of drugs, and out of nowhere, he went into remission. But he lived a year and a half believing he was going to die."

Carver spoke softly, "You think that's why he is reckless?"

Hicks laughed quietly. "I'm no psychiatrist, but I think that could be one answer."

Carver shot up his eyebrows. "That could go a long way to explain his driving."

Hicks nodded. "I've heard."

Carver turned back toward Byrd. "I'll make sure he gets some professional help when this is over. I assume he's cleared for as much leave as he needs."

"Absolutely. I'm willing to bet he won't want to take much time off, but we'll deal with that when the time comes. I'll make sure the shooting team keeps you in the loop on the investigation."

Hicks shook hands with Carver again. "Thanks, Inspector Carver."

Carver stood stock-still. "I'm sorry?"

Hicks smiled. "We need a new Inspector. You are the most likely prospect. If you want it."

Carver nodded, obviously in shock. "Whatever you need."

Hicks clapped Carver on the back. Then he placed his gray fedora squarely on his head. "Now, you stay in here while I have a few more words with the local Sheriff."

CHAPTER 21
SETTLING DUST

Daniel Byrd was hungover. The meds he had gotten at the hospital were compounded by the two large vodkas he served himself when he was dropped at his apartment. His mouth tasted like carpet. Old carpet. From a strip club where everyone smoked. All day.

He rolled off the bed and stood. Too quickly, he found out, as he dropped back to the bed and waited for the room to stop spinning. *Alcohol and drugs don't solve problems*, he thought. *Words spoken by someone who had never shot anybody.*

He stood more slowly and made it to the bathroom. He relieved himself, then brushed his teeth until his gums were bleeding. He rinsed his mouth and spit into the sink. *Better*, he thought.

He looked in the mirror and realized he was nude. He normally didn't sleep in the raw and was surprised he hadn't noticed earlier. He found a pair of briefs in a drawer and pulled them on.

He shook his head and headed to the kitchen to make coffee as strong as he could handle. It was bitter, but he needed it. He drank one cup and then poured a second.

Byrd could still smell the woods, the damp air, and a hint of gunpowder. He sat at his kitchen table—the same one he had shared with Montana such a short time ago. When he closed his eyes, he could see Lumpy laying on the ground trying to point the gun at him.

He clicked on the TV to find that the double homicide was the top story at noon. He turned up the volume and sat on his couch. Byrd watched as the Cherokee Sheriff was interviewed about his personal involvement in the case. The Reporter talked about the death of the two young people in the trailer on the gravel road. Video of the trailer with crime scene tape hanging in the front yard flashed briefly across the screen.

Then came a one-on-one with Sheriff Haggin himself. The off-screen Reporter started. "Sheriff, what can you tell us about these horrific murders?"

Haggin smiled broadly. "My team of Investigators worked tirelessly to find the group of people involved and to bring them to justice."

"Sheriff, we understand that one of the suspects died in a shootout. Can you tell us anything about that?"

"Well, the details of the shooting are still under investigation. The GBI has been called in to investigate the shooting of the one suspect. He is the same man who shot two Canton Police Officers. We are just pleased that all these killers are in jail or in the morgue."

The scene switched to video of GBI Crime Scene trucks and State Patrol cars blocking an area. Byrd recognized it as the shooting scene, his damaged Expedition front and center. The next shot was of the Canton Police car with the window shot out.

"I want the people of this county to know that these desperate men were captured or killed due to the hard work of the men and women of my office," Haggin continued in a voiceover. "And I will continue to work hard for them when I am reelected in 2004."

The Reporter wasn't satisfied. "Sheriff, I have been told the Officer who killed the murder suspect was a GBI Agent. Can you confirm that?"

The picture switched back to Haggin as he said, "I don't have anything to add."

Byrd leaned back on his couch and propped his feet on the coffee table. He watched a follow-up story about the shooting of the Officers on the side of Interstate 575. The Reporter had managed to get a shot from the station helicopter while the scene was still closed off. The two police Tahoes were also draped with the obligatory yellow tape, whipping in the wind.

He was surprised he felt so detached from the events of the day before. Byrd had only recently worked through the issues he had after watching a County Sheriff from up north get shot by a Superior Court Judge, who then turned the gun on himself. Byrd had had nightmares for months and was diagnosed as "hypervigilant." He just thought of it as being careful.

Byrd went to the refrigerator for something to drink and found a liter bottle of diet cola. He filled the glass with ice, then opened the pantry door to look for food. The smell from an open bottle of Pine-Sol hit him in the face. Suddenly he was back in the woods, diving for cover. His bare skin made a squealing sound on the vinyl floor.

Byrd was prone on his kitchen floor, laying in spilled cola and ice. The plastic cup had survived. Byrd was covered in a cold sweat, and his hands were shaking. His heart was pounding in his chest, and the room seemed dark. On wobbly legs, he picked himself up and stumbled to his bed. He decided it was time to nap a bit.

He stretched out on his bed. His heart was still thumping away like a drummer at a rock concert. Byrd saw the prescription bottle on his bedside table with his alarm clock. He eyed the clock and the bottle. He thought, *One of these I need, and one I do not. I choose better living through chemistry.*

He opened the bottle and took out a capsule. He swallowed it with spit and rolled onto his side. Soon his heart rate slowed, and he dozed off.

Byrd thought he had only been out a couple of minutes when he heard the pounding on his door. Suddenly he was wide awake. He grabbed his pistol and was beside the door in four long steps.

Byrd stood near the door in an area that would naturally stop most small-caliber bullets. "Who is it?"

There was a cough. Then a weak voice. "It's me. It's Montana."

He threw the door open, standing with his pistol hanging by his side. "Come on in."

Montana stood still. "Were you expecting me?"

"No. Why?"

"You meet me at your door with a pair of tighty-whiteys on, I have to figure something is up."

Byrd pulled his gun around in front of his crotch and backed away from the door. "Whoops. I'm still a little groggy from the meds they gave me at the hospital."

Byrd headed to his room, wrapped himself in a robe, and came back. "I guess you know we can't talk about anything that happened yesterday."

"Sure," she said. "They told me that I would be interviewed after I went through at least two sleep cycles."

Byrd nodded. "I think I just went through three or four in the last eight hours. How are you doing?"

She shrugged without thinking, then winced at the pain in her ribs and chest. "My whole chest feels like I got hit by a big truck. Breathing is painful out in the cold weather."

Byrd winced. "I bet climbing the stairs up here was no picnic."

She laughed and then coughed. "Damn. When I cough, I see stars, and I feel like I can't get my breath." When she was able, she continued. "And I spent the night sitting up with Milligan's wife while they worked on his arm."

"How is he doing?" Byrd asked.

"I think he's ready to get home. He has a young daughter, and he wants to get out of there and show her everything is okay."

"So, you didn't sleep? They doped me up so much that I've been out all night." Byrd asked.

"And most of the day it looks like."

"What?" Byrd asked.

"It's almost four in the afternoon."

Byrd looked at his watch. "I had no idea it was so late."

"That explains your attire."

He pressed the issue. "And you haven't slept since yesterday? Not even a nap?"

She shook her head. "I couldn't. I tried, but I keep seeing that gun pointed at me. When I closed my eyes, that's all I saw. And when my eyes were open, sometimes, I saw that bastard rolling out of that car like a stuntman."

Byrd motioned toward the couch. "Sit down." They sat at opposite ends of the couch.

Montana turned to Byrd. She frowned. "I can never repay you for what you did."

Byrd's eyebrows wrinkled. "Killing Lumpy?"

She nodded. "I can't get over how quickly everything happened. One minute everything was normal. Just another day on the job. The next I'm on the ground fighting to stay alive. He could have easily walked over and finished me."

Byrd hung his head. "You need to talk to someone about all this."

She started to cry. "I'm talking to you."

Byrd slid across the couch and hugged her. "I mean a professional. Someone who can explain the feelings you're having. Once before, the GBI sent me to a Peer Counselor. It's a good program, but you need to see a professional, too."

She shook her head. "What is a Peer Counselor?"

"Another cop who has used deadly force or been in a life-threatening situation. They help, but if I had a broken arm, I wouldn't want to talk to someone else with a broken arm—I'd want to see a Doctor."

The tears ran down her face, but she cried quietly. Byrd tried to wipe the tears away with his robe. Suddenly, she was laughing and crying at the same time.

Byrd smiled, too. "That was quite a switch."

She turned toward him, smiling. "You're flashing me, you idiot."

Byrd wrapped the robe tightly around his middle. "Sorry."

She leaned into him and hugged him back. "I guess we're both going to be a mess for a while."

Byrd put his head on her shoulder. "I thought I had left you for dead." Byrd began crying on her shoulder.

She stroked his hair. "You didn't do anything. I'm the one who couldn't wait for him to come out of the car. Maybe if I had waited, none of this would have happened."

He looked up, embarrassed. "Cops don't make suspects do things. They make that choice. We just play the cards we're dealt."

She started crying again. "I wish I could believe that."

"Do you believe in God?"

She nodded, looking puzzled. "Sure. I was raised by Baptists."

Byrd smiled. "What about Satan? The devil?"

She shrugged. "I guess. I mean, I hadn't thought about it."

Byrd continued. "He's as real as God. He fights for his side as hard as the good folks fight for justice. We are warriors. God made us this way. We just struggle sometimes. It's not an easy fight."

She hung her head. "It sure isn't an easy fight."

He smiled. "If it was easy, anybody could do it."

She held him close and whispered in his ear, "I love you more than you will ever know."

He leaned back and raised an eyebrow.

She continued, in a soft voice, "And less than you would like."

He pulled her close and held her as she shook. For a moment she sobbed, then she turned back to face him.

She stood up. "I've got to go. I need to rest, or I'll collapse."

He motioned to the guest room. She shook her head and walked to the door.

She turned back. "I need some time to think. I get what you're saying about fighting the good fight, but this may not be the job for me. I don't know if I can deal with all this."

"The PD needs to get you counseling."

She nodded. "I talked to a lady on the phone a little while ago. I have an appointment to meet her tomorrow. She does all the counseling for the agencies in this area. Everybody says she is good."

"What did she say?"

Montana laughed gingerly. "Stay away from you. I told

her we had gone on a date, and she said now was not the time to start a relationship with you."

Byrd frowned. "Like I need help running women off."

She shook her head. "She says that we are very vulnerable right now. And when I told her I might want to get out of law enforcement, she said I shouldn't make any big decision right now."

Byrd held her hand in his. "You're a good cop. No one can ever take that away from you. You put your heart into it, and the people out there need folks like you. Don't sell yourself short."

"Sometimes I do think God put me on this earth to be a cop. I like helping people and standing for something. But I guess I'm just trying to decide if this was a blessing or a wake-up call."

Byrd nodded. "Both," he said quietly. He leaned forward and kissed her head. "Take care of yourself."

Montana leaned toward him and kissed him on the lips. "Now, close that damned robe. The neighbors will be talking as it is."

He watched Montana walk stiffly down the outside stairs. He looked at the time, and then made a decision. He stumbled toward the shower. He figured a cold shower would wake him up.

Byrd pulled his personal truck into the parking lot of the Junction gas station, just inside Bartow County. His Expedition had been towed to GBI Headquarters, and he wouldn't be able to pick up a pool car until he was medically released to return to work.

As soon as he walked in, he saw Ramona Clark, the mother of Krystal, standing behind the counter. He had her work address from his interview notes. She was smoking a cigarette and examining the stock on the wall behind her. When she turned, her face looked as though she had aged ten years since yesterday morning. She locked eyes with Byrd.

She stood absolutely still. Then, before Byrd's eyes, she seemed to deflate. She sunk to the floor and hung her head. Byrd rushed over to help her, but a man working with her behind the counter got to her first.

Ramona was sobbing quietly. Her shoulders shook as the man tried to figure out what was wrong. The man looked at Byrd and said, "I don't know what came over her. I guess she's still in shock from losing her daughter yesterday. I told her not to come to work, but she said she needed the money."

Byrd nodded. He stood quietly while Ramona tried to get herself together.

When she stood up, she looked at Byrd. "I heard on the news that y'all got them that killed my daughter. Is that so?"

Byrd nodded. "The one who pulled the trigger is dead. The other two are locked up."

Ramona hung her head. "I didn't know how bad it would be. I've lost my daddy already, and I figured there wasn't much life could throw at me that I couldn't handle. But this feeling I've got in the pit of my stomach, this deep-down sadness, is the worst thing I've ever felt."

Byrd reached out to her. He hugged her like they were old friends. She laid her head on his shoulder and was quiet.

After a full minute, she raised her head and backed away. She wiped her eyes and looked at Byrd. "You just wait here. I need to get myself together for a minute. I'm going to step into the little girl's room and then I want you to answer some questions for me. Jeff, will you cover for me while I freshen up?"

Jeff, the man behind the counter, nodded and motioned her to go.

She turned and used her shoulder to push into the restroom. Byrd stood in the middle of the run-down service station, out of place in his business suit, and waited.

Byrd could hear the water running for a minute and then heard the toilet flush. He heard the water running again and then heard a crashing sound. Jeff looked shocked but waited for Byrd to move. Byrd forced the ladies' room door and found Ramona lying on the floor.

She looked slightly blue, and her breathing was labored. There were blue tablets around her hand on the floor. Byrd noticed that one of the pills had been crushed on the edge of the sink and most of the powder was gone.

He turned to Jeff. "Call 911. Tell them we have an overdose and need an ambulance right away."

Jeff ignored Byrd and ran for the door.

"Hey, what the hell are you doing?"

Jeff shouted back, "An ambulance just pulled up to get gas. They are outside."

Ramona was moaning, and her breathing was becoming more regular by the time the two firemen came into the service station. They helped her sit up and shot a liquid up her nose that seemed to improve her condition almost instantly.

Byrd was leaning over the firemen, watching. "What did you just do? It's like she just came back to normal."

The older fireman looked over his shoulder. "Naloxone. It's an opioid antagonist." Byrd's eyebrows shot up. The fireman laughed. "It will reverse an opioid overdose."

Byrd said, "I didn't know such a thing existed. It sure works fast."

The fireman nodded. "She was coming back anyway. We just, basically, flushed the drugs out of her system." The firemen took a closer look at Byrd. "Are you a cop?"

"I'm with the GBI. But I'll call Bartow County and get a Deputy out here. We sure are lucky you guys were in the parking lot."

The two firemen began to get their gear together. "Glad we could help. We don't save as many as we would like."

Byrd stood up. He pulled the phone from the wall and dialed 911. When the Operator came on the line, he asked for a Deputy to respond to the overdose. He carefully omitted his name and title. Once he knew a Deputy was on the way, he hung up the phone.

"Jeff, tell Ramona I'm sorry for her loss. A Deputy will come here and take a report."

Jeff looked surprised. "Are you leaving?"

Byrd shook his head. "I was never here. If my boss finds out I was out working, he'll skin me alive."

Byrd didn't sleep well that night. He kept flashing back to the moments in the woods. He tossed and turned, got up, and thought about taking another pill. He dismissed the idea, as he wasn't clear how many he had already taken that day.

He reflected that, if he died of an overdose, people would think it was intentional. Then he thought about Ramona and whether she was medicating the pain or trying to escape it.

He opted to do pushups, sit-ups, and squats until he was bathed in sweat. Then he climbed back in bed for another round of tossing and turning.

When sleep came, it was fitful. He had a vivid dream that caused him to sit straight up in bed. His heart was pounding.

He got out of bed and turned on the TV in the living room. He scrolled through the channels, trying to find something to distract him.

He found the end of an episode of *Gunsmoke*. He watched as Marshal Matt Dillon faced the outlaw. Dillon drew and fired at the same time as the bad guy. The suspect clutched his abdomen and fell to the ground. The US Marshal looked down at the bad man and frowned, then stalked off as the theme music came up.

Byrd laughed wryly. "That's the way to do it, Matt. Drop 'em and leave 'em lying in the street. No shooting investigation, no bad dreams, no recriminations. Just move on to the next case."

Then, startled, he said, "Damn, I'm talking to myself out loud. I may be more screwed up than I thought."

He poured vodka and a splash of tonic. After drinking it down, he headed back to the bedroom. He lay quietly for a few minutes, and then said a prayer for the parents of Mark and Krystal. He rolled over and closed his eyes. Then, as an afterthought, he did something he had not been able to do for the last two days. He said a prayer for Lumpy Cochran.

For the next month, Daniel Byrd and Montana Worley would meet for lunch or dinner. They were both on administrative duty, and Byrd was relegated to background investigations. Montana was assigned to a desk in the police administration building.

On the last week of the month, they were sitting at a table in a Mexican restaurant in Prominence Point, a shopping district on the south side of Canton. Byrd had chosen a table with a good view of both doors. Montana had given up trying to get the seat against the wall.

Montana sat down and pushed the menu aside. "I'm feeling more confident. The counseling is really helping. How are you doing, Danny?"

He shrugged. "The Counselor is good. And I'm doing okay."

"How about the drinking?"

The conversation stopped when the Server came to the table for their order. Montana knew the menu by heart, and the Server knew what she usually ordered. Montana smiled when the Server asked, "The usual?"

Montana nodded. "Yes, sir!"

Byrd gave the man his order, and then they waited for him to be out of earshot. "How have you been the last couple of days? I haven't heard from you."

Montana looked uncomfortable. "I've been working on a couple of personal things. I was trying to figure out the next step in my life."

Byrd said, "Anything I can do to help?"

Montana laughed. It wasn't a happy laugh. "Danny, you can't figure out the next step in your life. Why would I think you could help with my life?"

Byrd hung his head. "I'm sorry." He hoped Montana couldn't see how her comment had stung.

"Don't be sorry, get yourself together, and stop drinking away the rest of your life."

Byrd shrugged. "It's how I cope."

She shook her head. "No, it's the way you escape. I can't live like you want to live right now. I'm going on a few days' leave next week. I'm hoping this will be the answer to my search."

"What?"

"It's personal. And you didn't answer my question earlier. How much are you drinking at night?"

"I'm not on call for cases until the Grand Jury meets."

"In other words, there is no reason for you to drink in moderation. I guess you're getting drunk every night."

"Montana, I'll be back on the call rotation next month."

She took a sip of iced tea. "Don't waste your life."

CHAPTER 22

DOTTING THE T'S AND CROSSING THE I'S

MONDAY, APRIL 21, 2003
CANTON, GEORGIA
10:00 A.M.

Daniel Byrd stepped out of the Grand Jury room for what he hoped would be the final time today. Today he had been called to testify about the shooting death of Lumpy Cochran. He had testified to another Grand Jury in March about the murders of Mark Goodwin and Krystal Page.

Byrd was the last witness before the District Attorney would call for a vote on potential charges in the death of Cochran. A Grand Jury could determine, based on the evidence presented, whether Byrd's actions were within the law. Byrd had already testified earlier today, but after the Grand Jurors heard other testimonies, they wanted to ask him a few more questions.

Byrd came out of the meeting room and leaned against the wall in the hallway. After taking a deep breath, he looked around. The hall was empty except for a woman standing near the end. Byrd noticed she was a few years older than him, looked athletic, and was dressed in navy blue. He noted that she looked vaguely familiar.

Byrd was anxious as he paced the hall outside the District Attorney's Office. He had been assured by his

Attorney that there would be no charges for the justified shooting of Cochran, but he knew anything was possible. He was wondering how long this process would take. He had walked away from the Grand Jury room and toward the bank of elevators when he heard voices coming from near the law library.

Montana Worley came around the corner escorted by Canton Police Chief VanDower. They both stopped when they saw Byrd. VanDower thrust out his hand. Montana had been the second witness to testify about the Cochran shooting.

"Agent Byrd, good to see you," VanDower said. "We just came to see what the final word from the Grand Jury was."

Montana gave him a hug. "How are you doing? You look worried."

Byrd shrugged. "These things are never a slam dunk. There is always the chance somebody can find an issue with any police shooting."

VanDower nodded his head in understanding. "This should be a slam dunk, if there ever was one."

Byrd shook his head. "Don't jinx me, Chief."

"Call me Rob," the Chief replied.

Montana spoke up. "Can I call you Rob, too?"

VanDower smiled. "Pretty soon you can."

Byrd was confused. But before he could ask about the remark, the Assistant District Attorney came out. He pointed toward Byrd. "The Grand Jurors wanted me to tell you that you did an awesome job as a witness, and after your follow-up answers, they have absolutely no problems with the shooting of Mr. Cochran."

Byrd let his breath out. "Thanks, Jacob. I knew you could do it."

The ADA called back, "No problems. It was a slam dunk!"

Byrd shook his head. Montana hugged him again. "That's great news," she said.

Byrd turned toward a settee in the hallway. "You guys mind if I sit for a minute?"

Byrd dropped into the seat as the ADA walked over to the well-dressed woman he had seen earlier. He escorted her into the Grand Jury room. As she passed, Byrd remembered who she was. The woman was a former Captain with the Cherokee Sheriff's Office.

Montana walked him over to a bench, and they sat down together. "Wow," Byrd said clasping his hands. "I didn't realize how nervous I was."

Montana laughed. "Everyone told you it would be a slam dunk."

Byrd smiled, brushing his hair back with his left hand. "You just never know."

Byrd slumped back on the seat and took a deep breath. Then something he had heard earlier popped back in his head. "What did the Chief mean when he said you could call him by his first name soon? You haven't decided to quit, have you?"

She looked at the floor. "If you mean getting out of law enforcement, no, that's not what's happening. My Counselor told me some of the same things you did, and I have been able to work through most of my issues from that day. In fact, I am more committed than ever to this career."

Byrd looked in her eyes. "I hear a 'but' coming."

She tilted her head, looked at the floor then met his eyes again. "When we sat and talked, I listened to what you said."

"You shouldn't ever take my advice!"

She laughed and reached out to hold his hand. She exhaled and then said, "I'm going to be a Trooper."

Byrd was relieved. "That's great. Any idea what part of the state you'll be in? Have they given you any idea?"

She looked at the floor again. "Yes. They said I would be working on the border. That's where they need Troopers."

Byrd frowned. "The border with Alabama? I've never heard anything like that from the GSP."

She looked at him and smiled. "Not GSP. THP. Texas Highway Patrol."

Byrd was stunned. His heart sank. "You're moving to Texas?"

She nodded. "They made me an offer I couldn't turn down. More money, better fringe benefits. You name it, they threw it my way."

Byrd shook off the shock. "That's awesome. You deserve everything they offered you and more. You're a hell of a cop!"

She stood up and he followed. "I wanted to tell you in person," she said. "I have to be in Austin for Trooper School in two weeks, but I am moving my furniture tomorrow. I just wanted to get away from all this and get a fresh start."

Byrd nodded. "I wish we'd had the chance to get to know each other better."

She laughed. "You mean you wish we had slept together."

Byrd smiled and said, "That, too. But I enjoyed the time we did spend together. You're a hell of a cop. And will make one hell of a Trooper in Texas."

She looked deep into his eyes. "And you are either the bravest man I've ever known, or the craziest. And I may never know which it is."

He hugged her, and they walked to her car. He gave her a last hug and then watched her drive away.

Byrd walked over to the pool car he was driving. The navy blue Crown Victoria was worn out, but it was still reliable transportation. He fired it up and waited for the air-conditioning to cool the interior down. Late April was early summer in Georgia, and this year was no exception.

He checked his watch and realized that he was due at the counseling center in less than an hour. He had an appointment with the same Counselor who had been seeing Montana. He would have to rush to get there on time.

I don't want to be late, he thought. *She is a hard ass.*

Anne Kuykendall was waiting in her Woodstock office for Byrd to walk in. She stood and met him at the door with a hug. Byrd stiffened at the contact.

"Are you afraid of me?" Anne asked.

"No. I'm just uncomfortable is all."

"Get used to it. We have some time we need to spend together."

Byrd found a seat on her sofa. "Are you working me in among the junkies and drunks?"

"No name-calling. They pay the bills. And they have more in common with you than you're willing to admit." She sat in her chair across from him.

Byrd leaned forward. "Did you know Montana Worley was going to Texas?"

"I can't discuss another client. You should know that."

"So, yes."

"Do you want to spend your time talking about me or about you? I get paid either way."

Byrd laughed. "Damn, you're a hard ass."

She just smiled. "I get that a lot."

Byrd tried to get the conversation moving in a direction he was comfortable with. "I guess we'll be looking for Saddam Hussein for a while. Maybe we can send some of the same folks who can't find Eric Robert Rudolph."

Kuykendall stopped him short. "We're not here to talk about current events. We're here to talk about you." She paused. "I think the Olympic Park bomber is dead, anyway. I know the area in North Carolina where he is supposed to be hiding. There's no way he could live off the land up there. Not this long!"

Byrd laughed. "There's a country song there somewhere. 'Looking for Rudolph in All the Wrong Places.'"

She grunted. "Okay, enough. Back to you!"

Byrd grudgingly got back on topic. He hesitated, then he spoke in a low tone. "Rose Mitchell called me last week. She wants to go out again."

"The lady you had the relationship with from the District Attorney's Office in Ellijay? Do you think that's a good idea?"

"That's her. We talked about her last time." He shrugged. "And I guess it's better than some of my ideas."

Kuykendall groaned. "Is that where you want to set the bar in your life? One idea being only a little better than your last mediocre idea?"

He stretched his legs out, and they talked about the shooting again. And about the other time, when he first met Rose Mitchell. She listened, interrupting for clarification as though she wasn't familiar with most of the details.

Kuykendall had been to hours of training on stressful situations, and she explained to Byrd that he hadn't heard his own gunshots because of a phenomenon called auditory exclusion. Then she told him that smells were often triggers for anxiety attacks. He told her about the incident with the pine smell, and she nodded.

"Do you see his face often?"

Byrd blinked. He frowned as he said. "Nope."

Anne laughed. "You're a liar."

Byrd felt ashamed. "I see him occasionally, but not as much as I did in the few days right after."

She nodded. "That's normal. You saw a person die."

Byrd shrugged. "I'd be more than happy to kill him again if I had to."

She leaned in. "That doesn't matter. No matter how bad a person was, you took their life. And it will take a while to get over that."

"How long?" Byrd asked.

"How long will you live?"

Byrd thought about his answer. He leaned forward and looked her in the eye. "I guess it depends on who you talk to. My bosses think I'll be lucky to make it to the end of the month. I figure I'm good for a few more years. Who knows?"

They talked for several more minutes when there was a quiet knock outside. Anne leaned toward the door. "Yes?"

A voice on the other side of the door said, "There is a call for Mr. Byrd."

Anne Kuykendall looked at Daniel, who shrugged. She pointed at the phone on her desk, one eyebrow raised as she watched him.

He stood and went to the desk where the phone line was blinking red. He pushed the button and said, "Byrd."

"Teddy? You ready to get back to work?"

"Hey, Doc. What do you need?" Byrd couldn't deny the surge of excitement he felt at the sound of Doc's voice.

"We have a double homicide in Fannin County. Looks like a who-done-it. Can you come that way? Tina says you're off administrative duty since the Grand Jury met."

Byrd chuckled. "They just met this morning, Doc!"

Byrd looked to Anne. He put his hand over the bottom of the phone. "We need to cut this short."

Anne was already gathering her notes. She could see where this was heading.

He turned back to the phone. "I'll head that way."

Anne stood up. "I give up. Get your ass out of here and go do what you love. But you need to be back here in two weeks."

Byrd was smiling genuinely, for the first time in a while, as he rushed to his car and jumped in. He turned on the blue lights and siren and headed for the interstate. As the police car merged onto the highway, Daniel Byrd felt home again.

EPILOGUE

Byrd walked over to the Trooper retiring today. He reached out to touch the uniformed shoulder and noted the Major's gold oak leaves on them.

When Montana Petterson turned around, it was evident she was startled to see him. Her eyes were wide, and she wrapped her arms around him.

Byrd was uncomfortable returning the hug. "Is this what you want to be seen doing on your last day? A uniformed Major shouldn't be hugging some guy in a room full of her subordinates."

She stepped back and grabbed his tie. "I guess maybe I should strangle you then. Hell, I don't know what I should do."

She leaned close to his ear. "I think most of the people in the room know that I regularly sleep with a Texas Ranger. Clete can't keep his damned mouth shut!" She hugged him again. "It sure is good to see you."

He hugged her back. Then Byrd said, "I love you more than you will ever know."

She said, "But less than you would like." They both laughed.

Then he felt his eyes welling up. "Damn, I hadn't planned on crying."

She held him at arm's length, looking into his eyes. "My friend, there are never enough tears to wash away all the things we've seen. Even the things we've seen together."

Byrd laughed. "Yep. We've been down some rough roads, that's for sure."

The two stood, alone in a room full of people. They compared their lives since they had been together last.

Montana reluctantly walked away when she was called to the podium. She and her husband were the guests of honor at the retirement celebration. Byrd found a seat and listened as the Director of the Texas Department of Public Safety talked about the careers of the couple in uniform.

The Chief of the Texas Rangers stood to commend the work the couple had done in service to the State of Texas. Many commemorative plaques were offered to both of the retiring Officers. Byrd was amused to note that each one of the mementos was in the shape of Texas. The Chief of Police for El Paso lauded the accomplishments of the couple. Montana and Clete were appropriately embarrassed.

Then Clete stood to make some final comments. He teared up as he talked about his father and mother, both gone before he became a Major in the Rangers. He talked about the friends he had made in his career and even the wonderful woman he had found and wed.

When it was her turn, Montana Petterson made similar comments. She talked about the family she still had back in Georgia. She, too, praised the different Officers they had worked with and for. She talked about the pride she took in being a female commander in what was, still, a male-dominated profession.

She took time to talk about her family and how important it had been for her to find the right balance between family and career. Then she spoke about her love for her children and her husband. How they had stood with her in good times and bad. Then she stopped and pointed at Daniel Byrd.

"And there is a man here today who came all the way from Georgia to honor me today. He has been a friend and a coworker, both in Georgia and here in Texas. Many of you don't know that I started as a Police Officer in a little town in Georgia. This man was there for me when I needed him. Then a couple of years later, he saved a certain Texas Ranger. And as long as I live, I'll never forget him for that."

The room had gone quiet. Several people looked over at Byrd as he stood and shifted from one foot to the other. Questions were whispered among the other Officers.

Montana leaned toward the microphone. "And I've seen him in his tighty-whities. That something I can't unsee."

The room broke out in nervous laughter.

"Ladies and gentlemen," Montana continued, "help me give a Texas welcome to Special Agent in Charge Daniel Byrd of the Georgia Bureau of Investigation. I've worked with a lot of brave Officers, including the one I married. But Danny Byrd may be the toughest SOB I've had the pleasure to work with." She started to clap, and the audience followed her lead.

Byrd felt embarrassed as he acknowledged the applause and retook his seat.

When the speeches were over, Montana and Clete brought others over to meet Byrd. He was uncomfortable with the attention.

After Montana and Clete changed into jeans, Western shirts, and white cowboy hats, they found Byrd waiting back in the lobby. He thought he probably looked like he was running away from home, seated with his carry-on bag standing at attention beside him.

Montana pulled him to his feet. "Are we going to State Line for some barbecue or what?"

Clete spoke up. "He already asked about Cattleman's Steakhouse."

Montana laughed. "Red meat. All right, that sounds good. Do you want to get out of that suit?"

He did. They ran him by his motel in Clete's Texas-style truck. The couple of Texas Law Officers waited until he checked in and changed. He strode back out in jeans and a polo shirt.

Montana spoke up as he walked toward them. "I see you still don't own any cowboy boots."

Byrd looked down at his boat shoes and grinned. Byrd hopped into the back seat of their gigantic pickup truck. He looked over his shoulder at the greatest asset the high desert had—a magnificent sunset. In a few minutes, the city of El Paso was fading away, but the city of Juarez was still in the right-side window.

Montana turned in her seat to face him. "So, how are our friends Sturdevant and Westbrook doing? Last I heard, Westbrook was up for parole this year."

Byrd gave her a rueful smile. "Westbrook took a bad turn, health-wise. He died in prison from lung cancer. Sturdevant is still hanging on, but he got life without parole."

She shook her head. "I can't believe they ever considered paroling Westbrook. He put all that into motion."

"You were in Texas by the time we went to trial. His parents never did believe that he would be convicted. On the day it went to the jury, they showed up at the courthouse with a cake. It took the jury less than four hours to find him guilty."

"I guess the family wanted to believe he wasn't a bad man."

Byrd shrugged. "I'll never forget it. His mother sobbed as the verdict came in. Neither mom nor dad lived long after that. He ruined a lot of lives."

Montana looked Byrd in the eye. "He got what he deserved." Montana changed the subject. "You still working, I guess?" she asked.

He nodded. "Still fighting the good fight. Till they tell me I have to go home."

Her voice softened. "Is there anyone to go home to?"

Byrd hesitated. She was probably one of the few women in the world who could ask him that. "I'm single, if that's what you're asking."

She laughed. "Well, now that Clete is unemployed, I may be looking for greener pastures."

Clete laughed, too. "You won't find much green around El Paso."

Byrd smiled at the banter. He wondered what would have happened if things had been different. But they weren't.

Montana sensed that Byrd wanted to change the topic. "We sure do appreciate you coming out. How long can you stay?"

"I'm flying out tomorrow. Nobody does my job when I'm gone."

"I understand. I can't thank you enough for coming out. It sure does mean a lot to both of us."

Clete nodded.

Byrd leaned toward the middle of the truck. "You're getting out at a good time. Cops are under fire, literally and figuratively. I think about getting out more than ever."

Clete glanced back in the rearview mirror, catching Byrd's eyes. "We all did our part. We all stood for something. That means a lot."

Montana turned in her seat. "This job is what God made you for."

Byrd laughed uncomfortably. Montana tried to make eye contact, but he wouldn't allow it. "If that's true he would have made me better at it."

She didn't laugh. "He made you a warrior. He made you someone who runs toward the truth and who doesn't quit."

Byrd sighed and rubbed his face with both hands. "I think more about quitting every day."

Montana shook her head, clearly not buying it. "You don't know how to quit. It's not in you."

Byrd didn't know how to respond to that. He looked out the window at Mexico in the distance. He wondered if the airport just across the border was still there, but he couldn't bring himself to look.

Byrd looked over his shoulder at the setting sun. "Maybe I was just born a hundred years too late."

Montana looked straight ahead. "You may be right," she said.

ACKNOWLEDGMENTS

My wife, Grace, has endured the life of a cop's wife. She made sure the kids got to school or to a sporting event when I got called away to a murder or a drug deal. She was a loving mother to our children, and now to our grandchildren. We met—during the days when smuggling planes seemed to fill the skies—on a blind date. Then I had to cancel the next three dates in a row to run off to South Georgia. She must've seen something there, but I still haven't figured out what.

I must also recognize the Texas contingent: Zack, Erika, Addy, Rae, and Stetson, for their faith in me; and Shelia, Mark, Ashley, and Alexis for their sage counsel.

The biggest "family thanks" goes to Emma, who worked with me, corrected me, and encouraged me. Emma has been, and will always be, my sounding board, my editor-in-chief, and most importantly, my daughter.

To say I love each of the individuals listed above would be an understatement!

I must thank my first readers, who found the little mistakes and inconsistencies or were kind enough to tell me that what I wrote just didn't make sense. In particular, a shout-out to Jesse Hampton for being willing to take on that responsibility.

I have had the pleasure of meeting, talking with, and being encouraged by so many people, it becomes hard to list everyone. Thanks to the friends who encouraged me over Mexican food (the Simses, the Sinclairs, the Pages, and the Chandlers) and were the first to buy a copy of *Mountain Justice*. Thanks to the members of the mystery book club in

Kennesaw, and the staff at the Book Exchange. And thanks to the friends, coworkers, and acquaintances who made me feel I had something. Each of you are special to me. This book wouldn't exist without your kind encouragement.

And, last but not least, thanks to the staff at BookLogix who helped guide me through the process of getting my stories in print.

Phillip W. Price began his law enforcement career in late 1974. On January 8, 1978, Price was appointed to the Georgia Bureau of Investigation (GBI) as a Special Agent. Price served in various capacities with the GBI, from working in extreme South Georgia swamplands to the North Georgia mountains. SAC Price retired on October 31, 2006, with twenty-nine years of criminal investigative experience.

In 2010, Price was hired to lead the Cherokee Multi-Agency Narcotics Squad (CMANS), a drug task force in Canton, Georgia. Price re-retired on December 17, 2021.

Price has an associate in arts degree from Reinhardt University, a bachelor of science degree from North Georgia University, and a master's in public administration from Columbus State University.

He lives in Canton, Georgia.